Rebel Angels

James Michael Rice

James M. Rice

This one's for The Nightmares...

~One~

Someone was following her.

The mosquitoes and gnats didn't matter anymore, nor did the blisters on her feet, nor the fact that her car had broken down and she was stranded out here, in the middle of nowhere, all alone.

The only thing that mattered was that someone was following her, had been following her for miles, and now she was going to be raped, or killed, or both, all because she had been too frightened to trust her intuition not to leave the safety of her car behind.

Somewhere along the grassy shoulder of Route 11, Anna Hartsoe stopped, searching the darkness for her stalker, and found she was unable to tell one shape from another. Heart fluttering, it dawned on her that someone—or something—could be standing right beside her, and she would never even know it. Not until it was already too late.

Clutching the straps of her maroon Kelty backpack, she cocked her head and listened. There was only the dry hissing of leaves as the treetops caressed the cauldron-black belly of the eastern sky. Whatever it was she thought she had heard, it was gone now.

Probably just a squirrel, she reassured herself. *Or maybe a raccoon. Stop being so paranoid. Stupid, stupid! Besides, if there really was someone following me, they would have made their move by now. Nobody in the world could be that patient. It's only an animal, scrounging around for food or something. Don't let your imagination get the best of you...*

1

Wait...there it was again! That sound!

GO! a voice screamed inside her head. *RUN! GET OUT OF HERE!*

In her mind's eye she actually saw herself running; arms and legs pumping wildly, Birkenstocks slapping the pavement, long chestnut hair flapping behind her in the wind. But in reality she had not moved a muscle.

For several seconds she couldn't even breathe. Her body tingled to the core. She was shrinking. Either that or the world around her was expanding, because she suddenly felt very, very small.

All around her the darkness lunged forward, swelling above her, ready to drown her, to suck her down, down into its unfathomable depths. She wanted to sleep. Her eyelids were heavy, her fingers and toes tingled with pins and needles. Sleep, yes. For a little while, anyway. It was soothing to close her eyes, to let her mind drift away. *But what about that thing?* she asked herself. *That thing in the woods?*

As she struggled to keep her eyelids open the world began to tilt, and she realized for the first time what was happening to her: She was fainting.

It wasn't until she heard a familiar sound in the distance behind her that she could breathe again. It was an engine. A car engine! Jerking her head around, Anna saw two golden orbs floating toward her in the darkness, and a joyful sob escaped her. *Thank you, God*, she thought, watching the slow progress of the headlights.

Then, in the nearby forest, it moved again. Branches snapped like firecrackers in the still summer night. The footsteps were slow, deliberate. *Whatever it is*, thought Anna, *it wants to be heard*.

She whirled toward the forest, eyes rolling like big brown marbles as she scanned the dark wall of underbrush. The footsteps stopped. Leaves conversed in static, untranslatable whispers. Trees reached out with their clawed hands, as if to draw her into their shriveled arms. Mosquitoes landed on her arms and legs and drank their fill of her nervous blood. It was toying with her, this forest-thing. Trembling, she turned her attention back to the car, more desperate than ever for a savior.

On the side of the road, Anna Hartsoe stood with one arm extended and a red-nailed thumb pointing towards the empty night sky. After a moment she realized the car was further away than she had perceived, and let her arm fall limply to her side. Frustrated, she clenched one small hand into a fist, nails shoveling into the palm. The pain felt good; it seemed to help her focus.

Please, God, please let me get outta here alive. I won't ask you for anything for the rest of the week—no, make that the rest of the year—a long time, a long time, if you just answer this one little prayer, please God, oh, please...

She had never imagined something like this could happen in the real world. Not to her. Her goddamn car had broken down for the second time that month, her cell phone was out of range, and there was something in the woods that was following her. No, those kinds of things only happened in the movies...or so she had believed, until the footsteps had begun.

Crap, Deb was right, thought Anna. Debbie Allbright was her roommate at Boston College. She was also Anna's closest friend. *I should've waited until tomorrow. A few lousy hours, and I could've saved myself a lot of trouble. Hell, maybe even my life. It's gonna cost a friggin' fortune to fix that stupid car.* She squinted into the approaching headlights. *You're gonna be fine*, she told herself. *You're gonna be fine. You'll laugh about this later. You know that, don't you?*

Anna stuck out her thumb again, hoping to attract the driver's attention. She wiggled her toes inside her Birkenstocks, wincing at the pain that traveled up the back of her legs, tying her calf muscles into hard little knots. She doubted if she'd be able to walk another mile before the pain became unbearable, or before she'd go insane with fright. If only she hadn't taken that last exit to buy cigarettes. *Hey, Mom, you always said smoking would kill me someday...well, hardy-fucking-har, are you happy now?*

Route 11 was a lonesome, winding back road that meandered all the way from Bridgewater to Buzzard's Bay, where it then junctioned with Route 44 and later ended abruptly at the coastline. Long ago, Route 11 had been the main thoroughfare for the many vacationers who made Cape Cod and The Islands their summer

3

playground. There had once been restaurants, stores, and taverns all along the well-worn road, until the spring of 1987, when the completion of nearby Highway 495 drew the tourists away, quickly draining the area of its lifeblood. Those fortunate enough to have the means had long since packed their bags and migrated with the almighty dollar, while others stayed and floundered into bankruptcy. Entire neighborhoods were abandoned. Convenience stores, ice cream stands, and rustic clam shacks soon closed their doors forever, slowly consumed by the nearby swampland. All that remained was a dilapidated motel here, an empty foundation there, and the occasional driveway to nowhere.

After more than a decade of neglect, few motorists still navigated the pot-holed road called Route 11, save for a small clan of local residents who could not afford to move. They lived in dilapidated, century-old houses of weathered gray shingles, isolated by miles of cranberry bogs, forests, and pavement left scarred by the wrath of long ago winters. Before that evening, Anna would never have imagined such an ugly, desolate place could exist in the Commonwealth of Massachusetts, and so close to the hustle and bustle of Boston. Not counting the lonely, burnt-out streetlight she had passed over an hour ago, she had not witnessed a single trace of the modern world...until now.

The car slowed to a near crawl as it passed the attractive young hitchhiker.

It was an old tan Buick, freckled with rust. Anna could tell it was old by the shiny bumpers; they didn't make cars with chrome bumpers anymore, only trucks.

Her heart leapt as the right directional signal winked on and the car began to pull over, some ten yards away from where she was standing. The Buick's tires rolled off the pavement, crunching softly into the sand of a narrow embankment, as the forest settled in the muddy glow of its headlights.

With the nylon strap sawing into her shoulder, Anna adjusted the weight of the backpack as she walked slowly and cautiously toward the car. The engine's loud idle made it impossible for her to hear if the thing in the woods was still there, and she was grateful for that.

Her legs trembled as she approached the driver's side door. The interior of the car was so dark, the windows might as well have been painted black. The engine knocked, the exhaust chuffed. Several seconds passed, and still no sign of the driver. *This is way too creepy*, thought Anna. She took a tentative step back, away from the car. A sensible part of her wanted to bolt; she could feel the eagerness of her legs, but it was getting late, and it had been a long time since a car had come her way. The important thing was to get away, far away, from the forest.

At last, the driver rolled the window down. "Why, hello, there!" he beamed, his voice matching the congenial timbre of a television game-show host. The sound of jazz music wafted out through the open window, softening her nerves. "Do you need a ride somewhere, Miss?"

Stepping a little closer to the car, Anna bent over, examining the shadow-splashed face of the driver. All she could make out was the dark shine of bifocals resting on the bridge of a porous nose, the knot of a black necktie on a white Polo shirt, and a thin crop of silver hair slicked back from a high, bulbous forehead. From what little she could see she guessed the man's age to be around fifty, give or take a few years.

Glasses chuckled pleasantly. "I guess that's a silly question, huh?" He slapped his forehead in a pantomime of embarrassment. "Of course you need a ride. Why else would you be standing there with your thumb out?"

"My car broke down." She hated the way her voice sounded, like a skittish little girl asking her mommy for an ice cream. Clearing her throat, she tried again. "You might've passed it, about five miles up the road. Little red Escort?"

"I saw it, alright," he told her, nodding. "I'm sorry, Miss. I'd like to help you out, but I'm afraid I've never been much of a mechanic. All thumbs, as they say."

"Oh," Anna said softly. Her stomach flip-flopped. "That's okay. I don't suppose you could give me a ride to the nearest gas station, could you?"

"As far as I know, there are no gas stations open around here. Certainly not at this hour. I'm truly sorry, dear. I'd really like to help you out, but..." He shrugged one beefy shoulder, as if that explained away everything.

"Oh..." repeated Anna. "Well, thanks, anyway." She glanced around, from left to right. No lights, no phones, no houses, only that hateful, never-ending darkness, as far as the eye could see.

Alone, she told herself again. *You're out here all alone...except for that...that thing in the woods. If Glasses abandons you here...well, you can bend over backwards and kiss your ass goodbye.*

Glasses apologized one last time, shifted his car into drive, looked both ways to make sure no other cars were coming, and began to pull away, leaving her in the backwash of his taillights.

"Wait!" Anna shouted suddenly (that little girl's voice again). "Mister, wait!"

The brake lights came on, splashing bloody light across her face. Her backpack swung like a pendulum as she jogged to the car.

"Maybe," she panted through the still open window, "you could just...drop me off...at the nearest payphone? I can...I dunno, call for a tow truck or something, y'know?"

Glasses nodded thoughtfully. "I suppose that's a good idea. I don't think I could sleep tonight, knowing you were still stranded out here all alone. My wife would kill me if I told her that I left you. I have a niece about your age...you have to be, what, about eighteen?"

"Nineteen, actually." Anna smiled politely and the man with the glasses smiled back at her, thin lips stretching back to reveal his crooked yellow teeth. Upon seeing his creepy attempt at a smile Anna felt her own smile start to falter, and she could only hope he hadn't noticed.

"Nineteen," he marveled. "The perfect age. Ahh, to be nineteen again..." Any trace of an expression seemed to vanish from his face. Several seconds ticked by until his smile returned again. "Hop in," he offered at last. "I hope you'll excuse the mess, but I just got out of work, as you can probably tell." He lifted his tie and waved it at her.

As she sidestepped the Buick's blunt nose, Anna weighed her options once again. When she boiled it down, she decided she was left with only two choices: walk or ride. Before she had time enough to second-guess her decision, she had already gotten into the car, shrugged off her backpack, and surrendered herself to the much-welcomed comfort of the cushioned vinyl seat.

"Thanks, mister," she said. She closed the car door and set her backpack on the floor, by her feet. As her head met the headrest, it occurred to her that vinyl had never felt so luxurious. "I really appreciate this."

Glasses extended a large hand towards her. "You're very welcome, young lady. Now, where're my manners? I'm Alan. Alan Moody."

"Anna Hartsoe." His hand was cool and clammy but she accepted it just the same. She even tried to shake hands firmly, as her father had taught her when she was very young, but found it was next to impossible to do so. Shaking his hand was like trying to shake hands with a giant. Only now, sitting beside him, did Anna realize the full immensity of the man named Alan Moody, who was easily the size of a Patriots linebacker. Arms as thick as stovepipes, connected to broad shoulders that strained against the seams of his shirt; large, powerful hands that were at least twice the size of her own; a barrel-shaped torso; legs as thick as tree trunks. Sitting beside him, Anna suddenly felt very safe. Surely, a man that size wouldn't let anything bad happen to her. A man that size probably wasn't afraid of anything.

"Nice to meet you, Anna Hartsoe." After a few seconds he released her small hand, shifted into drive, and slowly accelerated into the crisp July night.

"If you don't mind my asking," he said, his voice almost fatherly, "where were you headed, Anna?"

I've been asking myself that same question all night, she wanted to say. Instead she shrugged, offering him a friendly smile. "My friend Debbie said she had a job lined up for me on the Vineyard, so I decided to give it a shot." She laughed a high, nervous little laugh. "My car hasn't been running so good lately, but I haven't had the time to have it looked at."

Mr. Moody nodded sympathetically. "Yeah, I hear you. I know how it is, not enough hours in the day. I was a college student myself once, believe it or not."

"How'd you know I was a student?" she asked suspiciously, squinting into the headlights of an oncoming car. As the two cars passed one another, she stole a look at Alan Moody's face, and saw he was wearing that strange crooked-toothed smile once again. Her mind began to resonate with the sound of bells, loud and sharp and full of warning. She didn't like his smile. It looked fake to her, almost too polite. *Fear*, she remembered. *Don't let your fear control you.*

"Your sweatshirt," Alan Moody answered, jutting his square chin towards her. "Boston College, my old Alma Mater."

"R-really? You went to BC?"

"Yep, back when I was just a pup. Hmpph! It seems like that was just about a million years ago." He half-chuckled, half-snorted, into the top of his fist.

It was a childlike gesture, and it made Anna feel at ease. She thought, *This guy ain't so bad after all. A little goofy maybe, but what the hell. I guess Deb's right; you can't judge a book by it's cover. Besides, this is a hell of a lot better than standing around in the dark, getting eaten alive by mosquitoes, waiting for some maniac to jump out of the woods and rape me.*

The warning bells fell silent, her heartbeat slowed, and she settled back against the seat. Ahead, a metal sign materialized in the gloom. Anna had time enough to read the reflective lettering:

Welcome To Hevven—Population 15,000.

And then it was gone in a blur.

"You must be one brave girl, Anna."

Anna looked at him uneasily. "P-pardon me?"

"Well, to have walked all that way by yourself...and at night." He glanced at her solemnly. "You know," he went on, "you should be more careful. Don't you watch the news? There're a lot of strange people out there. A lot of strange people."

Thinking back to the footsteps in the forest, Anna felt the blood rush to her face. They were far away from that place now, but she couldn't shake the memory of the terror she had felt.

After a moment, she said, "I have to admit, I was a little scared." She considered telling him about the thing in the forest and the noises she had heard, but quickly changed her mind. He'd probably just chuckle condescendingly, thinking it was all in her imagination. But it wasn't. She really had heard something, hadn't she? Or had her mind been playing tricks on her?

Mr. Moody was smiling—a thin slash of white that glittered in the shadows. "What do you say we listen to some nice, relaxing music? Do you like jazz?" Before Anna could respond, he was already leaning forward to turn the dial on his antiquated car stereo.

The speakers crackled softly with the sound of trumpets and saxophones, while in the background, a drummer ticked away the time with the detached precision of a metronome.

Two minutes passed before either of them spoke again.

At last, Anna swallowed uncomfortably. "I couldn't help but notice that sign back there. It said 'Entering Hevven.' Is that where we're going?"

Outside, the shadows fled from the Buick's headlights, only to return again to swallow the road behind them.

"Tell me, Anna," Mr. Moody whispered in a stony voice. He removed his small, silly glasses, tossed them carelessly into the back of the car. He looked at her with eyes as black as coal. "Do you believe in God?"

Anna was pondering the relevance of that question when a large, cold hand grabbed her by the back of the neck and mashed her face into the edge of the dashboard in one lightning-fast motion, instantly shattering her two front teeth. Something warm and salty exploded in her mouth. Stunned by the impact, several seconds went by before she realized it was her own blood she tasted.

Dimly, she raised her head and saw the man who had called himself Alan Moody staring back at her with glazed, lifeless eyes. He was still driving calmly, with one monstrous hand planted firmly on the steering wheel. In the background, a trumpet wailed with reckless abandon.

Before Anna could scream, his other hand returned and worked its thumb into the soft spot just below her larynx. Gasping through her ruined mouth, she thrashed against him, arms flailing, sandaled

9

feet stampeding against the carpeted floor. At last her long red nails found purchase on the side of his face, and the soft mound of his cheek fell away into her hand in a single, rubbery flap. Through the hollowed-out cavern of his face she saw the deep and delicate reds of striated muscle, the white flash of bone, the receding skeletal grin of something that was not entirely human.

Suddenly, that thing in the forest didn't seem so scary anymore.

~Two~

Scars, thought Rick Hunter as he walked in the shadows of the elmwood trees, *never really heal.*

He wasn't thinking about physical scars, like that pale and shiny line that had already begun to form around the sutures on the soft side of his left wrist. He was thinking about the scars people carry inside. Those kinds of scars, he realized, never stop hurting, never go away.

As the auburn sky slowly draped itself in a rich blanket of night, he stepped from the decayed, sand-washed pavement of Titicut Street and entered a dark and wondrous place known as the Hockomock Forest. Although his mind wandered elsewhere, his feet remembered the way. They led him through briars and ferns, between tall stands of elms and dense groves of evergreens, around rotted tree stumps, and over thick black roots that protruded from the mossy earth like the gnarled hands of corpses grabbing at his feet.

It was mid-July in the uninspiring town of Hevven, Massachusetts, and the evidence was all around him. Birds heckled one another from their leafy hideaways, their songs giving way to the rusty drone of crickets, the thrumming basso profundo of bullfrogs.

A cool breeze mingled the earthy smell of freshly cut lawns with the mouth-watering aroma of backyard barbecues, the sweet and

11

sour fragrance of wild grapes and honeysuckle, the sharp odor of skunk cabbage. If nothing else, the air tasted like summer.

As Titicut Street vanished behind him, seventeen-year-old Rick Hunter faced the biggest—and perhaps, the last—decision of his life. He could rendezvous with his friends, allowing them to offer him the help he so desperately needed, or he could walk back to his house, write another suicide note, and make certain he did the job right this time.

Live or die? Live or die? A tough decision, that.

Reflectively, he glanced down at the fresh gauze bandage that was wrapped around his left wrist. His white flag of surrender. He could not wait to be rid of it. As he slowly worked the fingers on his left hand, a sharp pain coursed down the length of his arm and into his chest. His hand began to spasm. He shuddered weakly, not so much from the pain as the memories it conjured.

The cold kiss of the razorblade. The way the skin had parted, so willingly, in its wake. The vicious, bloody smile of the incision. He had not felt the pain at first, but when it finally came it had rolled over him like a wave, embracing him like an old, dear friend.

He could never forget the way his mother had screamed that night—a shrill, involuntary sound that rose and rose until her voice finally broke—when she discovered him on his bedroom floor, lying in a puddle of blood as eternal darkness beckoned him. Nor could he forget how she, along with his father, had stood on opposite sides of his hospital bed, asking him over and over why he had done such a horrible thing to himself, even though they already knew the answer.

The answer. Oh, God, the answer.

Lori.

Stop that shit, he told himself. *Try to think about something else. Something good. Anything. Like what? I don't know, but make it fast!*

It was too late. The incessant rustling of the branches against his jeans had destroyed his concentration, allowing his mind to return to the very contemplations he'd been trying so hard to avoid. The scales of Life and Death, always unbalanced, always tipping in favor of the latter. From a distant part of his mind, a frightened voice beckoned him to hurry, HURRY! But the boy knew that no matter how much he hurried, he could not escape that which awaited him in the Hockomock.

(Her touch. Her smell. Her smile.)

He could not escape the past.

Over the years, Rick Hunter and his companions had spent countless hours there, in the seemingly endless forest that surrounded their hometown. The woodland was their play-ground, their refuge, and their kingdom. Even now it seemed as though every tree, every stone, every step, held a memory. He felt such great sadness as he pictured them there: A strange collection of scrawny, wild-eyed boys—mere shadows of the men they would inevitably become—hunting bullfrogs and lightning bugs on all those long summer nights, in a time that now seemed about as real as a fairy tale. But those magical times were gone now, gone forever, just like Lori, just like everything else he had once held sacred; gone to that mysterious place where all things must go when young boys become young men, and the past becomes a graveyard full of hopes and dreams.

Yet a part of him truly believed that, in another time and place, they would eventually return to those glory days; and they would remain forever as children; and in their virgin hearts there would always be dreams yet to be realized, dreams that would never come undone. He smiled at the thought. Perhaps he was a fool to believe in such things, but memories themselves were inherently foolish, weren't they? Nothing more than ghosts of the mind...

Just like Lori, sweet Lori.

Rick stopped. He'd arrived at the spongy bank of a stream. Its shallow water tinkled softly, swirling in the afterglow. After a while he was aware of something warm on his face. He touched his cheek, and his fingers came back glistening with tears.

He should have known better than to wander the past.

After his recent hospitalization, during which time he had just barely escaped being institutionalized only by the mercy of the chief surgeon, who just happened to be an old family friend, Rick was no longer consumed by the idea of killing himself. At least, not with the same intensity as a few short weeks ago. But that failed to change the fact that nothing in the world seemed to matter anymore. Well, almost nothing. He still cared about his loved ones, his family and friends. If it hadn't been for them he'd be dead right now, because they were all he had left, all that still mattered to him.

Damn them! he thought, fishing a box of Marlboros and a lighter from the inside pocket of his denim jacket. *Damn them for caring, damn them for worrying, and damn them for being so painfully kind, when God knows I don't deserve any of it!*

Rick lit a cigarette, and his first eager pull made his head swim. Then he looked at the lighter in his hand, the chrome Zippo his friend Kevin Chapman had given him last Christmas. It represented a time that he had, just recently, lost. A time of togetherness and happiness. A time when he had still enjoyed the simple thrill of being alive. As he returned the lighter to its place inside his jacket pocket, Kev's face smiled at him from the faded photo album of his mind.

Amongst the parents of his friends, Kevin Chapman was secretly referred to as The World Class Fuck-Up, which was not to be taken lightly since most of them were actually fond of the boy. Though he was good-hearted, witty, and well-cared for by his mother, he could not escape the shadow of his misspent youth.

Kevin Chapman had started smoking at the age of ten, mostly to impress the older boys who hung out at the bowling alley after school. At twelve, while most kids his age were still playing with their GI Joes, Kevin was discovering the wonderful world of alcohol. By thirteen, he'd already grown bored with alcohol and had moved on to marijuana. Eventually his mother caught on, and sent him away to the Mount Hope Rehabilitation Center in Plymouth. It wasn't the brightest move on her part, but it had seemed like a good idea at the time. It was there that Kevin had met Gino Pepsak, a rat-faced crackhead who sold drugs out of a shitty, roach-infested apartment somewhere on the outskirts of Boston, and who claimed to have the finest marijuana that money could buy. "I got a connection with this guy who grows his shit in Honduras," Pepsak had confided. "Best shit you ever had. Get you stoned in one puff. We can make millions selling this shit, man. Millions! Trust me.

We'll be wiping our asses with $100 bills. Just gimme the word and you're in. Just gimme the word..."

This went on for six weeks or so, at the end of which Kevin had finally given Pepsak the word. It was a decision that would haunt him for the rest of his life.

As it turned out, Kevin Chapman never wiped his ass with a $100 bill, or any other form of legal tender, for that matter. But he did end up with a shitload of weed. And like most young drug dealers, he typically smoked more than he sold. From that point on, Kev was almost always stoned. When he wasn't stoned he was drunk. Usually, he was both. With the possible exception of Max Kendall, whose recent preferences included ecstasy, acid, and cocaine, Kevin Chapman was the worst drug abuser with whom Rick had ever been acquainted.

Unlike Max, however, Kevin never got out of control when he was high. He never yelled profanities or smashed things or started brawls, as Max often did. Kev was no angel, but at least he was civil. He was mellow and quite intelligent, and could probably make it through college if he ever decided to straighten himself out a little.

And apart from his problems, Kevin was Rick's friend, whether he was a World Class Fuck-Up or not.

That Kevin Chapman was careless, however, was an irrefutable fact.

Nearly a month ago, while changing the sheets on her son's bed, Ms. Chapman had stumbled upon the stash of weed Kevin kept hidden under the mattress. As a result, Kevin was given two alternatives. His choices were 1) Get Help, or 2) Find Yourself A Place To Live, Kiddo. It wasn't a tough decision for Kevin, who worked part-time delivering pizza and selling weed (usually at the same time), and who had nothing to show for his labor but the twelve joints his mother had confiscated, a vast collection of Pink Floyd CDs, and one hell of a permanent buzz.

Kevin Chapman, the mellow fellow from Hevven, Massachusetts, had made the obvious choice. He agreed to Get Help...again.

So off he went.

"I miss ya, man," Rick whispered. He had not spoken for several hours, not since Mike Swart had called to invite him out for "some drinks with the boys." If it had been anyone else Rick would have refused the offer, but Mike was his best friend, and he would not take no for an answer. A persistent son of a bitch, that one.

Now Rick wondered what the hell he was doing here. Already he found himself wishing he hadn't answered the phone. Mike just didn't understand—about Lori.

Rick Hunter hadn't realized until after Lori Shawnessy had vanished from his life just how much of himself he'd given to her. He'd fallen in love with her so completely, he often wondered if there was anything left of himself to squander. What little remained of his heart was barely enough to keep the blood flowing through his veins.

Why? Rick asked himself. *Why can't I just get on with this miserable life?*

Because, a voice in his mind replied mockingly, *you loved her while she was alive, and now that she's dead you love her even more!*

He couldn't bear it much longer. Lori had been everything to him. He'd lived his life for her, and her for him. And now she was gone and there wasn't a damn thing he could do, by the godforsaken laws of life and death, that would bring her back into his arms. Nothing. He felt empty and lost. But above all, powerless.

He looked up at the sky. Through the trees he saw the Big Dipper, the Milky Way, and part of Orion's belt. *What's my purpose in this world?* he wondered. *Does my heart beat for a reason, or does it simply beat, unaware of itself, a prisoner of its own design?* After a few moments he looked away. There were no answers there in the heavens, only the ghosts of stars that perished long before mankind had ever thought to give them names.

He took another drag from his cigarette, wondering what might come next, wondering where the night might take him. So many thoughts were rattling around inside his troubled mind that it was hard to grasp a single one.

The stream shimmered in the bruised glow of sunfall as he stared at his own dark reflection, watching himself smoke. He was

16

five feet and eleven inches tall, darkly handsome, with a medium build and a naturally tan complexion. His raven-black hair was parted slightly off-center, with several loose strands tumbling over his dark, conscientious brow. On the stream's mirror-like surface, his mouth was almost invisible. But when he smiled (which was a rare occurrence these days) he looked like a movie star. The female seniors of Hevven High School had even nominated him to appear in the yearbook under the banner of Best Smile, although he had modestly declined the honor. According to the late Lori Shawnessy, however, his best feature was not his smile but his eyes; they were a brilliant blend of hazel and green, thoughtful and kind, wild and intense, strong yet full of compassion.

But now, after the accident, there was something else within those hazel-green eyes, something only he could see. Hatred. He hated himself, and this hatred burned like a fire within him, so hot it felt numbingly cold. He hated himself so badly he could taste it, like bitter ashes in his mouth.

If only there was some way to travel back in time, to the place where his life in Hevven ended and his tailspin into hell began...

It was a chilly April night when Lori Shawnessy, the only girl Rick Hunter had ever truly loved, lost her life to a terrible accident. Two days later, when they lowered her coffin into that dark and hungry hole at the Pleasant Pines Cemetery in Hevven, covering it over with the cold, uncaring earth, a part of Rick was buried with her.

Buried forever.

It had happened just three short months ago, though it seemed more like years to him now, when Rick and his tight-knit company of friends had made their yearly exodus to Sundown Beach for the traditional end-of-the-school-year bash. With the exception of Lou Swart, who was only a freshman, they were all graduating seniors. Their days as students at Hevven High were numbered, and they were determined, like most high school seniors across the country, to go out with a bang.

The party had begun like any other. Hordes of teenagers milling about a keg, drinking foamy beer from clear plastic cups, already fearful for that miserable moment when someone would cry out those dreaded words: "THE KEG IS DRY!" Stereos were blaring. Several bottles of hard liquor were being passed around, and dozens upon dozens of partygoers were staggering about, talking their usual drunk-talk.

Although the scenario was a familiar one there was something unique, something almost enchanting in the air that night. Perhaps they all knew, in the back of their minds, that after graduation day things would never really be the same again. Perhaps, in some strange, secret way, they had already begun to miss one another.

By nine o'clock, a few juvenile pyromaniacs had begun to set fires against the night. The seven friends—Rick Hunter, Lori Shawnessy, Max Kendall, Mike and Lou Swart, Karen Sloan, and Kevin Chapman—were swilling beers by firelight, telling each other tall, tall tales, and talking about the years to come. They spoke of the things only close friends could share: hot-red sports cars and mansions by the sea, tropical islands and golden sunsets, memories and dreams. And always, in these visions, they were together. Always together. Friends forever.

They had believed they were immortal, and nothing could have convinced them otherwise. Nothing, that was, save for the horror of the following day, which would shatter those beliefs, and alter their lives, forever.

The night moved on.

Soon, ten o'clock floated in like a misty dream.

Lou Swart, having had one too many mixed drinks, was reviving his most recent meal (a Whopper Junior and a large order of French fries, as he would laughingly confess on the way home) in the privacy of the duneland.

Mike Swart and Karen Sloan, with whom Mike had been going steady for almost two years, were also in the company of the cool, dark sand dunes, and if anyone had been sober enough to notice they were missing (which, of course, no one was) they would have known better than to disturb the two lovers.

Meanwhile, Max Kendall and Kevin Chapman, along with several others, were sitting around a large bonfire, passing around their Funny Cigarettes, whooping it up like a pack of hyenas. They were trying to sing an Ozzy Osbourne tune, but not one of them could remember the second verse, and so they repeated the chorus over and over:

"I'M GOIN' OFF THE RAILS ON A CRAZY TRAAAAIIN...GOIN' OFF THE RAILS ON A CRAZY TRAAIIIN..."

Rick and Lori were mingling with their classmates, discussing old times, both properly drunk for the occasion. Every now and then they would step away from the party and return to the dunes to check on Lou. On their third trip they finally coaxed the boy into returning to Mike's car, where he quietly slept off the rest of the night.

Eleven o'clock fell in a New York minute.

That was when the argument had started.

Lori, who was tired, drunk, and extremely unreasonable, suddenly remembered her twelve o'clock curfew. Afraid of being late, and even more afraid of what her mother and father would do if they found out she'd been drinking, she insisted it was time to make like a tree and leave.

Rick was drunk, not stupid. He knew they were in no condition to drive. He assured her they would leave just as soon as the both of them had sobered up a bit. They had been dating one another exclusively for eight months, and they had never even come close to having an argument. He never saw it coming.

Staring at his reflection on the pond, Rick couldn't recall how their discussion had become heated so quickly. Nor could he remember who raised whose voice first, or how long the whole thing lasted. In the end those things didn't matter, anyway. What he did remember, perhaps too well, was how the argument had ended.

"Asshole," Lori had muttered under her breath. There it was, the A-bomb. Her clear brown eyes looked glazed and bloodshot behind the long blonde curls of her hair. At that precise moment the discussion was severed, with such neatness it had stunned him, with that one sharp word:

Asshole!

Rick could hardly believe his ears. *Did she just say what I think she said?* he'd wondered. Not Lori; she never spoke that way.

19

Meanwhile, down by the water, Max Kendall and the Potheads were still performing a wasted rendition of *Crazy Train*.

Several yards away, where the cars were parked on the edge of the sand, a stereo was pumping out a hip-hop tune that had inspired a dozen or more people to start dancing by firelight. Between these sounds there were muffled conversations, drunken cheers, and crazed, unbridled laughter. In the distance, someone was doing a keg-stand.

Amidst the cacophony of the party no one heard Lori's final words, save for Rick. Nobody would ever know how she had left him. That painful memory was his and his alone.

With sparks shooting from her eyes, Lori stared at him for several seconds, as if daring him to reply. Then she turned and walked away, as if none of it really mattered anyway. She had not looked back.

It tore him up to remember her that way. It wasn't like Lori to act belligerent (he'd only heard her swear on one occasion, and that was when she'd found out she was getting a C instead of a B in Calculus). It was the alcohol talking, of course. Not her. He could not blame her. Even now, two months later and just a razor's edge away from suicide, he could not blame her.

At any other time he would have swallowed his pride and followed her, but after watching her disappear into a nearby crowd, he eventually wandered back into the party. It was their big night, their Big Senior Bash, and it had seemed so damn important at the time.

About an hour later, as he neared the twilight of sobriety, Rick began to search the party for his estranged girlfriend. After grilling a few of his classmates, he arrived at the conclusion that Lori had found someone to drive her home, because her mother's car was gone and no one had seen her for a long time. This conclusion seemed only logical to Rick, since she'd been so concerned about making her curfew. The fact that she had bailed without telling him made him angry, but he trusted her judgment. She was a good girl. A smart girl. She wouldn't have taken a ride with someone she didn't trust.

In an effort to cheer him up, Max conned him into drinking a few more beers...then a few more shots. Before Rick knew it, the night was over, and the first pink fingers of dawn were reaching out across the ocean.

The next and last thing Rick remembered was squeezing into the back of Kevin Chapman's mother's caravan with a bunch of kids who reeked of marijuana. He'd already forgotten about the argument, and his only sensible thought—his only thought at all—was to try and get home before his Dad woke up to go to work.

Rick could not remember the ride home, or how he had managed to find his way into his bedroom, but that was where he found himself next. He was still sleeping when the phone rang, and still half-asleep when he answered it.

"The-there wuh-was an accident, Ri-Rick!" a shrill, hysterical voice wailed into his ear. "MY BABY! OH, GOD, MY BAYBEEEE!"

The sheer volume of the voice shocked him awake, and he sprang from his bed in a panic. Standing in the middle of his room with the phone pressed to his ear, he could not remember how he'd gotten there. He was fully clothed, had a mouth that tasted as if he had eaten a bar of soap, and his room was spinning around him like a Tilt-A-Whirl from hell.

Something bad had happened the night before, but he had only the vaguest sense as to what that might have been. He only knew that it had to do with Lori, and that thought made him nervous because he had a peculiar feeling that she was mad at him for some reason.

Then he remembered why he had awoken. The telephone...he had answered the telephone, and he was still holding it in his hand. He held the receiver away from his ear and looked at it in horror, as if it were some repulsive little creature that had somehow crawled into his hand while he was sleeping. From the other end of the line, a voice continued to sob incoherently. Not just any voice. A familiar voice.

It was Lori Shawnessy's mother.

His knuckles turned white as he clenched the phone, slowly bringing it back to his ear. Mrs. Shawnessy was still rambling on in

21

a voice that was hardly decipherable, though her words would haunt him to the grave. Lori's car was found in Futawam, several miles away from the Hevven/Futawam border, twisted around a telephone pole and, "GAWWWD! OOOHH, GAWWWWD! MY LORIIII!"

was dead. Dead. DEAD.

Remembering that morning, above all else Rick could not forget the pain in Mrs. Shawnessy's voice, or the guilt he'd felt at that moment. In his mind, it was his fault. Lori was dead, and he had let her die. It was at that moment, that painful surreal moment on the phone, when the order and regularity of Rick Hunter's life had vanished like a ghost. It was also at that moment that his life had plunged into a great, dark well of despair and he knew, as well as his loved ones knew, that if he didn't manage to pull himself out in a hurry, he would surely drown.

Now here he was again, standing where he had stood so many times before, searching for the answers to the infinite questions that used to keep him awake at night. But so much had happened since those simple, carefree days, that those questions didn't bother him anymore.

And the answers didn't matter.

~Three~

Mankind's greatest enemy is time, thought Lou Swart, as he waited for his friend, and the night, to arrive. *Because time wants us to suffer.*

At the tender age of fourteen, Lou Swart was no closer to understanding his life (or life itself, for that matter) than he was at the age of ten. The answers he wanted were nowhere to be found. And much to his horror, as he neared fifteen, those answers seemed farther away than ever.

What's the meaning of life? Why do we live? Why do we die? Why was it that Mike and his friends always insisted on treating him like a kid? He was almost fifteen now, damn them, and that was old enough to be treated as an adult, wasn't it? What's the point in going to school, and busting your ass at a job everyday, and getting married, and growing old, when none of it amounts to shit when you die? *Tell me, God*, Lou begged silently. *Tell me: Why?*

Sitting in his gloomy corner, struggling to concentrate on the text of the *Video Game Weekly* magazine that lay open before him, the boy trembled with disgust. Was it possible that he was the only soul on earth who had ever wondered about such things? Lou thought it unlikely, although it certainly appeared that way sometimes. None of his friends seemed too concerned about their roles in the world. They knew who they were. *But who the hell am I?* Lou wondered.

Frustrated, he took a few deep breaths and attempted to return to the article he had been reading, but the dark typeface stared up at him like hieroglyphics, and he suddenly found himself unable to translate a word. Even in the soft glow of the Coleman lantern, which rested on the table in front of him, it was getting too dark outside to see anything but the pictures. Anyway, the cheat codes for Monster Hunter 2 didn't seem all that interesting anymore.

"Just remember, whatever you do, don't say anything that'll remind him of Lori," Mike Swart said from nowhere in his fatherly voice, bending over to pick up a *Hustler* from a stack of magazines on the floor. With a fresh can of beer in one hand and the magazine in the other, he flopped his lean body onto the tattered brown couch, kicked up his feet, and waited for his little brother to respond.

From the small, decrepit table across the room, Lou nodded and shifted uneasily in his chair. He lowered his red, white, and blue New England Patriots hat to conceal his eyes. "I'm not friggin' stupid," he muttered after a time.

Mike sighed, but did not look up. "You know that's not what I meant."

"Whatever. He's my friend, too, you know."

Since the funeral, the Swart brothers and their friends had been reluctant to talk about Lori Shawnessy. Her very name had become something close to a sacred incantation, as if saying it would somehow breathe unholy life into her charred and battered corpse. Lou thought about her often enough, and that bothered him tremendously, to think of her as though she were still alive. But to casually speak her name out loud? Well, that just didn't seem appropriate. Of course, he wouldn't tell Mike how he felt about this. Just as he wouldn't tell anyone how he'd gotten the chills just now, at the mere mention of her name. Because nothing ever really seemed to bother Mike. Nothing at all. Why should anything bother Mike, the patron saint of Hevven High?

Watching Lou squirm in his seat, Mike raised his head and said, "I miss her, too."

Lou blinked and swallowed hard, fighting back tears. Sitting at the table, ankles crossed beneath his chair, he looked even younger than his age. In white Reeboks, a saggy pair of Hilfiger Jeans, and a dark gray Old Navy T-shirt that was much too large for his thin, shapeless frame, he looked incredibly frail and defenseless.

Poor kid, Mike thought, his eyes returning to the magazine. *He's taking this harder than I thought. Maybe I should've had a talk with him, right after the accident, before the funeral. Maybe that would've helped some.*

Watching his older brother through the corners of his eyes, Lou was all too aware of their differences. Lou was five-six, 128 pounds, mostly skin on bones. Mike, who was three years his senior, was one inch shy of six feet, 180 pounds, mostly lean muscle. While Lou still had the blotchy, acne-prone skin of a teenager, Mike's complexion was glowing and smooth, and rarely revealed a blemish of any kind. Lou had cow-licked black hair and shit-brown eyes; Mike's hair was wavy and honey-brown, and his deep-set eyes were a calm, curious gray.

But what it really boiled down to, in Lou's mind, was this: Girls adored his older brother. Mike was good-looking, intelligent, and charismatic (Lou didn't know what that last word meant, but he'd heard somebody say it once, in reference to Mike, and he knew it was probably a good thing.) Of course, it didn't hurt that Mike had been the star quarterback and captain of the Rebels, and had almost single-handedly led them to a victory in the division championship. He had a rocket for an arm, and the accuracy of a laser-guided missile. He could run with the best of them, and pass on the go. But more importantly, he had poise. On the field, his presence had been so strong that the opposing team's fans often found themselves cheering for him. He was a leader. A warrior. A goddamn hero in the pocket.

Mike snapped the tab off his beer, the slender muscles in his chest and arms twitching beneath his plain white T-shirt, and drank greedily. Then he held up the *Hustler* by its dog-eared cover, letting gravity pull the centerfold down, revealing Miss July and all her naked, airbrushed beauty. He whistled softly in admiration.

So much for a pleasant evening, Lou thought bitterly. *I'm too scrawny to play football, too young to buy alcohol, and too ugly to find a girl. And still a virgin,* he reminded himself. *Yes, almost fifteen and still a virgin. Some friggin' life I have!* His eyes began to water. He chewed his lip. He wanted to scream. Eventually, he went to the cooler and grabbed himself a beer.

Mike felt sorry for his little brother. He barely remembered what it was like to be fourteen, to have nothing more serious than girls and pimples to fret over, although he vaguely remembered that girls and clear skin were rather high priorities for that age. Sure. Right up there with expensive sneakers, video games, and an MTV haircut. *Strange*, Mike thought, *how time sneaks by, transforming the present into the past.* Here he was, doing the same thing in the same place—only now he was a high school graduate with the world left to conquer—and where the hell did the years run off to?

The interior of the shack hadn't changed much since they'd last been there, before the accident. A thin layer of dust was the only sign of their neglect. The wooden paneled walls were mostly bare, save for the Budweiser mirror at the foot of the couch and the tri-level shelf above the table, on which there rested an assortment of empty liquor bottles, a candle, a tattered copy of Stephen King's *The Stand*, and an ancient Sears radio. A brown carpet covered the floor; it was dark enough to hide most of Max Kendall's cigarette burns, although it had become almost spaghetti-like along the edges where the threads had come undone. There was even a window, just above the couch. The glass was dirty, the screen was rusted, and it was a bitch to open, but the window allowed some sunlight and fresh air to enter without letting in the bugs. While the shack was far from being a palace by the sea it was their special place, their hangout, their home away from home.

More importantly, it didn't belong to their parents, it didn't belong to their teachers, and it didn't belong to the Hevven Police, who had it in for just about everyone under the age of thirty. And even though the Swart brothers and their friends had stolen the wood from a new construction site on Vernon Street, the finished product was theirs.

They were the ones who had dragged the wood from the site to the forest; they were the ones who had sweated, day in and day out, for nearly a week before it was finished; they were the ones who had hammered their thumbs and stepped on nails and itched with poison ivy for weeks thereafter. Truth be told, they had taken pleasure in every laborious moment, for when all was said and done they had finally found something they could call their own. And regardless of the fact that it reeked of stale beer, cigarettes, and Max's shitty weed, they were damn proud of their accomplishment.

"Where the hell is he?" Lou asked himself out loud, lifting up his Patriots hat in order to scratch his head.

"Huh?" Mike looked up, confused.

"Hunter," Lou sighed, pausing to sip his beer. "Are you sure he's coming?"

"That's what he told me on the phone," Mike answered calmly. "I asked if he wanted a ride, but he said he'd meet us out here instead. He's probably on his way."

"Do you think he'll be okay?" asked Lou. "What if he...you know—"

—*Tries to kill himself?* Lou was going to say, except he could not bring himself to utter those words. It occurred to him that his choice of words would not have been entirely accurate, anyway. The more accurate way of phrasing that question would have been: *What if he tries to kill himself again?*

"I wouldn't worry. Rick's a tough shit. He'll be fine."

A high-pitched silence rang through Lou's ears. The somehow ghastly sound of absolutely nothing happening. Lou thought about *trying not* to think about Lori, staring at the text of *Video Game Weekly* until his vision blurred and his temples throbbed. Mike sipped his beer, leafed through the magazine, and somehow managed to light a cigarette without missing a beat.

They waited as the longest ten minutes in history ticked by.

Time is torturing me, Lou thought. *It toys with us, speeding up when you want it to slow down, stopping when all you want in the world is for it to move a little faster. Time wants us to suffer.*

Lou looked down at the magazine on the table, slapped it shut. "You wanna listen to some music?" he asked. He would have said anything to disturb the stillness, because the stillness was sure as hell disturbing him.

"Sure," Mike murmured, not looking up. "If you can find a decent station."

27

Lou leaned forward, switched on the battered radio, and was greeted by static. Fumbling the dial, he quickly found the local college station. A Pink Floyd song crackled through the speakers. Lou looked across the room to get his brother's approval, and saw that Mike had already begun to tap his foot against the arm of the couch.

Lou turned up the volume, and the shack reverberated with the woeful conversations of electric-acoustic guitars. The name of the song was *Wish You Were Here*; the boys knew it well.

Absently singing along with the radio, Mike grabbed another *Hustler* and began to thumb through it.

Lou slumped back into his chair, watching the dust churn in the rusty sunlight that shone through the open window. Drawn by the soft glow of their lantern, a large moth flitted against the outside screen—once, twice, three times—and spun away into the twilight. Full dark was on its way.

Where the hell is Rick? Lou wondered, and he chased that thought down with the rest of his beer.

~Four~

"Fuckin-A!"

Fuck was—and had always been, for as long as anyone could remember—Maximus Kendall's favorite and most frequently used word.

Max reached a sweaty hand across the cluttered kitchen table, knocking over an empty can of Old Milwaukee, and turned up the volume on the Sony radio that rested on the windowsill. Bobbing his head to the beat of a Limp Bizkit song, he settled back into his chair. Resting his elbows on the table, he began to sprinkle marijuana flakes onto a rolling paper, cursing under his breath, something about the lingering heat. Despite the fact that it was still 70-degrees outside, he was dressed in his usual attire: faded blue jeans, a white Mighty Mighty Bosstones T-shirt with the sleeves cut off, and his trademark black motorcycle jacket.

"Gonna roll myself a fatty," Max rapped, making up his own lyrics for the song. "Yeah! Ba, ba, ba! Gonna get myself to Highville, fuckin' Highville..."

"DRANK MY GODDAMN BOOZE AGAIN!" Paul Kendall's voice boomed.

Oh, shit!

Max jerked his head in time to see the blur of something pass his face, then the room was filled with the sound of breaking glass. The Southern Comfort bottle grazed his nose (Max wouldn't remember this until later, because it had happened so quickly), and shattered

29

against the side of the Sony, which teetered on the edge of the windowsill for a single, agonizing second before gravity took notice and brought it tumbling to the floor. Max glanced down at the sorry-looking radio. The antenna was bent at an impossible angle, broken near the root. White noise drizzled from its speakers. In a rage, he yanked the plug from the wall, and the house went suddenly silent.

Max jumped up from the table, brushing fragments of wet glass from the shoulders of his leather jacket. He reeked of alcohol. His blue eyes flared. When it came to giving the Evil Eye, Max Kendall could make the Devil flinch.

They squared-off like boxers.

"What fuckin' booze?" Max demanded, eyeing his father viciously.

"That!" he screamed, pointing toward the shards of glass that now littered the kitchen from table to floor. As he leaned forward, his stomach spilled out between his boxer shorts and T-shirt.

"Ssss!" Max hissed contemptuously. "You probably drank it yourself, ya goddamn lush."

Of course, that was bullshit. It wasn't Max's fault that Daddy Dearest had passed out early last night, leaving his bottle of Southern Comfort unattended. If there was one thing Max had learned from his father, it was finder's keepers, loser's weepers.

"Besides," Max continued, "you stole two joints outta my room last week, didn'tcha?"

His father smiled boyishly. A sliver of drool hung precariously from his bottom lip. He shrugged, revealing his yellow, sweat-stained armpits. After a few seconds, he wiped away the drool with the back of one hand.

"Yeah," Max muttered, "that's what I thought."

"Ahh ken do anythin I wannoo, you undershtand?" Paul Kendall slurred in his own defense. He tapped a thumb against his chest, greasy gray hair tumbling down over his eyes. "Dish is my gatdam house. Yer livin' under my woof. And gat knowsh you don't pay no gatdam went."

"You want rent? Here's your fuckin' rent." Max flung the joint at his father, who wasn't in any condition to play catch. Paul could

30

only blink in dismay as the joint bounced off his beer belly and landed soundlessly upon the threadbare carpet. Max laughed and headed for the door, followed by his father's sunken, hateful stare.

"Wunna deesh dayz, Mash, I'm gone show ya hooz da bosh around heah!" Paul slurred after him, using a coffee table to balance himself as he bent over to pick the joint up off the floor. "I'm shtill ya fadda. I'll teachya to tweat me wit reeshpect."

Max gave him the finger over one shoulder, kicked open the screen door, and stepped out onto the porch. He walked a half mile or so down the street, hoping to hitch a ride. After a few unsuccessful attempts, he walked back to the porch and sat down on the stairs. It was quiet inside. No more radio. No more Limp Bizkit. Shit.

Max sighed as he lit himself a cigarette. He reached into the inside pocket of his leather jacket and removed a bag of marijuana, a bag of pills that looked like M&Ms, and a pack of Extra Wide rolling papers. The pills he'd save for later. What he needed right now was something to help him relax, to chill, and the weed would do just fine. Using one knee as a work table, he skillfully rolled another fatty.

"Fuck you, Dad, you fuckin' prick. Steal my fuckin' weed."

When he was finished, he flicked away his half-smoked cigarette and put the rest of his supplies back in his pocket. Then he lit the joint, took a deep hit, and held it in, relishing the burning in his lungs. A few seconds later he exhaled a small cloud, watched the smoke pour from his mouth.

Someday I'm gonna leave this place, he thought, looking up at the starry sky. He smiled dreamily. Kevin had hooked him up with some extra-good shit this time. Max was already feeling the tingle. It was too bad what had happened to Kev—but no, Max didn't want to think about that right now.

Closing his eyes, he went in for another pull, imagining what it would be like to be a bird, to soar high above his house, over the trees, and far, far away. As he held the smoke in his lungs a funny thought occurred to him, and he couldn't help but laugh out loud. He envisioned himself as a giant bird with a bad case of the runs, dive-bombing his father with reckless abandon.

31

"Bombs-awaaaay!" Max snorted, coughing out a mouthful of smoke. The image of his father's shit-shined face was almost too much to handle. He made a farting sound with his tongue against the inside of his cheek, and began to laugh hysterically. Unlike Kevin Chapman, whose own mother had forced him into rehab, nobody could stop Max Kendall from getting to Highville.

~Five~

As the last rays of sunlight drained from the forest Rick gathered up his thoughts and started, once again, toward the shack. Lighting another cigarette, he continued down the narrow path, remembering the countless nights he'd walked alone, with hopeful eyes turned skyward, wasting his breath on wishes that would never come true.

Eventually, he arrived at the odd-looking structure. Standing outside the doorway of the shack, staring at the weathered shell of his favorite childhood sanctuary, he realized for the first time just how small the place really was; not to mention, unattractive. Did it only seem that way because he was older now, and more mature? Or perhaps he had finally opened his eyes to the truth: That his suicide had been successful, and he was dead and alone and living in Purgatory.

Suddenly he realized he'd forgotten to look for Mike's car on the way into the forest. Then a sound pricked his ears and he listened. The low hum of music was coming from inside, and he knew the Swart brothers were already there. They were probably on their way to getting shitfaced, and he would join them soon. But not yet.

Several more minutes passed as he stood outside the shack, remembering all that had happened since that sweltering summer day when they had pieced it together, like the world's ugliest jigsaw puzzle, so many lifetimes ago. They were in Junior High then; still young, still somewhat innocent. *Summers seemed to last forever in those days*, Rick reflected sadly. *Mick Jagger was wrong: Time was never on our side.*

He looked at the door. He didn't want to think anymore—about anything. He yanked on the handle, the door flew open, and he quickly stepped inside.

"Jeezus!" Lou hissed, almost tipping over on his chair. He clapped one hand over his heart. "Dude! You just scared the crap outta me!"

"Sorry 'bout that," Rick said, closing the door behind him. He'd only been there for two seconds, and already he felt awkward, as though he was no longer welcome here. He'd never thought he'd feel that way, not here; not with Lou, who was practically his younger brother, and especially not with Mike, who had been his best friend since kindergarten. But despite the familiar faces and familiar walls, he felt himself a stranger in this place.

"Took you long enough," Mike said from the couch, and his eyes found Rick's bandaged wrist in an instant, all too visible below the left cuff of his beat denim jacket. He tossed the *Hustler* onto the floor, where it landed with the rest of the magazines. Sipping his beer, he watched Rick as he closed the door. It had been a long time since the three of them had all been together. *Too damned long*, thought Mike.

"I lost track of time," Rick lied. The truth was he'd spent the past two hours in his bedroom, watching the shadows darken the walls, trying to decide whether or not he was ready to face his friends, let alone the rest of the world.

"How're you doing, man?" Lou asked, studying the bandage on Rick's forearm. He couldn't help but notice the dark blotches where the blood had soaked through. As hard as he tried, he could not look at Rick without looking at the bandage. His eyes were drawn to it like moths to a flame. After a few seconds, Lou held out his hand expectantly.

Rick slapped him five and took a seat at the opposite end of the table, aware that all eyes, including his own, were now focused on his bandaged wrist. Had he thought that his friends wouldn't notice? Yeah, right. They were teenagers. They noticed everything.

Rick studied the place, absently scratching the bandaged wound. Feeling the urge to be doing something, anything, he reached into the cooler and removed two ice-cold beers. He put one down on the table and the other hissed as he lifted off the tab. *There's no point in being sober*, he assured himself. He tilted back his head and drank.

"Where's Maxi-Pad tonight?" he asked after a few seconds.

"We're supposed to be pickin' him up in about ten minutes," Mike said, and found himself glancing at his watch for what seemed like the hundredth time that evening.

Rick nodded and drank some more. He drummed his fingers on the table. Lou was spying on him from behind his magazine. He looked as though he thought Rick might whip out a gun and blow himself away at any moment. Rick stared at his beer can, pretending not to notice.

"Well," Mike said, finishing his beer, "Whattaya say we ditch this place?"

Lou jumped up from the table. "What're we doin' tonight?" he asked. He loved hanging out with the older kids, especially when they went to places where they'd all be seen together, like the mall, the movies, or an upperclassmen party. It made the other freshmen think he was the coolest. Well, okay, maybe not the coolest. But certainly they thought he was some degree of cool. Maybe semi-cool? Well, even that was better than nothing, he supposed.

"Dunno," Mike said, dipping his hand into the cooler. He snatched another beer. "Could call a few people. Maybe Maxi-Pad knows if there're any parties going on tonight."

"What's he been up to, anyway?" Rick asked, raising one eyebrow. What he actually meant was: Has Max done anything stupid lately?

"Did you hear what that jerk did?" Lou asked, confirming Rick's suspicions. "He told that Jenny Wallace chick that I wanna toss her salad. Really! Right in the middle of Donut Hevven! What the hell does that mean, anyway? Toss her salad?"

Mike and Rick looked at each other and chuckled. It was the first time Mike had seen his friend smile in a long, long time.

35

"It's not funny," Lou said, trying to keep a straight face, trying his hardest not to laugh with them. "Now she won't even look at me. She thinks I'm some kinda pervert or somethin'."

That made them chuckle even harder, and this time, Lou couldn't help but to join in the fun. "He's still an ass," Lou insisted with a grin. "Screw you guys."

"Nothing ever changes," Rick said as he rose from the table.

"Thank God for small favors," Mike said, always the optimist. He snatched his red and white varsity football jacket from a hook on the wall. "Let's get going while the night's still young."

Lou turned off the lantern, and the shack settled into darkness. He was the last one out, slamming the door shut behind him as he trotted to catch up to Mike and Rick.

"What's the plan for tonight, anyway?" asked Rick.

"No plan," Mike said. "We could go grab something to eat somewhere. Maybe see if there's any good movies playin'? There's that new Chris Rock movie. Looks pretty funny. Doesn't matter to me. Why, you got any ideas?"

"Pfff...I don't give a shit. Not like anything's ever going on in this lame-ass town of ours, anyway," Rick muttered bitterly as they walked. Finishing his beer, he whipped the empty can into the dark and listened intently as it clunked against a tree and fell to the ground with a hollow metallic thud.

"We'll find something to do," Mike said, and Rick envied his positive attitude.

He's always so certain, Rick thought. *He always seems to know exactly what's going on. But me...I'm always so...confused...and lost. Damn, Mike, I wish I could be more like you.*

The path ended, and they soon arrived at the hidden alcove where Mike had parked his car, a black Ford Thunderbird with chrome wheels, customized ground effects, and a WBCN sticker on the back bumper. In the murky glow of a nearby streetlight, the car looked sleek and mean.

Mike slipped on his varsity jacket and hopped into the driver's seat, unlocking the passenger door for Lou and Rick. Rick took his usual place in the shotgun seat and Lou hopped in the back, where he'd soon be joined by Max. A moment later the engine roared to life and they tore off into the night, leaving the shack with nothing more than dust, darkness, and the echoes of faded memories.

It was the last time the three of them would ever be there again.

Rick searched the glove compartment for an appropriate CD (his choices were Jimi Hendrix, Pink Floyd, Beastie Boys, an assortment of Godsmack, Third Eye Blind, The Offspring, and several others that weren't labeled), and finally settled on Godsmack, because he was in the mood for something loud and aggressive.

The engine purred, the music played, and the night came.

~Six~

Max Kendall was sitting on the crooked front porch of his converted trailer-home on Oak Street, when the black Thunderbird swooped into the earthen driveway and parked beside his father's rust-red pickup. A cigarette dangled from the middle of his mouth, and his head was tilted in such a way that his hair had fallen across his face in tangled strings. He raised his head slowly, almost defiantly, and smiled with the cigarette clenched between his teeth. His eyes gleamed mischievously.

Silence in the Thunderbird. Max was oozing a nasty vibe, and they all felt it. He looked deeply troubled, more so than usual. Maybe it was Lori's death. Or maybe it was the fact that the four boys had lost touch with each other in the weeks that had followed the accident. But whatever it was they saw in Max's face, the three boys sitting in the Thunderbird didn't like it. They glanced at one another uneasily. When Max had that look in his eyes it usually meant trouble—for everyone.

Max Kendall was the type of person who would sucker punch a stranger in the face (or sometimes even an acquaintance, if he was in a particularly shitty mood), just to see what kind of damage his fist could do to an unsuspecting nose. The only reason his friends put up with his bullshit, the only reason he still had any friends at all, was because they shared a common bond: They had all grown up together. They were bound by history. It was that simple. Not to mention, Max was a good person to have on your side when the odds were stacked against you. He was not as physically strong as Mike or as tough as Rick, but he was fast, real fast, and far more intimidating.

One look at his long arms, broad shoulders, and bluish-gray Don't-Fuck-With-Me eyes, and people nearly twice his size would back down from a confrontation with him. Those who didn't often lived to regret it. Some of them, just barely.

As usual, his long, caramel-colored mane was wet and dirty-looking, and several days' of dark stubble eclipsed the soft pinkish glow of his complexion, which was almost girlish in its natural smoothness. With his long hair, his small, angry mouth, and his eternally pissed-off expression, he looked like someone straight out of a Seattle grunge band.

Tonight his icy blue-gray eyes actually thawed a few degrees as the familiar vehicle pulled into the driveway, and a dopey smile cracked the hard surface of his face. But that bad vibe remained with him like a shadow.

Max got up from the porch and strutted slowly to the car. From somewhere inside the dilapidated trailer-home behind him came the sound of glass breaking, quickly followed by a loud, painful cry: "AWW, SHHEE-IT!"

It was a familiar scenario. Mr. Kendall was on another of his infamous drinking binges. It was now obvious why Max had looked so down when they pulled into the yard. Max could not afford a car of his own, had no job to speak of, or girlfriend to visit him. His best friend, Kevin Chapman, was still in rehab, and the rest of his friends had gradually lost touch after the funeral.

It was simple, really: The kid was lonely.

"What's up?" Max asked in his harsh, scratchy voice, ignoring his father's drunken cry. He popped his head into Mike's open window. "Rick? Holee shit! How's it goin', man? Long time no see."

"It's goin'," Rick answered with a one-shoulder shrug, and sipped his beer, hoping to end the conversation before it started.

Max bobbed his head unconsciously, the way he always did when he was stoned, as if keeping time with an endless song only he could hear.

"What's up?" Mike asked.

Max's head stopped bobbing. "Oh, just the usual," Max said. "My goddamn dad is wasted. Again. Fucker's in a real shitty mood, too." He took an intense drag from his cigarette and then flung the butt onto his weed-infested lawn. The bobbing resumed, and his long bangs fell forward, covering his glossy eyes. Tilting his head, he raked the hair back from his face with both hands. Max Kendall was too cool to brush his hair; all he needed was his ten-finger comb. He exhaled a small cloud of smoke. "You got any alky-haul?"

Mike nodded and raised an eyebrow. "Got any weed?"

Max didn't answer Mike's question. Not that he had to, really, because the answer was written all over his face, in his bloodshot eyes and goofy grin. The long-haired boy smiled incredulously, opened the car door, and slithered into the back seat.

A minute later, they were back on the road.

"Is this all we got for booze?" Max asked, grabbing a can of beer from the cardboard case that rested on the floor of the back seat.

"Quit yer whinin'," Mike said cheerfully. "You didn't pay for it, did you?"

"Seriously," Max said. "Is this all we got for booze?"

"There's a twelve-pack of Bud bottles and a bottle of vodka in the trunk," Mike said into the rearview mirror, hoping beyond hope that that would be enough to shut his friend up.

"All's I got is a couple of bucks," Max said, opening the can and taking a gulp. "We'll spark a few jibbers and call it even, okay?"

Max had about a million different nicknames for marijuana: hooba, ganja, dubage, dubies, and Caribbean Kazoos were just a few of his favorites. But for now he settled on jibbers.

"Like I have a choice," Mike groaned, unable to conceal his easy grin.

Trees lined the road in huge, shadowy masses, concealing the secrets of the infamous Hockomock Forest where, some 300 years ago, the blood of heroes and villains had been spilled in what historians now referred to as King Phillip's War.

41

"God, I hate him," Max said suddenly. He was talking about his father. It was a touchy subject, one that they avoided as often as they could. "I wish he'd just...aw, man, I'd love to just kill the fucker." There was an uneasy silence. There was little doubt, in any of their minds, that Max meant it.

"Any parties going on tonight?" Lou asked a few seconds later, trying to change the subject.

"Naw, not 'til tomorrow night," Max said, easing up a bit. "It's Thursday, what the fuck do you expect? Thursdays suck. Our chances of getting pussy on a Thursday are like a billion to one."

Mike grinned. "Your chances of getting pussy are always a billion to one."

Max politely responded with his middle finger.

Mike turned a corner onto Roller Coaster Road. The first two houses were dark and dead. The third was a large raised-ranch with one light glowing in an upstairs window, and an outside porch light that shone upon an empty driveway. After that, the nearest house was in Futawam, some three miles away.

There were no other cars in sight. Just a dark and open road, begging to be conquered.

"Think I can do a buck?" Mike asked. They had traveled Roller Coaster Road many times in the past, and they had once reached 95 mph before they were forced to slow down at the area most commonly referred to as "The Bend," an elbow-shaped curve about a mile from the Hevven/Futawam line.

"Fuck, yeah!" Max shouted with newfound vigor, showing the side of himself that they knew best. "Drive like you mean it. Punch it!"

Mike punched it.

"Get me another cold one!" he ordered. Another beer appeared by his right shoulder and he took it. He handed the can of beer to Rick, who opened it and passed it back to him. Mike couldn't afford to lift his eyes from the road.

As the speedometer needle punctured 75 mph, the four friends began to laugh wildly. Mike tapped the PLAY button on his stereo and cranked up the volume until the speakers threatened to blow. Rick chuckled and grinned mysteriously, taking small sips of his

42

beer. Lou held his breath and buckled his seatbelt with trembling hands. Max drummed his hands on the headrest of Rick's seat and bobbed his head to Mike's CD, hair flapping wildly in the wind. They were going to make this a fun Thursday night if it killed them.

Up and over a blunt hill. Their stomachs dropped. Mike drove faster.

85 mph...

No one saw it coming.

Amid the noise and excitement, not one of them noticed the partially concealed cruiser on the side of the road ahead of them.

All at once, the blue and white Punk Catcher came to life in a frenzy of sirens and lights. Mike saw the cruiser in his rearview mirror, and his heart tried to run for the hills. They were speeding, drinking, and (it was safe to assume, with Max on board) probably in possession of more than just marijuana. To put it in Max's own terms: They were fucked.

Officer William Bailey had seen the Thunderbird coming from the moment it had turned the corner, and had clocked it doing 65 mph in a 35 mph zone. And he had watched, with a gleam in his eyes, as the car accelerated past him. And so what if it was just a routine stop? He was only 26, lanky and baby-faced, with a blond crewcut, and he was tired of being called a damn rookie.

Hot diggety damn! he thought, plucking the microphone from its hanger. *My very first car chase! Weeeeee!*

He spoke in a calm voice, trying hard to conceal his eagerness. "Alpha-3 in pursuit of four suspects in a new-model Ford Thunderbird, traveling west on Roller Coaster Road. Color: black. Mass. license plate number 697-VLF. Suspects are white males, approximately 20 years old, driving erratically at a high rate of speed. Copy?"

He was answered by the annoying crackle of static, and realized that his radio wasn't responding again. The last time it had burned out he was breaking up a keg party at the Cherry Street pits. It hadn't really mattered then and he supposed it didn't matter now, except that the Chief would give him hell for taking out a car with a busted radio again. Officer Bailey wondered if the dispatcher had been trying to reach him, and decided it was best not to think about it. He was in pursuit, and he needed to focus.

He could do this on his own. Screw dispatch. Screw the Chief. Rookie or not, these punks were his.

"Piece of shit!" he grunted, slamming the microphone back onto its hanger. Despite his frustration, he couldn't help but smile. He was gaining on them.

"Aww, shit!" Mike said. It occurred to him that maybe he should pull over, but in a split second he decided that the Punk Catcher hadn't been close enough to get his plate number. So instead he sped up, and in his mirror he saw that the cruiser was already starting to fall behind.

"What're you doin'?" Lou whined from the backseat. "Are you crazy? Slow down!"

"I can take 'em," Mike assured them. Then, aloud to himself, "Get off my ass, you fuckin' whore!"

"At the bottom of the next hill there's a dirt road on your left!," Max hollered from the backseat. "Take it!"

"What?"

"Just trust me!"

Mike nodded and put the pedal to the floor, watching as the cruiser in his rear-view mirror became nothing more than a distant, twinkling light. He dimmed his headlights as they raced up and over the hill, foot hovering anxiously over the brake.

"WHERE?" he yelled.

"RIGHT THERE!" Max screamed, pointing his finger over Mike's shoulder.

Barely visible, the mouth of the dirt road appeared out of the darkness. Mike cut the wheel and hit the brakes. The car bounced sideways as the tires searched for solid ground, missing a small grove of saplings by a few bare inches, kicking up clouds of pebbles and sand as it skidded to a halt. Something loud and heavy slammed against the inside of the trunk. Mike braced himself against the wheel with both hands. Rick conked his head on the ceiling and saw stars. Lou's beer foamed over, spraying him in the face, and gushing down onto his lap. Max fell back against the seat with his feet in the air and howled with pure delight.

44

Mike threw the shifter into PARK, cut the headlights, and killed the engine. They watched and waited as the dust settled around them.

The siren grew louder and the lights brighter as Officer William Bailey traveled in pursuit of the black Thunderbird. His boyish face was tight with anger. Now it was more than just a routine stop. Now it was personal. *Those punks*, he thought, *those goddamn punks! What were those bastards thinking, trying to run?* The cruiser bounced on its shocks as it passed up and over the steep hill.

Inside the Thunderbird, muscles tensed. Silent promises were made to God. All at once, it seemed, the four boys collectively held their breath.

A bright flash of red, white and blue came speeding closer, closer, closer. And with one loud whoop, it was gone. The lights disappeared as the cruiser continued toward Futawam, its siren already fading.

A few minutes later, Officer Bailey's moment of glory ended as he realized he had somehow lost the punks. For the second time, he was thankful that his radio had gone dead. It saved him from the humiliation of trying to explain himself to Chief Asshole, who was always so eager to critique the shortcomings of others...and punish them for it. He'd forgotten the plate number during the chase, but that didn't matter now. Even if he remembered it, he wouldn't have reported it to the station dispatcher. But he'd remember that car, all right.

The little bastards were safe for now, but there would always be next time. No, he would not forget that car.

Officer William Bailey, a.k.a. The Rookie, crossed over into Futawam's backroads and quickly made his way back toward the center of Hevven, hoping to exchange his patrol car before anyone noticed his radio was dead. After that, he decided he would head downtown to grab a coffee, and see if any townies were out raising a ruckus.

"Where the hell did they go?" he muttered to himself. "I was right behind them. I had 'em. I know I had 'em. What the hell kinda engine they got in that thing, anyway?"

Officer Bailey was glad there was no one there to answer him.

~Seven~

The pool told him what to do. Right now, it was telling him to hurry...HURRY!

Somewhere close by, a police siren wailed hysterically into the cool summer night. Judging by the increase in volume it seemed to be moving in his general direction, but he felt there was little need to be alarmed. What business could the police possibly have out here, in the middle of the forest? More than likely the cruiser was on its way toward Hevven center, because that's where the teenagers hung out on summer nights, smoking their tires, laying patches of black rubber in the parking lots of Donut Hevven and Hockomock Farms Plaza, sitting on the beds of jacked-up pickups, cranking up their stereos, looking to brawl with the kids from Futawam High who sometimes came around trying to score some action with the Hevven girls. That's where the trouble usually started, with the high school Punks trying to prove to one another who had the biggest balls. What filth!

Still, the pool was calling him, telling him with mad, static, whispering voices:

(like the sound of a thousand angry wasps)

HURRY! HURRY!

The girl was a heavy one, all dead weight, but he was more than capable of the task at hand. As he lifted the body her head bobbed and her mouth popped open, spilling maggots onto the dusty, bloodstained floor. He held her the way a child holds its favorite doll, at arm's length, with her legs dangling. Though her nakedness excited him, her dumbfounded expression struck him as being rather comical. It was almost life-like, that expression. But there was nothing else life-like about her, he'd made certain of that. Oh, yes! The full swing of his muscular legs, armed with a pair of steel-toed boots, had made certain of that.

He heaved the body up and over one shoulder and began down the hallway, toward the staircase. On his way he heard a soft whispering-whimpering sound coming from one of the other rooms, but he ignored it. *All in due time*, he thought, and continued down the stairs.

Out the door, and he crossed through the dead grass and ducked through a wide hole that he had made in the barbed-wire fence that protected his hiding place, careful that the body didn't catch on the protruding metal twists.

Thorns nipped at his bare forearms, face, and neck, sometimes snagging the limp body that rested on his shoulders, trying to steal her away. Mosquitoes swarmed around him, buzzing in his ears, drinking freely from him. Branches lashed out at him angrily, tearing at his flesh, twisting their malformed fingers in the hair of the corpse. But he ignored these things. Nothing could stop him from what he had to do.

Nothing.

Seemingly out of nowhere, the dark pool of water appeared in a clearing of pines, its surface gleaming in the moonlight. His spine tingled at the sight of it. Muscles working like the gears of some magnificent machine, he hoisted the body above his head and held her there. He breathed calmly through his nose.

It's deeper than it looks, he thought. *Much, much deeper. As soon as I throw her in, she'll be sucked under. Just like the others. Sucked down to that cold dark world beneath the surface, where she'll be still. Where everything is still, and everything is saved.*

He loved how the water seemed to take control of the bodies as he tossed them in, as if cleansing them of their sins. It seemed to devour them, to suck them down out of view for some purpose he could not comprehend. Yet it gave him such pleasure to watch the process. It mesmerized him. He knew it was good, because the voices told him so, and the voices wouldn't lie.

If anything, he would continue to kill just to be witness to that unnatural occurrence, just to feed the pool and keep it...

Happy?

Now that he thought of it, the pool always seemed a bit more pleasant after he fed it. The swirling surface, the smiling, ghostly faces that beckoned him for more offerings, the sweetly seductive voices that promised he could join them soon. *We want more company*, the ghost-voices told him. *Bring us more. The time has come that you will join us soon. Yes, very soon. Here, you will be beautiful. Here, you will be saved.*

The pool spoke to him in voices that only he could hear, voices that were both frightening and soothing at the very same time. Even his reflection looked different on the surface of the water...younger, almost beautiful, like a statue.

The pool told him what to do. It promised him a better life as long as he kept feeding it the bodies. And if that meant he would have to kill again and again, so be it. Killing was one thing he'd always been good at. And he took pleasure in his work.

The pool told him what to do.

(in mad, whispering, waspish voices)

He had to listen, had to obey. Or and he dreaded to think about it—the pool might choose another to take his place. It might even decide that he was a sinner, that he should be killed, that he should be the next to be buried in the tomb of its unfathomable depths. Perhaps, then, the pool would disappear, and never show itself to anyone again.

But he would not let that happen, could not let that happen.

All he had to do was keep sending the bodies down there. As long as he remained obedient, the pool would keep him in its graces. But he had to feed it flesh, had to keep it satisfied. But not just any flesh. The flesh of the damned, the flesh of sinners, those who would taunt him and call him a monster.

He tossed the body like a ragdoll, all 130 pounds of her, watching as the pool claimed its prize. All at once, the voices stopped. He stood with his head down, feeling very pleased with himself, gazing into the hollowed-out eyes of his reflection. On the nervous water, his face was transformed into something that resembled a Picasso painting.

Somewhere faraway now, the sound of the police siren was fading, fading...gone. He'd been right, after all. It was heading toward the center of town.

"Bye, bye, my bad little angel," he whispered in a gravelly voice. As the surface of the pool smoothed over where the body had been, he stood frozen, eyes wide, seemingly hypnotized by his own black reflection on the moonlit water.

He smiled, and his reflection smiled with him.

~Eight~

Max was the first who dared to speak.

"Whew! Shee-it, that was way too close!" he howled, still gripping the headrest of Rick's seat with both hands. He reached over and patted Mike on the shoulder. "Nice drivin', Mikey! You're my fuckin' hero."

"Yeah," Mike said, grinning as he released a sigh. "Thanks."

"Holy," Lou said breathlessly, "shit." He glanced around nervously, and was suddenly aware of something wet between his legs. *I friggin' peed myself!* he realized. The thought terrified him. Then he remembered the beer can in his hand, and smiled with relief. *How embarrassing would that have been?* he wondered uncomfortably. Imagining what the stain would look like, he realized his friends would probably assume the worst, anyway. Just to make sure he said, "Aww, man, I spilled my beer."

"What're we gonna do now?" asked Rick, already sounding bored.

"Let's just lay low for a little while," Mike said.

"Sounds good to me. Pull down the road more," Max said, cracking open another beer. "Just in case that Punk Catcher comes back."

"What's down there, anyway?" Mike asked, flicking on his low beams and starting up the car.

"You guys've never been to the Moody house?" Max sounded genuinely surprised. Mike shook his head. "You're gonna shit when you see this fuckin' place."

The driveway they were on cut a narrow, winding path through the forest. The black Thunderbird bucked on its shocks as its tires dipped in and out of an endless procession of potholes and stones. A few moments later, as the sky reappeared through the dense mesh of foliage, they found themselves looking at the face of a dark and ominous structure.

The Moody house squatted menacingly in the moonlight, its long shadow reaching out to them like an unpleasant welcome mat. Its once-white paint had peeled away, revealing the spongy, timeworn gray of rotten wood. Two long, narrow planks had been nailed over the doorway in the shape of an X; each of the four front windows were also boarded over in that same peculiar way, as if to ward off evil spirits. To Mike, they somehow resembled the eyes of a dead cartoon animal. Except he found them more repulsive than funny.

"Pretty creepy, huh?" Max grinned. He wasn't kidding. The aptly named Moody house looked like something straight out of a 1960s horror movie, back when horror movies were actually scary.

At Max's suggestion, Mike parked his car behind a tall thicket of weeds, as close to the house as they could possibly get, just in case their friendly neighborhood policeman was still looking for them. Mike cut the lights and the engine. As they emptied the car, Max reached back and grabbed a 12-pack of beer from the floor. "C'mon," he said excitedly. "There's a way in around back." He handed the box to Lou. "Make yourself useful, dork."

Lou was about to tell Max to go screw himself, but before he could open his mouth Max was dumping the twelve-pack into his arms. Instead he settled on saying, "What is this place?"

In the moonlight, Max stopped and looked at him somberly. His eyes shined with raw meanness. "It's the doorway to Hell," he whispered without humor.

Lou froze, his shoulders sagging beneath the weight of the 12-pack. "That's not funny."

Two more seconds went by before Max burst out laughing. "Haaa! Man, I had you!" Max cackled. "I had you good. Admit it. The doorway to hell. Aaaaaaah, you're such a little pussy sometimes."

"You're such a dick," Lou muttered beneath his breath.

Max's jaw dropped in surprise. Then he grinned. "I heard that, you fuck-puppet."

"Butt Pirate."

"Anal Avenger."

"Pickle Puffer."

"Cut the shit," Mike said quietly, looking from one boy to the other.

Max and Lou exchanged a silent glance.

"Jeesh," Max said, "I was just havin' a little fun with the kid."

"Cut the shit," Mike repeated. "I mean it."

"Okay, okay." Max began toward the house, and the others followed.

"So," Rick said, "what's the deal with this place?"

"Me and Kevin used to come here a lot," Max told them. "You know, to smoke weed and shit. Especially when my dickhead dad was on my case. We cleaned it up some, but that was, like, five years ago."

Max was leading the way into a giant moonshadow, and the others were stumbling through the thorny underbrush, trying to keep up with him. One by one, they arrived at the rear of the house. The back door consisted of a solid, windowless rectangle with rusted hinges, and a circular hole where the knob used to be. Max stuck his fingers in the doorknob hole, and the hinges cried in pain—an ungodly screeching sound, not unlike fingernails on a chalkboard—as the heavy door came open. Once inside, they continued through what appeared to be a large foyer, which then funneled into a narrow, pitch-black corridor.

"Where the hell are you taking us?" Lou demanded, clutching the heavy 12-pack against his chest. "Is this place even safe? Are there rats? I think I hear rats."

"Wait here," Max told them. The others stopped and watched him dematerialize in the perpetual darkness ahead of them, his footsteps echoing into oblivion.

"What the hell is he doing?" Rick asked.

"Rick?" Lou asked. He squinted his eyes, trying to discern human shapes in the room where he was standing. But the darkness was a shapeless, shifting thing.

"I'm right here," replied Rick. "Hey, Mike, where are you?"

"I'm over here," Mike answered, unable to conceal his displeasure. The air sizzled as something sticky touched his face. "I think I just swallowed a goddamn spiderweb."

As he said this, a speck of light appeared at the opposite end of the corridor. A few seconds later, as the light grew brighter and brighter, Max reappeared holding a thick red candle, whose small flame sent the shadows running.

"C'mon," Max said, grinning like a death's head. "Let's go upstairs. His last word echoed: "stairs...stairs...stairs."

"Alright," Mike sighed, almost reluctantly. "After you."

Max led them to a staircase on the far side of the house, and the others followed the bobbing candle flame as he began his slow ascent.

"This place smells," Lou announced in a disgusted whisper.

Only silence agreed.

When they finally reached the second floor Max continued forward down another corridor, pausing occasionally to let the others catch up with him. Even with the candlelight, it was impossible to see more than a few feet ahead of them. After passing eight or so doorways (Mike counted eight, but he was sure he had missed some), Max eventually stopped at the open doorway of a small square room.

"This is it," he said, when his friends had all caught up with him. He turned and shuffled into the room, where he placed the candle in an empty Campbell's Soup can he found lying on the floor. As his friends gathered around him the room settled into the eerie yellow glow, revealing the contents of its interior.

Broken bottles, faded beer cans, and an assortment of cigarette butts littered the floor, along with a moldy stack of *Playboy* magazines, and what appeared to be wrappers from a McDonald's Happy Meal. There was a water-stained poster of a red Porsche tacked to one wall, and beside it someone had written the words PUSSY PATROL in black spray paint. On the opposite wall, in that same drippy writing, were the cryptic words NIGHTMARES FOREVER.

Lou set the 12-pack down on the floor, and Max tore into it like a wild dog. Popping the tab, he held his beer can up in the air and frowned. "What're ya waitin' for?" he asked the others. "Let's get cocked!"

Mike grinned. More than likely, it was the closest Max would ever come to raising a toast. "I'll drink to that."

Max was already guzzling his beer, the foam running down his chin and neck. When he was finished he wiped his mouth with the back of one hand. Then his crushed, empty can clinked to the floor. "Hey, does anyone got a smoke?"

"What happened to yours?" Rick asked, mildly annoyed.

"I'm runnin' low. 'Sides, I forgot 'em in the car."

"How convenient," Rick said, tossing him a cigarette. "I suppose you need a light?"

"Nope, got my own," Max muttered, using the candle to light his cigarette, cocking his head to one side so as not to burn his long, dangling hair.

"Anyone else want one?" Rick asked, holding up his pack of cigarettes.

"Me," Lou said, raising his hand as an automatic response, and Rick handed him one. Lou put the cigarette between his lips. "Can I borrow your lighter?"

"I'll have one, too," Mike said, and they all looked at him questioningly.

"What?" Mike snapped.

"Tsk-tsk," Max teased. "Now what would Karen say?"

"She won't say anything, dickhead," Mike warned. "Because no one's gonna tell her. Got it?"

"Alright, alright," Max said, raising his hands in submission. "I was only kidding, man. What the fuck? Chill the fuck out."

Side by side they eased their bottoms onto the dusty floor, sitting with their backs against the wall, each drinking and smoking in silence, each searching for some meaningless bit of dialogue. Their run-in with the police was behind them now, though still fresh on their minds. But they were safe for the time being.

Although the night hadn't started off the way he had hoped, Rick was beginning to feel somewhat relaxed. Whether it was the alcohol or a natural feeling, he could not tell, nor did he care. Either way, they were together again (except for Kevin, Lori, and Karen of course) and that's what mattered most to him. He hadn't realized just how much he had missed being with his friends until tonight. And, last but certainly not least, there were still plenty of beers left. In the aftermath of his earlier thoughts, it seemed as though it would be a decent night, after all. Perhaps even a good night. Not that he'd forgotten about Lori, or Kevin, but this was something to take his mind off those things.

"So, where is Karen tonight?" Rick found himself asking.

"Home," Mike answered. "I might swing by and get her later."

"You should bring her to the party tomorrow night," Rick said. He sipped his beer. "Feels like I haven't seen her in a million years."

"Maybe I will," Mike said, nodding in agreement. "I know she'd love to see ya."

"Whose party is it?" Lou asked.

"Amanda Johnson," Max said. He grinned mischievously in the flickering light.

"You gotta be shittin' me!" Lou said. "How come nobody told me about it?" He hadn't spoken much since they'd left the shack; he had been too busy wondering why Rick, whom he had always thought of as a second brother, had tried to take his own life. Now that thought was temporarily swept aside and replaced by an image in his mind: Amanda Johnson! She was sweet, petite, and dirty blonde, with an ass that made his mouth water. And those breasts! So large, so firm, so perfectly perky! There wasn't another girl in Hevven High whose body could compete with Amanda Johnson's. And tomorrow night, he (Lou Swart, freshman virgin) would be at her house, at her party. And what a party it was going to be!

56

"What, do you honestly think she'd go for a scrawny little fuck-puppet like you?" Max sneered. "Hey, Mike, you remember the last party she had? That dress she was wearing? Man, would I like to sink my teeth into that..."

"Yeah," Mike chuckled in mid-sip, cutting him off. He pointed an accusing finger at Max. "I also remember you making out with that fat chick from Futawam. Don't try to deny it. I saw you grabbin' those mud flaps. What was her name, anyway?"

"Bertha Plimpton," Rick chimed in.

"Bertha-fuckin'-Plimpton!" Mike doubled over with laughter. "With a name like that, she was"

"C'mon, don't even bring that shit up," Max pleaded above the laughter, unable to conceal his Cheshire Cat grin. "Besides, she wasn't that fat...was she?"

"Are you kidding me?" Mike chuckled. "You're just lucky we dragged your skinny ass out of there before she used you for a dildo."

They all burst out laughing, including Lou, who hadn't even been there at the time, and didn't have the slightest idea what his friends were talking about. Max buried his face in his hands in a pantomime of shame.

Unfortunately, the moment was short-lived.

"I got accepted to UMASS," Mike interrupted, quickly following his announcement with a swig of beer. Just like that, their laughter evaporated.

They looked at him, speechless.

Mike had expected this reaction. "I'll be leaving in September. My parents are gonna pay for an apartment, until I can find a job or somethin'. There's a chance I'll even get a football scholarship. Just thought you guys should be the first to know."

"Congratulations, man," Rick said in a somber voice, wishing that Mike hadn't brought up THE FUTURE. If anything, he'd rather talk about Amanda Johnson, or even Bertha Plimpton. Anything but college. He couldn't bear the thought of them losing one another. THE FUTURE—one lousy fucking joke that he wanted no part of, because he didn't get the punchline, and he doubted very much that there was one, and because sometimes he felt like he was the only one not laughing.

Rick had received letters from two local colleges—Bridgewater and Stonehill—and had promptly transferred each of the two unopened envelopes from his mailbox to the trash. After losing Lori, higher education was the last thing on his mind.

"Yeah," Max muttered, shaking Mike's hand. "Congrats, dude."

For the next few minutes they drank their beers in silence.

"Are we gonna jet soon?" Lou asked finally. He didn't care for the company of the old house. Not one bit. It felt unnatural. The feeling he had, trespassing here, brought his mind to a horrible place. The sounds of the creatures outside (which he didn't think anyone but himself had noticed) were growing louder by the second, causing the fine hairs on the back of his neck to stand on end. His young mind was conjuring thoughts of slimy, bloodsucking swamp creatures; creatures that would take a great deal of pleasure in devouring a handful of human boys. Never in a million years would he talk of such things (his friends would surely make fun of him if he did), but his imagination escaped him nonetheless.

"In a couple of minutes," Mike said. "After I finish the rest of this beer. What's your hurry, anyway?"

"I thought we were gonna smoke," Max whined. "I wanna get roasted-toasted."

In Max vernacular, roasted meant getting high. Roasted-toasted, on the other hand, meant getting stoned beyond belief. Max usually opted for the latter.

"We are smoking," Lou stated in a puzzled voice. He raised his cigarette and considered it in the candlelight.

"Der, ya little retard. I'm talkin' about a joint, shithead."

"Oh." Lou lowered his cigarette, took two short drags, and deposited the butt into an empty beer can.

"Don't worry, we'll spark," Mike said. "But not right now. Later, when we know that cop ain't out there waitin' for us. The last thing I need is to get busted for possession and lose my friggin' license."

Lou got up and began to pace the room. "Hey, guys, I gotta take a wizz. Where's the bathroom in this place?"

"There's a room at the end of the hall," Max said, thumbing the direction.

Lou nodded and started for the door.

As an afterthought, Max sang after him, "WATCH OUT FOR THAT LITTLE DINKY OF YOURS! THE ROACHES MIGHT WANT A SNACK!"

Lou shook his head, grinning in spite of himself, as Max's laughter reverberated throughout the dry skeleton of the abandoned house. Lou turned left outside the room, running his hands along the damp walls in search of a door, slowly moving toward the black void where the corridor seemed to disappear. After a few agonizing seconds, his head finally succeeded where his hands had failed.

"Arrghh! What the..." Lou grunted as he collided with the heavy door. Instinctively he began to rub his forehead, but he was more agitated than injured. He gave the door an angry shove and it swung inward with a reluctant moan.

Undoing his jeans, he stepped into the room. While Lou relieved himself, listening to the sound of his urine splashing onto the bare wooden floor, his eyes gradually adjusted to the darkness.

At the opposite side of the room, highlighted by shafts of moonlight that flowed between the cracks of the boarded windows, was something that resembled a person sleeping. Lou finished pissing with a contented sigh and, zipping up his pants, started across the room to investigate the object.

Something was definitely there—but what? Most likely an animal. A big one. A dead one. Hopefully a dead one. What if it's not? What if it's rabid?

Lou Swart was about to find out.

Mike tossed his empty beer can on the floor, a sign that he was ready to go. His friends rose with him, eager to return to the car, where the rest of Mike's Godsmack CD was begging to be heard. Max picked up the candle, and the room shifted sideways in the nervous light.

"Where's that brother of yours?" Max asked impatiently. "Prob'ly jerkin' off somewhere."

"Come on," Mike said. "The two of you are driving me up the friggin wall. This is supposed to be a fun night out. Can't you just call a truce?"

"I'm only jokin'. Hey, where you goin'?"

Mike didn't answer him. He stepped into the dark hallway. Rick went next, and Max followed him with the candle.

From somewhere far away, they heard a strangled gagging sound.

Rick stepped up behind Mike. "Sounds like your little brutha's puking."

Mike took a deep breath and sighed through his nostrils.

Rick's observation was met with little concern, and even less surprise. Lucien "Lou" Swart was only fourteen, and they had all had their share of hangovers at that age. They knew the routine. Get him cleaned up, take him to Donut Hevven for a coffee and some greasy food, and he'd be as good as new in no time. Ready to start drinking again within an hour. At the worst he'd wind up crashing in Mike's backseat for the rest of the night, which would probably be the better for him anyway. It wouldn't be the first time, either.

"Good! More beer for us!" Max chuckled.

"Hey, Lou, are you alright down there?" Mike called into the long, dark hallway.

No answer.

Mike released another loud, disgruntled sigh. "Let's go find him."

Max Kendall's chuckles echoed eerily throughout the blackened hallway as they followed the sound of heavy vomiting to the far room. "Whoa, do you smell that?" he asked, pinching his nose between two fingers. "Awwr, who farted?"

"Smells like roadkill," Rick said, and tried to breathe easy. His eyes began to sting. The smell was that strong.

They found Lou standing with his back to them, panting like a dog, balancing himself against a doorjamb with one trembling arm. He was still adding to the large puddle of vomit that littered the floor around him, and it was already beginning to fill the upstairs of the house with a strong, acidic stench.

"One too many, huh?" Max cackled, slapping him on the back. "Yeee-uck! What the fuck did you eat? Looks like dogfood."

Lou closed his wide, glossy eyes and spat onto the floor. He shook his head, tried to speak, could not make a sound.

"Knock it off," Mike said, shoving Max aside.

"Alright, alright," Max muttered. "Let's just get the fuck outta here, okay?"

"Are you alright?" Mike asked his brother.

Lou shook his head, doubling over in agony.

Mike ignored Max's plea. He brushed past Lou, who remained just inside the doorway, trembling like a frightened puppy, and began to move toward the center of the room. He was looking for something. Mike didn't know what he was looking for, but he knew that whatever it was, it had scared the hell out of Lou. He also knew that it was in this room. In the dark.

On the floor beneath a crudely boarded window, where the moonlight trickled and gathered like puddles of Elmer's Glue, lay a large, motionless...thing. Yeah, a thing. In the shadows. He could almost see it clearly now. Mike knew it would only take a few seconds for his eyes to adjust, but in the dark it felt like longer.

He took a few steps closer to the thing, dimly aware that one of the others had followed him. Outside, a cloud passed before the moon. Shadows chased moonbeams across the floor, dancing over the object that now lay directly in front of him, and the moonbeams fled through the window cracks.

God, the darkness.

Mike stopped, then shuffled forward, slowly, blindly, trying to feel his way through the void.

A few seconds later, the moonlight returned, squeezing through the cracks of the boarded window, and reached out across the floor, as if meaning to touch the thing at Mike's feet, the thing he had almost stepped on in the darkness, caressing it with long, ghostly fingers.

It was then that Mike saw it, though he could hardly believe it...at his feet, he had almost stumbled over it...a young girl lying naked on her back, not moving, not breathing, eyes wide open,

61

pleading...flies buzzing on and around her. And dear God that smell!

Death.

She hadn't died pretty. Her face was a cruel caricature of her suffering: bruised cheeks, swollen lips, and broken teeth, her mouth open, forever frozen in a final, silent scream. Reflecting moonlight, her eyes, wide and unblinking, stared up at the ceiling. Stared at a world she could no longer see. Stared at nothing.

Stared at him.

Her head lolled at an unnatural angle from her body. Her neck had been broken and partially severed, the flesh peeled back like the skin of a rotten fruit, exposing her insides. Her long chestnut hair was a tangled nest of flesh and debris. Bloodstains covered her pale, naked body, like splatters of black paint. Her breasts, as with the rest of her body, had taken on a soft, bloated look: the nipples were shriveled and dark, a cold-looking, bluish-purple color that reminded Mike of a really bad bruise he'd once gotten while playing football. The fingertips on her left hand were jaggedly torn, where small protrusions that looked like splinters of pink wood found their way out of her flesh. No, not splinters. Bones. The bones of her fingers.

Life had vacated her body like a married man vacating a sleazy motel in the dead of night, leaving her to the mercy of maggots, flies, and decay. And as Mike stared down at the bloated corpse, it suddenly occurred to him that she was more than just a body. She was the remains of a person, a human being. A girl whose parents probably loved her, and missed her. Parents who didn't know their little girl had become food for the flies in the grimy room of an abandoned house. Parents who were probably wondering, at that very moment, where their daughter might be. Parents who were probably praying that their little girl would come home safely. Though Mike was certain he had never seen her before, she might have lived in Futawam, the next town over from Hevven, and possibly attended high school there. Maybe she even had a boyfriend. A boyfriend who would also miss her, who might even love her. Friends who would miss her, too.

She was more than just flesh and blood and bone. She was a
human vessel that had once contained a spirit, a soul, a life, before
some sick bastard had robbed her of these things.

Okay, Mike thought hysterically, *I can wake up now.*

But he didn't. He couldn't.

Because he wasn't sleeping, wasn't dreaming.

It was real.

While Mike and Rick stood inside the room, trying to cope with
the reality of what they were seeing, Max was standing at the
doorway, bombarding Lou with questions he could not answer. Lou
stared into space with a blank expression, unable to utter a coherent
word. He looked as though he wasn't even aware of Max's presence.
As Max would later say, Lou was acting like a fuckin' vegetable. It
wasn't that Lou didn't hear him; Max was far too annoying to ignore.
Lou wanted to answer, he truly did, but he simply couldn't find the
words. All he could think of was the body, the butchered, hacked
body he'd discovered in the room.

What the hell kinda nightmare is this? Lou wondered. Then a
name flashed in his mind: The Hevven Hacker! Could that be
possible? No. That was just an urban legend, wasn't it? But what
about all those missing people? All those missing girls...the
newspapers said they were runaways, but...

Maybe it was a monster, a terrified voice came forward in Lou's
mind. *No*, he reasoned. *There's no such thing as monsters. That's
baby stuff! What the heck are you thinking? There's no such thing
as...*

Monsters? But what kind of man could commit such a murder?
Shuddering, Lou spat the stinging taste of vomit from his mouth.
His stomach burned from the inside out. His eyes watered.

"Shit!" Max said. "Answer me, you dick!"

Lou barely noticed him.

Mike turned away from the corpse, unable to look at it any
longer, and wasn't surprised to see that Rick was standing behind
him. Blinking slowly, Rick looked up from the body, and deep into
Mike's eyes. After a moment, he looked down once again. But
Mike would not forget what he saw in Rick's eyes. And it scared
him. The rage!

63

"C'mon," Mike murmured, and began for the door. After a moment, Rick followed him.

Max was holding the collar of his shirt over his nose. He took two steps toward them, eyes shifting from Mike to Rick, from Rick to Mike. "What's going on?" he asked in a muffled voice. "It smells like shit in here."

"We're gettin' the fuck outta here," Mike commanded in a shaky voice. "Right now!"

The vegetable nodded in agreement, beads of sweat rolling down from his hairline. He spat again, hands clenching his stomach. He moaned.

"What the fuck?" Max growled, angered by the thought that there was something the others weren't telling him. He turned and waved the candle at Lou, trying to provoke a response from the mute boy. "Will someone please explain to me why this kid's actin' like a fuckin' vegetable? What's in there, a dead animal or somethin'? I ain't no pussy like the Vegetable Man over there. I can take it."

Mike's eyes flared with sudden anger, partly because he was sick and tired of Max giving his little brother shit all the time, but mostly because he was terrified. "You don't understand. We gotta get outta here. Right now!"

"What the f—" Before Max Kendall could finish, Mike Swart grabbed two fistfuls of his leather jacket and pinned him to the wall like a decoration. Max's eyes bulged, stunningly blue in the candlelight. For the first time that evening he looked very, very sober.

"Right now!" Mike said through clenched teeth, as if talking to a disobedient dog, resisting every urge to punch Max in his square, stubbly jaw. "We'll talk later. Now put out the fuckin' candle."

For a moment, as the shadows toyed with Max's already-stoned mind, Mike didn't look like Mike anymore.

He looked like a monster.

Even Max could see the insanity of arguing. He winced a little and raised his hands in the air, as if to say: Okay, okay, I'm cool now. Mike held him that way for a little longer, until he was certain that Max understood who was in charge. Then, slowly, Mike released his grip, and his twisted, maddened face returned to normal. The anger left his eyes. The monster was gone. He was Mike Swart once again.

Max pinched the wick, and the flame sizzled out beneath his fingers. The smell of smoke and wax mingled with the smell of (flies and maggots and decay) the dead girl, as the boys emptied into the hallway.

Lou was the first to reach the top of the staircase, with such speed that the others had to jog to keep up. They were about to head downstairs when Rick stopped suddenly, blocking Mike's path.

"What is it?" Mike asked.

Rick raised his hand to silence him, but in the darkness Mike couldn't see it.

"What is it?" Mike repeated.

Max and Lou had paused on the stairs. "Come on!" Max insisted quietly, desperately.

"Shhh," Rick said in a low voice. "I thought I heard something."

"It's nothing," Max said. "Probably just the wind or somethin'. Come on!"

Rick lit the Zippo, and in the dancing light they could see the fear spreading across his face as his eyes scanned the shadows. To the left of them there was another corridor. The sound seemed to be coming from somewhere down there.

"Hold on," Mike said. "He's right. I hear it, too."

"You heard it, too?" Rick asked somberly.

Mike nodded. "You stay there with Lou," he said. "Rick and I are gonna go check it out."

Max nodded and looked over at Lou, who was hanging onto the railing for dear life.

Mike tapped Rick on the shoulder and the two boys started off down the shadowy corridor. They followed the sound for what seemed like an eternity before they came upon yet another corridor, which seemed to run adjacent to the one they had just left. Whatever it was they had heard, it was getting louder with each step.

"What is that?" Mike asked in a barely audible voice.

65

"Dunno."

At the end of the corridor they arrived at a closed door. Rick gave Mike a morbid smile as he pocketed the Zippo. In the darkness, they listened.

"It sounds like..." Someone praying, Mike was going to say, but he didn't have to. They could both hear it clearly now: A soft feather of a voice, reciting the Hail Mary in a fast-forward whisper.

Rick rested his hand on the cold brass doorknob. "I'm gonna open it."

"Great," Mike whispered flatly.

Rick turned the knob and pushed the door open a crack.

"...blessedartthouamongstwomen,blessedisthe fruitofthywombjesus..."

Rick opened the door a little more, the sound becoming louder.

"...holymarymotherofgod..."

The two friends entered the room, Rick in front and Mike following closely behind him.

"...prayforoursinnersnow—"

The prayer ended abruptly.

Rick pulled out his Zippo and struck a flame.

Before his eyes could adjust to the sudden burst of light, a phantom face lunged at him from the shadows. It shrieked into his face, a single high-pitched noise that made his blood run cold...and then it was gone, back to the shadows from which it came.

Rick dropped the Zippo. His lungs stopped working. His heart stopped beating. Every nerve in his body was a live wire. He stumbled backward, collided with Mike, and the two boys tripped over one another and toppled to the floor.

"What the fuck was that thing?" Mike yelled.

As they scrambled to get back on their feet, the praying began once more.

"...andatthehourofourdeathamen. Hailmary..."

Rick felt around on the floor and found his Zippo. He struck another flame and waved the lighter through the air. Then he saw her.

She was naked and kneeling on the hardwood floor, ankles and wrists shackled to a thick chain which hung from a loop on the ceiling. Her head was bowed toward the opposite wall, the thick tendrils of her auburn hair spilling down across her bare shoulders, hands clasped before her, as if begging for forgiveness.

Suddenly, the heat of the Zippo brought Rick to his senses. He quickly handed the lighter to Mike and dashed to the girl's side.

"Shit! God, are you okay?" was all he could muster, his voice sounding distant and not quite his own. The auburn-haired girl kept chanting the Hail Mary in a continuous run-on sentence. Rick lifted her chin. She was about his age, attractive, with drowsy blue eyes, full burgundy lips, and well-defined cheekbones. Her eyes were vacant; they stared right through him.

"It's alright," Rick whispered in his soft, gritty voice. "We're gonna get you outta here." He glanced over his shoulder. "Mike! Give me a hand with these chains!"

Mike gave the chains a rattle, trying to test their strength, and didn't like what he saw. Each link was almost as thick as his pinky finger. He clicked the Zippo shut, and tucked it away inside his back pocket. The shadows returned with a vengeance.

"On the count of three," Mike said breathlessly. In the darkness he groped, found a hold. "We'll both pull at the same time. Put all your weight into it."

"Okay, ready? One, two, three!"

They both pulled, muscles working and straining together. Chunks of plaster tumbled from the ceiling, but the chains held fast.

"Again!" shouted Mike. He started nervously at a sound behind them, and fumbled for the lighter. In its flame he saw Max standing in the doorway with his mouth gaping and his eyes bugging-out. "Get over here and help us!" Mike ordered.

Max ran over and wrapped his hands around the chain. Mike put the lighter away again. In the perfect darkness, the three boys readied themselves.

"On three!" Mike grunted. "One, two, THREE!"

At last the chains crashed down in a spray of dust and sheetrock.

The girl winced at the sound, and continued with her Hail Marys.

"She's not all there, is she?" Max managed between breaths. "What's wrong with her?"

67

"She's in shock," Mike said, remembering the body at the opposite end of the hall. He could not even begin to imagine what kind of horrors this girl had endured in the old house.

Mike ignited the Zippo again, revealing the girl amid a tangle of chains. "How the hell are we gonna get these things off her?" asked Rick. They had succeeded in freeing her from the ceiling, but the shackles on her ankles and wrists remained intact.

"We don't really have a choice," Mike said. "We'll have to take them with us."

Rick knelt down and scooped the naked, babbling girl into his arms. Thankfully, she stopped in the middle of her prayer and wrapped her arms loosely around his neck. "Somebody grab these chains," he ordered.

Mike doused the light, tossed the heavy chains over one shoulder, and followed Rick out of the room. With Max shouting directions from the rear they worked their way back through the labyrinth of rooms and corridors, and found Lou still standing where they had left him. Upon seeing his friends he turned and hobbled down the stairs, his glassy eyes barely registering the naked girl in Rick's arms.

Together they stormed through the choking darkness of the abandoned house, feeling their way like the blind. Several lifetimes later they burst outside and into the starlight, where they continued toward the car.

As they trampled through the tall thickets of yellow grass, Rick stopped suddenly in mid-step. Something was stirring in the forest, near the side of the house. Near them. He wasn't the only one who had heard it.

"Quiet..." Mike whispered.

Behind him, in the darkness, his friends came to a clumsy halt. They were less than 20 feet from the car.

Before anyone could question why they had stopped, Rick pointed to the dark forest and they listened. Branches cracked and snapped beneath the weight of an unseen force. Someone, or something, was out there, in the forest.

There's only one thing worse than the sounds that come from a dark forest, Rick reflected nervously as he strained to listen, and that's when the sounds stop without warning. Something's wrong. Something's very wrong.

No birds. No peepers. No frogs. Everything was still. Then the forest was alive with the ominous cracking and crunching of branches—the unmistakable sound of something big moving through the underbrush, coming closer, closer.

Frantically, Mike motioned for Rick to continue towards the car, but it was already too late.

A hulking figure emerged from the treeline, a shape somehow darker than the darkness itself, and the four boys dropped into the tall grass, Rick with the girl still in his arms, Mike pulling Lou by the collar of his shirt. Lying still, their hearts pounded.

With long strides, the figure treaded ever-closer to their hiding place, moving into the center of the moonlit yard, where his thin white hair seemed to glow with an almost ghostly incandescence. When he was a little more than halfway to the house, he stopped without warning. Wearing dark coveralls, he stood motionless, except for his hands, which opened and closed into large tight fists at his sides. He wore a strangely evil expression; they could see it plainly, even from their distance.

He was grinning like a jack o' lantern, eyes burning with insanity.

Mike was sure whoever it was hadn't seen them, but soon would if they didn't act fast. Fear, like the fear he had felt while looking at the body, clutched him once again. But this time he ignored it. He had to. This time he wasn't looking at a motionless body, he was looking at someone who was alive, someone who was moving. A dangerous looking someone, moving toward them. Mind racing, heart pounding like a fist against the inside of his chest, Mike signaled the others to break for the Thunderbird.

Rick half-carried, half-dragged the naked girl as he followed his friends to the car. Though they were all taken by immense fear and excitement (yes, in danger there is always excitement), they were all aware of one thing: Their chance was now, or maybe never.

Rick quickly and quietly opened the passenger side door. With Mike's assistance, he pushed the girl and her chains into the car and slid in after her. On the other side of the car Max and Mike hopped into their respective seats, Max in the back and Mike in the front. *Come on!* thought Rick. *We gotta get the fuck outta Dodge.*

It did not, however, appear that the hulking man had seen them, thanks to the combination of the darkness and the immense tangle of weeds in which they had parked.

Lou brought up the rear, and as he rose to find the safety of his brother's car he felt something slide from the back pocket of his bulky jeans and into the grassy carpet below. Without a second thought he dove into the back seat. Whatever it was he had lost, it didn't matter now. Certainly it wasn't worth dying for.

Mike quickly keyed the ignition and the Thunderbird's engine roared with delight, giving them away. Startled, the white-haired stranger jerked towards them. Mike flicked on the headlights and gunned the gas pedal, skillfully maneuvering between the man and the house, swerving just in time to avoid several piles of junk that had somehow materialized in the darkness. As the headlights flooded the night, shining upon the face of the man—the craggy, emotionless face of a killer—Mike's skin crawled as if he were covered with insects.

What Mike saw was not a man. Sure, it resembled a man; it had two eyes, a nose, a mouth, and hair. It even walked like a man. But its face was not the face of a man; at least, not any man Mike Swart had ever seen. Its face was pale and almost skeletal, with scattered little teeth, and eyes that seemed as bottomless as a black hole.

It was there in the headlights, and then it was gone. Later, when he had more time to think about it, Mike would try and convince himself that what he saw was just his imagination getting the best of him; perhaps even some trick of shadow and light. But deep down inside he knew the impossible truth: He had seen a monster.

A cloud of chewed-up soil arose as they sped across the field, down the old dirt driveway, and onto Roller Coaster Road once again.

~Nine~

"You gotta be fuckin' shittin' me!" screamed Max, when they reached the beginning of Vernon Street. He punched the back of Mike's seat. "We are sooo ffffucked!"

"I'm s-sorry," Lou said.

Panicked by the sudden outburst, the naked girl whimpered and tightened her arms around Rick's waist. He stroked her greasy auburn hair, but nothing he said or did seemed to soothe her. He turned his head to Mike. "We gotta get this girl to a hospital," he said.

"I know," Mike said, throwing him an uneasy look. *But first things first*, he thought. He glanced up at the rearview mirror and found his little brother staring back at him with petrified eyes. "Lou, listen to me. Are you absolutely sure you had your wallet on you?"

"Yeah," Lou mumbled solemnly, his lips quivering. "I'm p-p-positive." He couldn't stop trembling, but he didn't care. For all he knew, his friends were trembling, too. It was too dark to tell for certain.

"You had your school ID in there, didn't ya?" It was Max again, his voice high and accusing, his lips frozen in a snarl.

Lou made a half-strangled sob. "Oh, sh-shit. Yeah, I had e-everything in th-there. Name, address, ph-phone number. Everything."

"Fuck!" Max droned.

71

"Don't worry about that now," Mike said. "We're goin' to my house, calling an ambulance for her, and then we're callin' the cops. After that, it's out of our hands."

"You bet your fuckin' ass I'm worried!" Max yelled. "I can't believe this! I can't fuckin' believe it! And you're telling me not to..." Max stopped himself abruptly, as if some troubling thought had just occurred to him, and in the darkness he squinted his eyes into mean little slits. Then he turned his accusing glare on Lou Swart and said through clenched teeth, "You had my name and address and all that shit in there, too, didn't ya? Didn't ya?"

Moonlight filtered down through the foliage and through the Thunderbird's windows, scanning their faces with horizontal bars of light. One such band now ran up Max's chest, gliding quickly up his neck, then his chin, flickering over his angry little mouth, slowing as it reached his nose, and pausing, it seemed, as it reached his cold blue-gray eyes, as if to emphasize the malevolence of his stare.

Lou saw Max's eyes in the light, and raised his trembling shoulders. "I-I th-think so. S-s-sorry. I-I-I d-d-didn't d-do it on pur-purpose..."

The light was gone in a sudden flash, and Max's face was all darkness again. "Tsss. Thanks a lot, you little fuck. If someone painted a fuckin' stripe on my ass for all the times you were sorry, I'd look like a fuckin' zebra by now."

"Max?" Rick said, turning to face him, his eyes wild and void of patience.

"I didn't even get to see the fuckin' body, you little shit!"

"Max!" Rick repeated, louder this time. Max stopped and looked at him questioningly. Seizing Max's attention, Rick leaned over from the front seat, until their faces were almost touching, and Max knew right away that he meant business.

"What?" Max Kendall snapped.

"Shut...the fuck...UP!" Rick growled into his face, and stared him down without blinking until Max looked away.

Max flinched involuntarily, and with a look of shock and anger he leaned back into the shadows, with his hands balled into fists he dared not use. He remained motionless, seething, his eyes gleaming like fragments of blue-gray glass through his long, untamed hair.

Still leaning over the seat, Rick turned his attention to Lou, whose eyes flickered like strobelights as the tears surged down his face. Rick rested his hand on the young boy's tensed-up shoulder and said, "Don'tcha worry, man. It'll be alright. We'll be there soon."

Mike narrowed his eyes and drove a little faster.

The Swart house stood on Sunset Ave, four houses down from the corner of Sunset and Vernon. It was a pleasant white Garrison with black shutters, a horseshoe-shaped driveway, and a small front lawn with neatly manicured hedges. Mike relaxed a little as the familiar street sign appeared in the headlights of his car. Not that he needed a sign. He'd lived his entire life at 52 Sunset Ave, and he could have found his way just as easily without the landmark.

But even from a distance, he could see that there was something different about the old neighborhood. Something terribly wrong.

His driving hand clenched the steering wheel. His other one clenched the armrest. He eased up on the gas pedal, staring through the windshield in disbelief.

Three patrol cars were parked in his driveway, and a fourth was at the curb that bordered his front lawn. Their flashing lights had transformed the front of his house into some kind of crazed impressionist's version of the American flag. Two uniformed officers were standing at the front door, while several others scanned the perimeter in a tangle of flashlight beams. One of them was standing in Mrs. Swart's flower garden, trying to shine his flashlight through the kitchen window.

Panic was unique in the sense that it could be shared. It only took one person to panic, but in situations where more than one person was present, it was oftentimes contagious. Anger, on the other hand, was a deeply personal emotion. Mike could think of a thousand reasons why the police were at his house, none of which gave them the goddamn right to trample his mother's flowers. His anger had rendered him breathless.

"Keep going," Rick said.

His voice somehow cooled Mike's temper. Mike let the T-bird coast by the mouth of Sunset Ave and continued down Vernon

73

Street. When they were a safe distance away, he set his foot on the gas pedal once again. He couldn't see his house anymore, and he was glad.

"Um, Mike, where the hell are you going?"

"Somethin's not right," Mike murmured as he drove past his street and continued down Vernon. "What're the cops doing at my house?"

"What do ya think they're doing?" Max said. "They're looking for us."

"No...Mike's right," Rick said quietly. "Why would they be looking for us already? Don't you think that's strange? Nobody knows what happened. We haven't told anyone yet."

"Maybe they're still looking for us from earlier, when we ditched that pig on Roller Coaster Road," Max offered, sounding rather unsure of himself. "What's the difference, we were gonna call 'em anyway, right?"

"Then why do they have their guns out?" asked Rick.

Mike thought about that for a moment. "There's only one way to find out," he said. "Reach under the seat and grab my cell phone."

Rick dipped his hand under the seat, fumbling through papers, CDs, and empty beer cans. After a few seconds, he handed Mike the phone.

"Who're you calling?" asked Rick.

"I'm gonna call the police station," Mike informed them, not yet sure of what he was going to say. "And find out what the hell's going on." He dialed 911, and his call was routed to the Hevven Police Department's emergency line.

"Hevven Police Department, this is Sergeant Gleason speaking, this line is being recorded for your protection. Can I help you?" answered a weary, authoritative voice.

Okay, Mike. Be calm. Tell him exactly what happened.

"My name is Michael Swart," Mike said, trying to maintain an air of composure. Instead, it came out sounding like a semi-hysterical confession. "Some friends and I...we found a body in the old house on Roller Coaster Road. We got a girl with us, she... "

"Where are you calling from?" Sergeant Gleason broke in. "Tell me where you're calling from, son, and we'll come and get you."

74

"I'm sorry...I don't under—"

"We don't want any trouble, Mr. Swart. Let me talk to the girl."

"What? I don't think that's even possible right now, sir. Look, she can't talk right now, she..."

"The smartest thing for you and your friends to do right now is to let the girl go, and turn yourselves in. Now tell me where you are and we'll send a cruiser to pick you up. We just want to ask a few questions, that's all. Don't make this difficult for yourselves."

This can't be happening, Mike thought, feeling the blood rush to his face. He pressed the POWER OFF button and tossed the phone onto the dashboard. He suddenly felt the urge to drive off the face of the earth. If such a thing were possible he would have given it a try. It was all a bad dream, anyway. It had to be. He was beginning to feel like a rat in a cage. Where the hell was his alarm clock to wake him up and free him from this madness?

"What'd they say?" Rick asked.

"He said he wants us to turn ourselves in."

"WHAT?" Max half-screamed, half-whined. "Turn ourselves in? For what? We didn't do nuthin'!"

Mike looked at Rick, and the expression on his face said it all. Mike told them quietly, calmly, "I think we should get the hell outta here."

"You mean, like, skip town?" Rick asked.

"Waitafuckinminute," Max interjected. "What about the police? What're we gonna do about ..."

"SHUT UP! JUST SHUT UP AND LET ME THINK FOR A MINUTE!" Mike screamed sharply, angrily, and his friends, and the girl, all jumped in surprise. He rarely ever raised his voice. He rarely ever had to.

Silence.

After a few seconds, Mike regained his composure. "Okay," he said calmly. "I think I know where we can go..."

"The Hevven ha-ha-Hacker," Lou said in a distant voice.

"What?"

"The Ha-acker! It's the Hevven Hacker! We have to leave, or The Hacker will find us. He'll find us." Lou spoke those words in a murky voice, as if mesmerized by the very thought.

75

The others looked at him with dismay and horror.

"That's just a story, you dipshit!" Max protested. "It's one of those legends, like the guy with the hook on his hand. They never found any bodies."

"Wait a minute. What if he's right? What if it's not just a story?" Rick wondered out loud. "What about all those missing girls?"

"How come nobody's ever found any bodies?"

"What difference does it make? Just because they never found the bodies doesn't mean those girls are still alive."

"Mike," Max said, almost pleadingly. "What are we gonna do?"

"I had an uncle that lived in a town called Willow's Creek, way up in New Hampshire," Mike continued. "He died a long time ago, but I'm pretty sure his cabin is still there."

"So...what are you fuckin' sayin'? We run? We just leave, like we're fuckin' guilty or somethin'?"

"You're the last person I thought would have a problem with that. You trust the cops? I sure as hell don't. If we leave, we'll be safe. So will our families. We need to get some money and...and some clothes. Lou and me can't go back to our house, and we can't circle back to your house, Max, because we'd have to go by the cops again, and it's obvious they're looking for us now. Rick, your place might be safe right now. Do you have any money? Maybe we can buy what we need."

"Yeah, I got a few hundred at my house."

"What if the fuckin' cops are already waitin' for us?" Max asked.

Mike didn't answer him. He didn't want to think about that. He drove on.

In the back seat a flame popped to life, filling the car with the smell of sulfur, as Max struck a match to light another cigarette. "We're so fucked," he mumbled, squinting through a cloud of smoke.

Silently, the others agreed.

Five minutes later they arrived at Rick Hunter's house on Titicut Street. Fortunately the neighborhood was darkly quiet, at least for now. Mike parked his car at the curb.

Rick slipped the trembling girl's arms from around his waist, and she allowed him to do so without protest. She stared at him with lost, lovely eyes. Then she brought her knees up to her chest, her hair spilling across her face, and began to rock slowly back and forth. Although she had not spoken in the car, Rick felt as if she had some awareness as to what was going on around her.

"I'll be out in a minute," Rick told no one in particular, and darted from the front seat of the car, jogging down the long dark driveway. He reached the front door, fumbled the key from his pocket, and suddenly realized that his mother's car was in the driveway. *Shit, shit, shit!* With a deep breath, he let himself in.

Once inside he was immediately greeted by the pleasant aroma of his mother's Italian cooking. The kitchen light was on and he knew that she was in there, probably warming dinner for his father, who often worked until 9 or 10 at night.

"Rick? Is that you?" his mother called out in her singsong voice.

Rick cleared his throat. "Yeah, it's me."

"I was worried about you," she said. "I came home and you weren't here." There was a brief clanging of pots and pans.

She poked her head from around the corner and smiled. She was still pretty for a woman in her mid-40s, and despite all the recent traumas he'd put her through; tall and olive-skinned, with the same raven-black hair as her son. "Try and remember to leave a note, will you?"

"I will. I'm going out with Mike and the guys. I just gotta grab some things."

"That's good," his mother smiled, genuinely delighted. She had always liked the Swart brothers. "You should spend more time with your friends. Oh, and you got a letter from Dartmouth today. I left it on the table for you."

"That's great," he said. "I'll look at it later."

Before his mother could go any further, he scurried upstairs to his bedroom. He flicked on the light, and his eyes moved quickly about the room as he surveyed the piles of dirty laundry, the unmade bed, the round ceramic ashtray stuffed with cigarette butts that rested on his nightstand, the larger-than-life images of Jimi Hendrix, Eddie from Iron Maiden, and a dozen scantily-clad swimsuit models, whose posters adorned his bedroom walls.

Crossing the room, he knelt down on the floor and began to rummage through his closet, tossing clothes over his shoulder and onto the floor. Eventually his fingers found what he had been searching for. Grasping his Army-green backpack by one strap, he yanked it free from the hodgepodge of clothes, camping gear, and old board games, and began to stuff it with the clothes he'd tossed onto the floor. He worked in an almost a dream-like manner, and only seemed to regain himself when the task was completed and the backpack was straining at the seams.

When he was done he knelt on the floor beside his bed and slid his hand beneath the mattress, where he felt the bulging paper surface he was looking for. Thoughtfully he removed a bulky envelope, and after a long pause jammed it deep into the already-overstuffed backpack. The envelope contained $672, all that remained of his life savings, which he had withdrawn from the bank a little over a month ago. He'd been saving up for his first car, and the envelope had originally contained well over $900, but over the past few weeks he had pissed much of it away on liquor and cigarettes. But the plans he had once made for this money still burned like dying embers within his mind's eye, carrying him off to another time, another place.

"We'll fill my T-bird and Kev's caravan and we'll cruise the country up and down," Mike had said one summer's night. They'd been parked in the Cherry Street pits, the two remaining people (except for Lou, who didn't really count because he was passed out in the backseat) at a keg party that had begun with a bang, and had died with a whimper. Mike and Rick were sitting on the hood of the Thunderbird, each working on a bottle of skunked Coors (which, after catching a good buzz from the keg beer, suited them just fine). "We'll ditch this shitty little town, Ricky."

Rick had responded with a nod and a grin, knowing that Mike was smashed, because Mike only referred to him as "Ricky" when he was drunk.

"Just the bunch of us and our dreams," Mike had gone on to say. "That's the way it should be, Ricky."

That was before the accident, when life was better.

Before Kevin Chapman's mother found his hidden stash, buying him a one-way ticket to the Mount Hope Rehabilitation Center, which was nothing more than a soft little prison where children learned to become better criminals. Before the hopes and dreams of two young lovers ended with a simple argument on the cool sands of Sundown Beach. Before the phone call from Lori's mother, her anguished voice tearing at his heart like a razor with every trembling word. Before the funeral, and the hazy days (or was it weeks?) he'd laid on his bed in a drunken stupor, staring at the shadows in the corner of the room, praying that they would somehow come alive and deliver him into sweet oblivion. Before the failed suicide attempt, the following days spent in the hospital, trying to figure out how his life had taken such a dreadful turn, trying to convince his mother and father that their only son wasn't crazy, that they hadn't failed as parents.

Rick realized these things all too well, because the image he'd had during that conversation with Mike was still fresh in his mind's eye. He and Lori in a red convertible, cruising the coastline in the afterglow of a surreal ocean sunset, like the last scene of some romantic movie. Her long blonde hair was flowing behind her in the salty air, and she was smiling that tight-lipped smile that made her cheekbones rise and her eyes twinkle, and he was smiling the shy, playful smile that would have surely landed him a slot in the Best Smile section of his yearbook, had he not been too damn modest to accept the honor. They were both smiling. Forever smiling, but only in his mind. Only in his memories.

Before Lori Shawnessy died, Rick Hunter used to smile without a care in the world. But not anymore. Not like he used to. Maybe never again.

Standing in the middle of his bedroom, face glistening with sweat, Rick knew he had never really doubted Mike's ability to make that dream a reality. But his vision was tainted now, because Lori had died...and somehow, the dream had died with her.

All at once Rick shook free of his daze. Tossing his backpack over one shoulder, he began down the hallway. He was almost to the stairs when he passed his parent's bedroom. The door was open. It was dark inside, but he could see the vague outline of their bed, a dresser, the reflection of a mirror in the moonlight. For the first time it occurred to him that he might never see his mother or father again, and he suddenly found himself overcome by sorrow.

I can't even let them know what happened, he thought. *After all they've been through in the past few weeks...the horror of finding me half-dead on the floor, a razor blade still in my hand...the hospital bills...the nervous way they look at me, as if they think I might go ahead and kill myself the second they look away...all the burdens I've laid on them...the promise I made that I'll never, ever put them through that kind of hell again. They won't have a clue as to where I am, and I can't let them know. I can't. I'd be risking all of our lives if I did.*

Then, as if driven by an unseen force, he quietly ducked into the darkened room and found himself kneeling before the large wooden chest that rested at the foot of his parent's bed. As if a thick fog was lifting before his very eyes, he realized what had brought him here, and he knew what he must do.

He gave the lid a tug. It was locked, but he had expected that. He tipped the heavy wooden chest on one edge and reached his hand underneath. Immediately he felt the key his father kept taped to the bottom of the chest, and pulled it loose. After a few seconds he found the keyhole with his fingertips, and inserted the key.

Carefully, he lifted the lid of the chest, removed a few neatly folded blankets, and found himself staring down at his father's pistol-grip shotgun, which had been given to him four years earlier, on Christmas, by an old Army buddy who had a strong belief in home security.

The very sight of the weapon seemed to hypnotize Rick; it seemed to glow, almost begging him to touch it, to hold it. Carefully, he lifted the shotgun from the chest and set it down on the floor beside him. After a few more seconds of searching he removed a small box of ammunition. He held the box close to one ear and shook it. Judging by the rattle, he guessed there were at least five or six shells inside. He stuffed the box of shells inside his backpack, locked the chest, and returned the key to its hiding place.

Before he left he paused in the doorway, the backpack over one shoulder, the shotgun aiming at the floor. "I love you Mom and

Dad," he whispered aloud to the empty room. With that he turned and started for the front door, concealing the shotgun as best he could inside his denim jacket.

"When will you be home?" his mother called out from the kitchen.

"Tomorrow," Rick said, wincing at the lie. "I'm staying over Mike's tonight."

"Okay," his mother said. "Take care."

Rick left in a hurry.

When he reached the car, he saw that someone (probably Mike) had taken the liberty of opening the trunk. He carefully put the shotgun inside, then covered it with his backpack.

"Got everything?" Mike asked immediately as Rick got into the car.

"What the hell took you so long?" Max hissed nervously. "Did you get the money?"

Rick nodded and took one more look at his house. "Yeah, I got it."

"See this shithole town later, right?" Max said, patting Mike on the shoulder. His eyes were wide and alert, but he sounded more nervous than excited.

Mike sighed apologetically. "There's one more stop we have to make, guys. I swear, it'll only take a minute."

"I thought you said we were leaving!" Lou squeaked.

"Karen?" Rick asked. Rick knew that Mike would rather be arrested, would rather risk his life, than to risk hurting the girl he loved. Even though he was gambling with all their lives, not just his own, Rick supposed he couldn't blame Mike for following his heart's compass. Rick knew damn well that if Lori was still alive, he would have done the exact same thing, as reckless as it was.

Max opened his mouth to protest, but decided, rather wisely, to keep his thoughts to himself.

Mike nodded calmly, squinting into the darkness ahead, occasionally checking the rearview to see if they were being followed. He drove on, his thoughts on Karen. What was he going to tell her? He wondered how she'd react to their story, and once again the harsh reality of their situation slapped him in the face.

Five more minutes passed, but to each of them it felt like hours. Silence wouldn't leave them be, and it was driving them into crazy thoughts. Things were happening too fast. Almost too fast to comprehend.

"Are her parents home?" asked Max, as they arrived at the Sloan house.

"Naw," answered Mike. "She said they were going to the movies. Can someone run up and see if she's home?"

Lou silently volunteered himself, anxious to escape the confined space of the Thunderbird. He got out of the car and sprinted across the driveway, the walkway, and up the three front steps. He rapped twice on the door and waited. A moment later the door flew open, and Karen Sloan stood before him in a rectangle of light.

"I knew you guys would come," she said breathlessly. She reached out, fumbling at the lock, and hurried him inside.

Dressed in tan shorts, sandals, and a pink tank top, Karen should have been a vision of beauty. She was near Lou's height, petite, with long, straight hair that seemed to shimmer like a black waterfall. Her skin was the color of caramel, her eyes the color of chocolate. The thing Lou liked best about Karen was her easy smile, but she wasn't smiling right now. Then again, neither was he.

"Lou," she sobbed. Her cheeks were flushed and shiny, and there were dark gray circles around her eyes, where she had unknowingly smudged her mascara while wiping away tears. And she was trembling. God, was she trembling.

She tossed her arms around the boy's thin frame, and he all but wept as he held her.

On Mike's request Max squirmed out of the backseat and raised the Sloan's garage door with a tug. Mike pulled the car inside, maneuvering between the various piles of junk that cluttered the dusty interior, and Max slammed the door down behind them.

Mike jumped out of the car and headed for the door.

"I'll stay with the girl," Rick called after him.

Mike gave him a solemn nod and disappeared inside.

Max followed Mike inside, where they found Karen and Lou in the foyer, both of them sobbing hysterically. As they entered, Karen tenderly withdrew from Lou. She looked at Mike, confused, and all

82

he could offer her at the moment was a subtle shrug. Then he went to her and held her.

"What's wrong?" Mike whispered into her ear. At this point, he wasn't really sure he wanted to know. How much had Lou told her?

She pulled away a bit, looking deep into his eyes. "What's going on?" she demanded in a hoarse voice. She leaned into him, crying hard against his shoulder. He tightened his arms around her lovingly, and sighed a long, tired sigh. Mike loved her, and he knew she loved him in return, loved all of them in some strange, sacred, maternal way. She cared for them, nurtured them, and Mike knew she would make a great mother someday. She'd had a lot of practice, after all.

"What did Lou tell you?" he whispered.

"I didn't tell her anything," Lou said, sniffling. "She already knew."

Karen closed her eyes tightly. "She told muh-me that you're all involved in a..." She opened her eyes, mouth working but unable to find the words.

"A what?" asked Mike, with an urgency Karen had never heard before.

"Ma-murder," she said at last.

Mike looked up at the ceiling, terrified, as an unfamiliar expression passed over his face: uncertainty. The others stared at Karen in disbelief at what she'd just told them.

Mike swallowed hard. "Who told you that?" he asked, still looking at the ceiling.

She raised her head, revealing her tear-filled eyes. Even with tears in her eyes she was still beautiful, with straight mocha hair, large brown eyes, and an unusually friendly smile (Mike had always thought she held a strange resemblance to the actress Demi Moore). But right now she was not smiling. "Ta-Ta-Trisha S-Saunders," she blurted out. "Her fa-father has a police scanner. The-they were l-looking for all of yu-you. They sa-said they saw your c-c-car and...and...the...they ...f-found a body...and...oh, God..."

"Why the fuck are they blamin' us?" Max yelled, enraged.

"I don't know," Mike said. "Maybe they found the wallet. Maybe that Punk Catcher found his way back there and found Lou's wallet with all our names and numbers in it. Then he discovered the body and reported it back to the station. Or maybe it was him... you know, that guy we saw. Maybe he found the wallet and then called the cops on us."

"Why would he do that?" Max asked. "That doesn't make any fuckin' sense."

"He knew we'd go to the cops, so he beat us to it. Now they'll be after us instead of him," Mike said. "Did anyone see his face besides me? Max?"

"Sorry, man. All's I saw was a blur."

Lou shook his head. He could barely remember anything after the body.

"He was big," Rick said, walking in from the garage. "That's all I remember. Everything jus'...just happened so fast...I can't really say for sure. I was looking at the girl."

"She still in the car?"

Rick nodded uneasily. "I managed to get the chains off her, but she went out like a light. I think she might've fainted."

"Girl?" asked Karen. "What girl?"

Just then the phone rang. Lou jumped as though he'd been electrocuted.

"Let the machine get it," Mike said.

They waited, but whoever it was hung up before the machine came on.

Mike's expression was grave. "Like I said, I think we gotta get out of here. If that's all we have for a description, who's gonna believe us?"

"Wa-waitta minute. What girl? What in the hell's goin' on here?" Karen begged. "What happened at that puh-place? Tell me. Now! Please...tell me..."

Mike took a deep breath as he prepared to speak. He wondered how she would handle such a bizarre story. Would she believe him? He wasn't even sure if he believed it himself.

Finally, having faith in her, he told her everything. Everything, that was, but the nasty little details about the body, and the man-monster that only he had seen; those were details she could live without.

"I can't believe this is happening," she said when he was done. She half fell, half sat, on the arm of a nearby leather sofa, taking steady deep breaths in order not to pass out.

"That makes two of us," Max muttered.

"So this girl you found, she's in your car right now?"

Mike nodded.

"So, why don't you take her to the police station...have her tell them what really happened?"

Mike shook his head. "She's..."

"Comatose," Rick finished, though the word tasted awful to him. It sounded so permanent, so final.

Mike turned to Karen. "Karen, we have to go. If we stay we're putting ourselves and our families in danger. We'll have to sort this thing out later."

"Wha-why don't you just ta-turn yourselves in?" she sniffled, wiping her tears away with the back of one hand. "Puh-please, just go to them and tell them what happened." She seemed to be going through a series of breakdowns, composed one moment, hysterical the next. Her words came out in machine-gun bursts. She was breathing rapidly, and trembling all over. "If...you run...what then? How will that look ...to them?"

"They're cops. Cops never believe anybody," Max said.

"And even if they did believe us," Mike said, "the police might not find this guy right away. He saw my car. If he found the wallet, he knows our names. If he knows our names, then he can find out where we live. That's why we have to go. We'll call the police and tell them what happened as soon as we're all safe. Then we can sit back and wait for them to catch this bastard." With that, Mike caressed her tear-stained cheek.

"Then you have to take me with you," she pleaded. "He might know who I am. What if he knows I'm your girlfriend? Everyone knows it. Everyone..."

Mike glanced around the room, not needing to speak, not needing to ask, and found approval in the eyes of his friends. He also saw that, like him, they were anxious to depart. "Okay. You'd better bring some clothes. And some blankets. Just hurry, okay?"

Karen sniffled and nodded, tears squirting from her eyes.

"None of you have to come with us," Mike told them in a soft and confident voice. "I want you to, because I think that's the safest thing to do, but I can't make that choice for you. I got $20 in my pocket and a full tank of gas and I'm asking you to trust me."

Mike waited for an answer. He could feel his heart beating in his throat.

No one said a word.

"Understand, hon?" Mike asked Karen, and she nodded. He kissed her on the forehead, and lifted her chin with his hands. "Alright, then. Better get your stuff together. 'Cause once we're gone, there's no turning back."

~Ten~

Shortly after nine that Thursday evening, five friends snuck out of Hevven with a girl whose name they did not know, and headed north on Route 24, beginning their journey for a remote New Hampshire town called Willow's Creek.

Karen Sloan had packed a few of her belongings—several changes of clothes, three heavy blankets, a sleeping bag, and some toiletries—into three green trash bags, working like an automaton, seemingly in her own strange little world. Rick had wrapped a blanket around the unconscious naked girl and placed her in the back seat beside Lou, who had stared at her timidly until he finally fell asleep with his head against her shoulder. Max sat quietly on the other side of Lou, his head against the window, staring into space. Hevven vanished behind them, swallowed by miles of darkness.

As they passed through Boston, Rick retrieved the pack of Marlboros and the Zippo from his pocket. He removed two cigarettes from the pack and lit one. Mike snapped his head in Rick's direction, surprised by the sudden burst of illumination.

"Smoke?" Rick asked, and handed his friend a cigarette.

Mike looked over at Karen, who was sitting between them with her chin against her chest.

"Don't worry, she's asleep. They're all asleep, I think."

Mike placed the butt between his lips and Rick lit it for him.

Mike inhaled, squinting into the night through a puff of smoke. "Is that the lighter Kevin gave you?"

"Yep."

"Hmmph. I miss that dude."

"Yeah, me too."

Outside and to their right, lights twinkled on the calm surface of Boston harbor, where waves lapped softly at the shore. Meanwhile, on their left, neon flashed and glowed, lighting up the city like rainbows in the night. Above the water, a dark cross with blinking red lights descended quietly from the heavens as a plane prepared to land at Logan Airport.

"I wonder what he's doing right now. Kevin, I mean."

Rick shrugged, looking out his passenger window, observing the various out-of-state license plates of the cars that were clustered ahead of them before the car tunnel. Connecticut, New York, Maine, New Hampshire ...

"Whatever it is, it's gotta be better than this," answered Rick. "This is one time he'll be grateful he's in rehab."

Mike chuckled a little.

"Mike?"

"Yeah?"

"What'll happen if he follows us somehow?"

They slipped inside the tunnel, where their faces appeared disease-stricken in the dim yellow glow of the fluorescent lights.

"Who? You mean...him?"

"Yeah. The Hacker, or whoever he is."

Mike looked at him seriously, exhaling through his nose. "There's no way he'll find us there."

Rick could only pray that Mike was right.

Just as Mike said this they emerged from the tunnel, and their features were once again eclipsed by the shadows that roamed over through the Thunderbird's interior in slanted rails.

Rick stared out the window for a minute more, losing himself in the heavens as the traffic let up and the city became a blur. "Sometimes...I wonder if things will ever be the same as they used to be. Sometimes I wonder if any of this bullshit is real. Like maybe this is all a dream, and...someday, I'm gonna wake up and find out everything is fake. I remember how easy it used to seem just to...just to live." He paused and looked at Mike, who turned to him with a grim expression. Mike didn't speak; his silence alone spoke volumes.

"I wonder if, when we die, we get a chance to start all over again," Rick continued, "to fix all the shit we fucked up in this life..."

"I dunno," Mike said. "Sometimes I wish I could be Lou's age again. Sometimes there's almost nothin' I wouldn't give just to forget the things I know. Just to have everything be simple again."

"It was a little easier back then, but it was never simple. Not really," whispered Rick. "It only seems that way 'cause we're older now."

"Yeah, maybe you're right, but it's been one hell of a ride, hasn't it? I mean, part of me never thought we'd make it this far."

Rick smiled grimly. "Yeah, me either."

Karen sighed in her sleep between them, and Mike put an arm around her lovingly. Although he wished she had stayed awake to talk, he felt some sleep would do her well. He couldn't help wondering if he was making the right decision by taking them to Willow's Creek. They would be safe there for a while, but for how long? To this question, Mike realized, there was no definitive answer. Only time would tell. And what if they ran out of money?

His thoughts began to creep and crawl, asking him over and over again, *Are you making the right decisions?*

He stared straight ahead, where the world seemed to end in darkness. The voice in his mind continued. *Are you making the right decisions?*

Boston's light-speckled towers disappeared behind them, but the traffic persisted all the way to the Wilmington exit. After that Mike sped up a little, eager to reach the border. Rick was staring out the window again. Mike drove on in silence, trying to deal with all that had happened, trying to make sense of it all. Was there something he had missed?

Are you making the right decisions?

He could not ignore the question (or the voice in his mind).

89

I'm making the only decision that seems sane, Mike told himself. But the bothersome voice that spoke out his worries was not satisfied with that. It put forth another question, one that troubled Mike far worse than the first.

Are you sane, Mikey? Do you really think you lead a sane life? Lookit you. Lookit your friends.

He couldn't ignore the question, nor could he answer it. Since Lori had passed on and Kevin was sent away, Mike didn't know what sane meant anymore, and now this...He began to think about Rick. If anybody was insane, it had to be him. He had, after all, tried to kill himself. As if to confirm this, Rick mumbled something inaudible as he continued to stare out the window and into the night.

Yeah, Rick's probably crazier than that psycho at the Moody house, the voice informed Mike. *He tried to off himself! Your best friend!*

The thought of Rick wanting to kill himself made Mike's stomach turn. Even in the darkness, he could see the ghostly white of the gauze bandage as Rick folded his arms across his chest.

No wonder we live in a world of fantasy, thought Mike. *Reality is so fucked up sometimes; maybe it's the fantasies that keep us sane. So we lie. We lie to ourselves. We tell ourselves everything's fine, but it's not. But is that really wrong? Can it be wrong to believe, to trust, to love? No*, Mike decided, *we do what's necessary to survive.*

Yeah, you and all your friends, his thoughts continued. *One of 'em tried to kill himself. One of 'em is locked in a loony bin. One of 'em needs to get wasted just to make it through the day. You're all so fucked up you don't even know...*

"Stop it," Mike told himself out loud. Karen sighed again and drew in closer to him, searching for warmth. *God, I love you, Karen*, he thought, and he had never felt it more than at that moment.

Rick snapped out of his daze and turned to Mike. "You fallin' asleep, man?"

"No," Mike said. "Just thinking too hard, I guess."

"I'll drive if you want."

"Naw, I'll be fine."

Rick nodded and returned to whatever it was he'd been looking at outside.

Inevitably, Mike began to think about death and loss. How easy it is to lose, and to be lost. That's exactly how he felt: lost. More lost than anyone could know. *Nothing is forever*, he suddenly realized. *Not love, not money, not society's silly little dreamland, and certainly not this clump of dirt and water we call Earth. Nothing. So why the hell are we here, then?*

He lit another cigarette. That was all he could do to keep himself busy, to keep himself from thinking until his head throbbed.

Thirty minutes later they passed a blue and yellow sign that read: Welcome To New Hampshire, and Mike felt as though a great burden had been lifted off his shoulders. They were out of Massachusetts, and hopefully their problems wouldn't follow them over the border. It was a slim hope at best, but it was better than nothing.

Mike rolled down his window a few inches, letting the cool northern air fill his lungs and dance through his hair. *Maybe*, he thought, *things will work out just fine. Maybe this is what we needed, a chance to be together. Maybe.*

He tightened his arm around Karen, thinking of how much he loved her. If all went wrong, she would still be his dream come true. Although Mike had loved Lori like a sister, he silently thanked God for not taking Karen from him. He said a silent prayer for Lori, in which he told her how much they all missed her. He also told her to watch out for Rick, because Mike was still worried about him. For some reason that escaped him, Mike was certain Lori could hear him, and that she was not as far away as it seemed. It was a warm, comforting feeling, as if he had an angel on his side. *Right now*, he thought, *I need an angel. We all do.*

He managed to drive for two more hours, watching the road, thinking of the body, before he finally had to stop at a rest area to vomit. He returned to the car half-sick, with the vision of the dead girl still lingering in the wastelands of his mind.

"You okay?" Rick asked, as they pulled back onto the highway.

"Yeah," Mike answered. "I'm fine now."

Another hour of silence passed before they came upon a sign reading:

Willow's Creek/Potter's Bluff Exit 10 Miles.

"Almost there," Mike whispered, and he glanced warily at his best friend. But Rick, with his head resting against Karen's shoulder, was now fast asleep. By the expression on his face it didn't appear to be a comfortable sleep, but nevertheless, Mike thought it would do his friend some good.

Just a few more miles, and their many problems would be far behind them...at least, for a little while. As the land became familiar to him, rolling upward into hills and climbing into steep walls of granite, Mike remembered the times he had traveled to Willow's Creek with his family. Although he had been only eight or nine the last time he had seen Uncle Jack, he could picture the man quite clearly.

Uncle Jack was a rugged-looking man, his features rough and well-defined. He was in his mid-40s the last time Mike had seen him, and time had already begun to carve deep lines that redefined his jawline, and forked out from the corners of his eyes. His eyes! They were as blue and honest as the clearest summer sky. And they always seemed to...well...to glow. They were almost like the eyes of a child, a child who was looking upon something he had never seen before. Something new and exciting. Uncle Jack had always had a most peculiar way of looking at the world.

When Mike was very young, Uncle Jack once told him that if you listened close enough, you could hear the mountains whispering to you. Giants, Uncle Jack had called them. He said the mountains were sleeping giants, buried and forgotten by mankind. He told young Mike that it was the giants' duty to watch over the land and its creatures, to make sure that everything was going according to God's plan. But as hard as he tried, Mike could never seem to hear the giants talking. For Mike, they were defiantly silent. Still, he believed in Uncle Jack's story, because Mike knew how strongly Uncle Jack had believed in the story himself.

When his thoughts slowly shifted back to reality, Mike wondered what his parents were thinking after all that had happened back in Hevven. Did they know yet? Had they come home to the sound of sirens and the flashing of lights? Surely they must know by now. He wished he could have told them what had really happened at that old place on Roller Coaster Road, but that was almost impossible now. Mike and his friends were on their own. Whether they liked it or not, they had come too far to turn back.

They were on the run.

So Mike followed the highway and his memories, and they led him back to a familiar place, to a postcard-perfect town called Willow's Creek.

A place where sleeping giants were supposed to live.

~ꙮleuen~

Rick Hunter awoke with a violent jerk, as if from a nightmare.

Squinting into the bright light of the Friday morning sun, his vision was fuzzy at best. Purple and orange spots danced before his eyes. The warmth of the sun continued to beat down upon him as he tried to sort reality from the dream world, and he found it was all a blur. The very last thing he could recall that was real (at least, he thought it was real…it had seemed real enough), was talking to Mike as they sped along the highway. The others had been fast asleep, and he guessed he must have joined them in dreamland shortly after they had crossed the border into New Hampshire. Upon awakening, he thought his memories—the dead (hacked) body, the naked girl chained to the ceiling, the police standing at the front door of the Swart's house, and the killer with the evil jack o' lantern grin—were little more than remnants of a dream. But as his eyesight slowly returned to normal, Rick looked out of the passenger window of Mike's car, and he knew that he'd been wrong.

Ahead of them, buried beneath a fine weave of rust-colored pine needles, a narrow dirt road wound its way through a dense forest of evergreens and birches. Above the trees, swathed in a fine white mist, row after row of mountains surrounded them, their stony faces glowing proudly in the rising sun.

All around them: trees, trees, and more trees. They were driving through a natural tunnel, the branches low and densely woven.

Disturbed by Rick's sudden movements, Karen yawned and slowly opened her big brown eyes. She ran her fingers through her hair and brushed it away from her face with the kind of slow, unconscious grace that only women seem to possess. Her deep red lips were parted, as if she was about to say, You wouldn't believe this crazy dream I was having! But these words never came, for she quickly realized that the crazy dream was real.

Mike glanced over and grinned at her confusion. He rubbed out his cigarette in the ashtray before she could see it. She didn't care for him smoking, and there was no need to argue. Not here. Not now. They had enough to worry about as it was, that was for sure.

The others were still fast asleep in the back seat, but judging by the way the T-bird was bucking up and down on the rough road, shaking them about like rag dolls, they were due to awake at any time.

Twenty minutes earlier, while the others slept, Mike had begun to feel a not unpleasant chill of déjà vu creeping over him. Above the trees, he had seen the battered shell of the Northville paper mill standing like a sentinel on the otherwise uninhabited outskirts of Willow's Creek. Beyond the paper mill, up and over the Maple Street hill, he had soon found himself looking down upon the minuscule center of The Creek, glittering hopefully in the rising sun.

At the bottom of the hill, Mike had turned east onto Main Street, where the houses and stores crowded the sidewalks like spectators waiting for a parade. Among them, Atkins' General Store, a lopsided shanty of weathered gray shingles and maroon trim in desperate need of a fresh coat, was a welcomed landmark. Slowing down, he had caught a brief glimpse of the "I Love New Hampshire" and "Don't Take New Hampshire For Granite" T-shirts hanging in the dark windows (the superficial keepsakes of tourists everywhere), along with a variety of fishing gear, and the same neon Schlitz sign he remembered from his youth.

Less than a block away, he had also recognized the dutiful brick facade of the Willow's Creek Public Library, as well as the humble white countenance of Our Lady Mary's Catholic Church, where Mike and his family used to go to pay their respect to God. Behind the simple white church was a small cemetery, where the mossy statues of angels contemplated the quiet morning amidst a maze of decaying gravestones and wrought-iron fences. So distant were the memories of hot summer days as a child in his Sunday's best, looking up at the statue of Christ above the pulpit, listening to the grownups sing like angels, that Mike had suddenly felt as if some greater power had beckoned him here. Why else would he be returning after so much time?

If Karen and I ever get married, Mike had promised himself as he drove along, it will be in that church. This is where we'll raise our family. This is where we'll find happiness ...if we manage to get out of this mess. Shit, don't think like that. Gotta think positive. Everything's gonna be fine...

Continuing down Main Street he saw Jasper's Arcade, The No-Name Bar And Pub, and the Lil' Sunshine Restaurant, still there after all those years, although Rocky's Soft Serve Ice Cream had been converted into Art's Bait and Tackle, and the old Five-And-Dime was now Anne's Used Books. Still, there was not a single fast food restaurant, or shopping mall, or stadium-sized movie theatre in sight; only the humble country establishments that gave Willow's Creek the placid charm of a Norman Rockwell painting.

Now they were almost at their destination, and Mike's mind was simmering with memories, his heart beating more rapidly with every inch they traveled. He wondered if his uncle had left anything behind, something Mike could keep in remembrance of those long-lost summer days spent at the cabin, something more than a child's scattered memories.

"Almost there?" Rick's voice crackled. He licked his lips, hoping it would help some, but his tongue was as dry as sandpaper.

"Just a few more minutes, I think," Mike told him, and flashed a weary smile in his direction. He motioned with his eyes. "How are they doing back there?"

Rick turned just as Max was opening his eyes. He nodded at his friend. "What's up?"

"Not much," answered Max, yawning.

"They still sleeping?"

"Yup. Are we there yet?"

"We'll be there soon."

"Cool."

97

Eventually the road broadened, and sunlight began to trickle down through the gaps in the treetops. Mike drove the Thunderbird through an aperture between two enormous cedars, and moments later they emerged from the forest tunnel and found themselves at the uppermost corner of a wide, sloping meadow.

Lou woke up just as Mike brought the T-bird to a halt. Ahead of them, the rutted dirt road wove its way across the meadow. At the end of the dirt road, flanked by several small evergreens and hunkering in the shade of an enormous oak tree, stood the fabled cabin they had come so far to find. From their vantage point at the edge of the forest, their view was less than impressive—one corner of a farmer's porch, two upstairs windows, the top of a stone chimney—but it was enough to get their attention. The view beyond the cabin, however, was nothing short of spectacular.

The meadow dipped down to touch the banks of a lazy river, which shimmered like mercury in the newborn sun, and then rose up again to form a jagged cliff that hovered precariously above the water below. In the distance, where earth and sky became one, majestic mountains poked their crowned heads through the morning mist.

As they continued farther down the overgrown driveway, the two-story cabin emerged from behind the drooping limbs of the massive oak. Thick veins of ivy crisscrossed the stone and mortar foundation, rising up in places to scale its weathered walls. Even with the boarded windows and mossy shingles it was still a delightful little place, and the deep shade that fell from the old oak tree only added to its charm.

Finally, Mike put the transmission in park. Their journey was over. Without waiting for the others he got out of the car, his legs and buttocks tingling with pins and needles. The others followed his lead.

Once outside they stretched and yawned, exhilarated by the sudden chill of the mountain air. Karen went over and stood beside Mike, resting her head on his shoulder. Rick shrugged off his denim jacket and tossed it back onto the front seat. Inhaling the fragrant mountain air, he looked at the cabin and the valley that stretched before him, deeply saddened by the thought that Lori was not there to share the beauty of this place. Lou surveyed the countryside with his mouth hanging ajar. It reminded him of a Tolkien novel, the kind of secret place where Hobbits dwelled. After some consideration, Max lit a cigarette.

Silence remained with them for a few final moments before tiring itself, broken by the eerily beautiful cry of an unseen hawk.

"Well, let's go check it out," Mike said cheerfully.

"What about her?" asked Karen, hugging herself for warmth.

They looked back at the girl, who was still sleeping soundly in the back of Mike's car, her body curled into an almost fetal position.

"We can come back for her after," suggested Mike.

"'Sides," Max chimed in, "I don't think she's gonna be running any marathons. Not in her condition."

Mike took Karen by the hand and began to lead her toward the cabin. "How are you feeling?"

"I'm alright," she said, shrugging, as they stepped up onto the porch. She could tell by the look in his eyes that this place was special to him, so she did her best to conceal her worries about the events of the previous day. The killer who might or might not be hunting them down at this very moment, the police who would be searching relentlessly for them night and day, all for a crime they did not commit, and her parents, who would be worried sick about her. It was better to let those things rest for now.

Mike guided her across the porch, where the floorboards cursed in bitter tongues beneath their weight, and to the cabin door. He paused, looking out across the valley, remembering so much of the childhood he'd left there. In the distance stood the green iron bridge that connected Willow's Creek to its neighboring town, Potter's Bluff. From where they stood, the bridge and the cabin were the only visible signs of civilization. He looked out across the greenish-gray mountains and the voice within his mind returned, except this time it was not alone.

Are you making the right decisions, Mikey? his conscience asked of him. As he stared at the surrounding mountains, remembering what his Uncle Jack had told him long ago, Mike finally realized where these voices were coming from.

It's the giants, he realized, with a blend of fear and fascination. They knew I was coming. What do you want from me? I'm doing what I think is right. Why are you bothering me?

We're not bothering you, Mikey-wikey, the mountains (giants) answered. *We're here to help. Uncle Jack is dead, his life is gone, you'll join him soon if The Hacker comes...*

"D'ya got a key?" asked Max, yawning into the side of his fist.

"Naw...we'll probably have to bust the lock," Mike said as he approached the door, the voices still echoing in his head, while the floorboards continued to protest their arrival.

Max bent over and scooped up a rock. "How's this?"

"That'll do."

Max cocked his arm back, as if winding up to pitch a baseball, and swung the rock down in a graceful arc. "How about that?" he said, tossing the rock aside. "Pedro Martinez, eat your heart out."

Mike pulled the remains of the broken, rusted padlock from the door and dropped it to the porch. "After you," he said to Karen, giving the door a push.

She smiled at him as she crossed the threshold.

Inside, the cabin was saturated with the smell of dust and pine. As the sunshine spilled around her back, a narrow staircase appeared before her, ascending into darkness. She stepped forward and looked to her left, scanning the contents of a spacious living room: a large stone fireplace, a sheet-covered couch, a round coffee table (actually a large wooden spool flipped on its side), and a faded imitation-leather recliner. The floor was made of clear-coated wood, with a thick oval rug in the middle. It wasn't the Four Seasons, but it sure was cozy.

Mike stepped up behind her. The cabin looked smaller than he remembered it. He supposed he felt that way because he was bigger now, had grown two feet or so since the last time he'd been there, but it was more than just that; with all that had happened the night before, the world itself seemed smaller.

After a brief inspection of the living room Karen stepped away to the right, where she found herself standing in a small kitchen, complete with a sink and several cupboards. She ran her finger across the countertop and pouted.

"Well, what do you think?" asked Mike.

"It could use a woman's touch," Karen said, wiping the dust from her finger.

"Come on," Mike said, "I know it needs a little work. But once we get these windows uncovered, brighten up the place a little... "

"I don't see a television, but I think it's the balls!" Max said with a grin, and flopped down on the couch. He crossed his legs on the coffee table. "Rick?"

Rick nodded in agreement. He liked the place just fine.

Lou, on the other hand, only wished he could share their enthusiasm. Like Max had said, there was no television, which, of course, meant there would be no video games, no DVDs, and no Internet. He walked over to the stone fireplace and stood there by himself, with his back to them. As hard as he tried he could not remember this place, any more than he could remember what his Uncle Jack had looked like. After a few seconds he turned around, a look of dismay on his face, and watched the others silently.

"There's two bedrooms upstairs," Mike told them. "Karen and I will take the one on the right, and you guys can fight over the other one. There's a bathroom, too, but I doubt if the toilet flushes."

"That's great," Max said glumly. "I think I feel a shit coming on."

"How are we gonna get the boards off these windows?" asked Karen.

"There's a toolbox in my trunk," Mike said. He took out his keychain and dangled it in the air.

"I guess I'll go," said Rick, remembering the shotgun. He wasn't sure if his friends had seen it (if so, they had not mentioned it), and he did not want to cause a panic, especially so early in the day.

Mike tossed him the keys. "We'll be here."

On his way back to the Thunderbird, Rick paused for a moment to feel the sun on his face. Closing his eyes, he listened to the birds and again he wondered if Mike had made the right decision in bringing them here, to the cabin. Rick knew the cops were probably looking for them, had probably already gone to question his parents, and the thought of the police in his house, with their dead eyes, notepads, and fake courteous smiles made him angry. But he believed in Mike, because Mike was his best friend, and because Mike had never let them down in the past. Besides, it wasn't as though someone had put a gun to their heads. They'd been given a choice, and they'd chosen to flee. Whatever came as a result of their actions, Rick knew they would have to share the consequences.

As he walked to the car, Rick paused at the side window to get a better look at the girl. The blanket had fallen from her shoulder, revealing the delicate pink of one nipple on the soft white curve of her breast, and although he felt guilty for spying on her, he found it next to impossible to look away.

She was about his age, fair-skinned and slender, with dark auburn hair that cascaded down her shoulders. Her face was delicately heart-shaped, with high cheekbones, sensuous lips, and a noble chin. Her eyelids twitched while she slept, the lashes long and dark, the eyebrows pulled down in a look that resembled either anger or frustration. She slept with both hands tucked under her head and one leg up on the seat, her body trembling slightly as she breathed (as if, in her dreams, she could still see herself chained to the ceiling of that horror-house.) Her legs were long and shapely, her toenails painted like little red mirrors. There was a tattoo on her left ankle; some kind of tribal design, by the look of it.

It wasn't until now that Rick realized just how beautiful she was, like a princess from some fairy tale. Watching her sleep, he was overtaken by the sudden, protective urge to cover her exposed body.

He carefully opened the passenger door, so as not to disturb her. Quietly, he knelt beside the sleeping girl. So soft, so gentle was her every breath. Balancing on one hand, he leaned closer to her. God, she was even more beautiful close up.

He grabbed one corner of the blanket, pulled it up to the base of her neck, all the while imagining what it would feel like to run his fingers through her hair, to kiss her parted lips, to hold her small feminine hands in his own, to put his arms around her waist. For a brief second he imagined it was Lori Shawnessy sleeping there, but he quickly shook that image from his mind. She barely resembled Lori, and besides, Lori was gone. *Gone forever*, Rick reminded himself.

As if to confirm this, he reached out one hand and gently caressed the side of the girl's face, finding her skin far softer and warmer than he had anticipated; so much so that he gasped, heart flexing with newfound vigor. For fear of waking her, he sucked in a breath and held it.

With a strangled whimper, her eyelids flung open wide to reveal a wild, electric blue. She sprang from her resting place, clawing at him with her long, spade-shaped nails.

Startled, Rick tried to stand, slamming his head against the car roof. Before he knew what was happening the girl was upon him, flailing and screaming.

"Jeezus Christ!" was all Rick could manage as he tried to fend off the attack. Something sharp caught him just below the eye, and he heard his own skin ripping as she dragged her nails down the side of his face.

"I'M NOT GONNA HURT YOU!" he hollered in desperation, but the attack persisted.

Grabbing both wrists, he managed to pin her back against the seat. For several seconds they remained that way, sweating and panting into one another's face, he with his weight on top of her and she still struggling to break free.

"I'm not gonna hurt you," he repeated, softer this time.

Her eyes were wild and unreachable. She growled at him helplessly.

"I'm not gonna hurt you," he repeated yet again.

Then, all at once, she fell silent. Her body went limp. The muscles in her jaw relaxed. She looked at him questioningly, the rage having fled from her eyes. They looked at one another for what seemed like an eternity, one unable to speak, the other not knowing what to say. A moment of quiet understanding passed between them.

What did he do to you? Rick wondered. Searching her eyes, it occurred to him that this girl was not entirely sane.

As if responding to that thought, she began to wail uncontrollably.

Not quite knowing what to do, Rick let go of her wrists and gently pulled her head against him. Clutching his shirt in both

103

hands, she buried her face into his shoulder, and cried until the tears soaked his skin.

"Noooo..." she whimpered in a muffled voice.

"Shhhhh," he told her over and over. "Everything's okay. You're safe now. No one's gonna hurt you. You're safe now. You're..."

"Hey, we heard—oh, shit, what happened?"

Rick turned his head and saw Mike and Karen standing outside the car, their eyes wide with concern. "She's awake now," Rick said, and only after he'd said the words did he realize how stupid that sounded.

"No shit, Sherlock." Mike said. "I can see that."

"Well, give me a hand here."

Karen leaned into the car. "Is she okay?"

"I don't know," said Rick. He looked down at the girl. "Are you okay?" he asked. "Do you want to get out of the car?"

The girl whimpered and locked her arms around his neck, like a frightened child being torn from her mother.

"Come on," Rick said, securing the blanket around her.

She looked up at him, trembling. Their eyes met.

"He...he..."

"Who?" asked Rick. "I don't understand."

"HE'S COMING BACK!" she screamed, and fainted dead away.

"Shit!" Rick said.

Karen covered her mouth with her hands. "Ohmygod...is she...?"

Rick lifted the girl out of the car. "She fainted."

Karen pursed her lips and sighed.

"Man," said Mike. "What the hell happened to your face?"

Rick gave him a confused look. It took him a second before he remembered the scratches on his face. "Oh," he said. "She, uh...it's my fault. I was trying to pull the blanket over her, and she just freaked."

"Jeez," murmured Karen, softly touching his cheek. "It looks pretty bad. Does it hurt?"

"Naw. Not yet, anyway. I'm gonna take her in the house." He spun around with the girl still in his arms. "The keys are on the floor, I thi"

"I'll go with you," Karen offered.

Rick only nodded as he started for the cabin, the half-naked stranger still cradled in his arms, her long, slender legs dangling lifelessly.

With his hands in his pockets, Mike watched them go.

~Twelve~

Officer Bailey was hunched over his desk, chewing on a pencil and reading the morning edition of *The Hevven Gazette*, when Chief Moriarty appeared in front of him.

"Officer Bailey," Chief Moriarty rumbled, pronouncing the name as though it were an insult. "I'd like you to meet Agent Ferren."

The pencil fell out of Bailey's mouth. He crunched the newspaper into a ball and stuffed it inside the already-overflowing basket beside his desk. He stood up quickly, his boyish face blooming red.

Moriarty loomed over him. He was a mountain of a man, his face a topographical map of bumps, creases, and folds. A large welt on the side of neck only added to the chaos of his features. His graying brown hair shone silver in the fluorescent ceiling lights. From somewhere deep within his cavernous sockets, two eyes glowed dully like little black pearls. After a moment, he stepped aside, made a sweeping gesture with his hand, and the man standing behind him stepped forward, as if on cue.

Wearing a black suit with a black necktie, Agent Ferren looked as though he had wandered off the set of an old black and white movie. Maybe *Citizen Kane*, or even *A Streetcar Named Desire*. But aside from the stylish suit and the squinty black eyes, the likeness ended there. He looked to be in his early 40s, short and stocky, with a round face and thin black hair parted neatly to one side. He smiled pleasantly, showing off his perfect white teeth. *A*

smile that could have been stolen from a textbook on good manners,
thought Bailey.

"Nice to meet you, sir," Bailey said.

They shook hands briefly.

"Agent Ferren is here to, uh, assist us with last night's...how
shall we put it? Incident." Moriarty looked at Bailey steadily, his
cold black eyes boring holes into his head.

Bailey nodded thoughtfully. He hadn't told anyone about last
night's chase, nor did he intend to. The fact that his radio had shit
the bed was actually a blessing in disguise. Because of it, nobody
knew how close he'd been to catching those punks, those murdering
little bastards. On the same token, nobody would ever know how
easily they had eluded him. "I wasn't aware the FBI had an interest
in this case."

"I'm part of the STF division," Ferren said.

"STF?"

"Serial Task Force."

"So, basically, you hunt serial killers?"

Agent Ferren nodded. "Well..."

"Agent Ferren is here as our consultant," Moriarty interrupted.
"He also understands that we have jurisdiction, and that we'll have
the situation under control momentarily."

Ferren closed his mouth and smiled wanly.

"Well," Bailey said, "if there's anything I can do..."

"Actually," Moriarty turned to face him, "there is. I'd like you
to take Agent Ferren over to the crime scene. Detective Cannon is
already there, so please alert him before you arrive. And not one
word of this to the press. They're already trying to compare this to
the goddamn Hacker."

"I'd also like to interview anybody who knows the suspects,"
Ferren said. "Their families, teachers, any friends they might
have..."

Moriarty lowered his bushy eyebrows. "The families have
already been interviewed. Our detectives are writing the reports as
we speak. As for their friends, that may difficult."

"How so?"

"Our main suspect, Michael Swart, runs a close-knit group. All but one of them has disappeared. We're not sure if the others are involved, or just happened to be in the wrong place at the wrong time. Right now, we're treating them all as suspects."

"You said all but one of them has disappeared?" The pleasant smile was gone. He was all business now. Chief Moriarty stared at him for several seconds, but Ferren did not look away. If Moriarty wanted to have a pissing contest, then so be it. Agent Ferren had never backed down from anyone in his life. And he certainly wasn't prepared to let some small-town cop with a hard-on for authority get the better of him.

"The Chapman boy," Bailey interrupted.

"Has he been interviewed?"

"Not yet," Moriarty replied. "Mr. Chapman is currently a ward of the state. The Mount Hope Center for Rehabilitation at Plymouth. This would be his third or fourth stay there. Probably not his last. I escorted him there myself, in fact."

"I'd like to speak with him," Ferren said.

"I'd rather you waited. As soon as they can complete all the proper paperwork, he'll be discharged. Monday, I believe. By my request. I think he'll be more cooperative if we conduct the interview at his home."

Ferren nodded. Moriarty was smarter than he looked.

"Okay," Bailey interrupted in earnest. He grabbed his cap from a hook by the door. Smiling politely, he said, "Follow me."

Ferren shook Moriarty's hand, once again noticing the bruised lump on the side of the larger man's neck, and thanked him for his time. Moriarty was halfway to the door when Ferren stopped him. "Oh, yes, Chief? Just one more question."

Chief Moriarty stopped and turned. "What is it?"

"The tip you received, the one that led you to the body. Do you have any idea who made the call, or where it originated?"

"The call originated from a pay phone, near the center of town. Our detectives have secured a perimeter around the phone booth, and are collecting fingerprint samples as we speak."

"I'd still like to hear a recording of the call, if possible."

"I'm afraid it isn't. The tape in question was accidentally recorded over before we were able to examine it. The officer responsible for the oversight has been reprimanded, I assure you."

"And the caller?"

"Anonymous. But the voice was that of a young woman, probably a teenager. Possibly that of the suspect's girlfriend, or possibly that of the young woman they allegedly abducted. Whoever it was, she sounded terrified for her life."

"And you're sure the caller identified the Swart boy and the others?"

"Positive. I should know, Agent Ferren. I took the call myself. Now, if you'll excuse me..."

"Of course."

The Chief slipped out of the office and closed the door behind him, while Agent Ferren stood with his arms crossed, staring at the floor. His brow was furrowed, his jaw tight. After a few seconds, he whirled around to face the young officer. "So...is this your first homicide?"

Officer Bailey glanced down at the floor and then up again. His round, boyish face turned several shades of red. "Yes, sir. You don't get too many of those around here. Homicides, that is."

Bailey turned and Ferren followed him toward the door.

Ferren smiled to himself. Chief Moriarty was toying with him. The mere fact that he had assigned a rookie to act as his liaison was proof enough of that. Had he wanted to, Ferren could have squashed Moriarty's precious authority like a bug, but he had dealt with small-town cops before, and he'd long since grown accustomed to their lack of cooperation. Rather than hinder the investigation, the best way to handle men like Moriarty was to give them the illusion that they were still in control. Of course that trick only worked for so long. But hopefully, by then, the case would be solved.

As they entered the reception area, Bailey threw a wave to the dispatcher, a plump brunette whose hair was pulled into such a tight bun that it kept her eyebrows raised in a constant look of surprise. She glanced up from the switchboard, mouth moving rapidly as she spoke into a headset, and gave them a wink as they stepped outside.

The sun was bright, the air already humid. As he followed the young officer, Ferren surveyed the town center. The Hevven Police Department, which occupied the first floor and basement of the Town Hall, was situated at one end of a small oval-shaped rotary. From there he could see the busiest part of town. The buildings were small, mostly one or two levels. With the exception of a McDonalds, a Dunkin' Donuts, and a Citgo station, most of the businesses appeared to be of the "mom 'n pops" variety. With its shady sidewalks and wide boulevards, Hevven didn't look like the kind of town that bred cults or killers. In fact, it looked like the kind of place where one might go to escape such hazards. But Agent Ferren knew better.

"So," Bailey said as they crossed the parking lot, "how long have you been with the Bureau?"

"Nine years," Ferren answered without hesitation.

"Yeah? Do ya like it?"

He grinned. "It's a paycheck."

"Yeah, I hear ya."

"Let me ask you something," Ferren said. He cocked a thumb over his shoulder. "Is he always so pleasant?"

"The Chief? No," Bailey said with a boyish smile. "Usually he's in a bad mood."

Ferren smiled. The two of them would get along just fine.

Bailey led him around the back of the building and through the gated entrance of a chain link fence. "Well, this one's mine." He motioned toward a new Ford Taurus.

They got into the patrol car, and Bailey did a U-turn out of the parking lot and started driving toward Roller Coaster Road, where the crime scene was. "Where are you staying?" he asked after a few minutes.

"The Holiday Inn in Middleboro. I arrived early this morning."

Early? thought Bailey. He glanced down at the digital clock on the dashboard. It was 7:30 a.m.

Leaning over to turn on the air conditioner, Bailey said, "If you don't mind my asking, why would the FBI bother to investigate one dead girl?"

Ferren raised an eyebrow. "What makes you think there was only one?"

~Thirteen~

By 10 o'clock that morning, the task of settling the cabin was near completion.

Karen and Lou had each chosen the uneasy task of cleaning the interior, evenly dividing the chores between them. He cleaned the spider webs from the cupboards; she dusted and scrubbed the countertops. He swept the two upstairs bedrooms (which were mostly empty but for a couple of folding chairs, a dismantled bed, and a stack of crusty newspapers dating back to the early 1980s); she swept the living room and kitchen.

Meanwhile, Mike and Rick systematically worked their way around the outside of the cabin, prying loose the heavy plywood sheets that covered each window and handing them to Max, who then placed them in a stack beside the porch. The most difficult task, however, was finding access to the second floor windows. Out of pure laziness, Max had suggested that they leave those windows boarded, but Mike, in his usual determination, swiftly solved their dilemma, with his discovery of an old wooden ladder that was hidden in the underbrush by the foundation of the cabin.

All this, and still their auburn-haired guest slept upon the couch where Rick had laid her hours ago. She had not moved, but to breathe.

Now the sun was directly overhead, burning a white-hot hole in the blue summer sky. The morning mist had long since evaporated,

revealing the details of the mountains in the distance, their jagged
granite faces and piney scalps.

Sitting on the porch steps, Rick felt at one with nature.
Dragonflies flitted across the meadow, rattling their brittle wings,
while butterflies glided silently, like leaves dancing in the breeze.
He sat alone, watching two young squirrels play hide-and-go-seek in
a nearby grove of balsam firs, listening to the birds play their
pennywhistles as they flapped about their daily routines. His gray
T-shirt was stained black with sweat under his armpits and between
his shoulder blades, and his dark hair was sprinkled with dust.

"Looks like we're done, man," Mike said, stepping out onto the
porch.

Rick looked up at him, took a long drag from his cigarette, and
nodded.

Mike went over and stood at the railing, eyes tracing the course
of the river in the distance. A moment later the others joined them
outside.

"Can I bum a smoke off someone?" asked Max.

Rick gave him a funny look, tossed him a pack of Marlboros.

"Thanks, dude," Max beamed, lighting up a cigarette.

"So...what now?" asked Karen.

"Hmmm," Mike started. "Well, to start, I think we should take
turns going into town for supplies. It will be harder to identify us if
we're not in a group."

"Assuming anyone's even looking for us," Max said.

"Oh, they're looking for us, alright."

Rick stamped out his cigarette on the walkway. He looked up at
Mike. "How can you be so sure?"

Mike shrugged. "I dunno. The way that cop acted on the
phone...like he was talking to a criminal. The fact that they were at
my house before we even called them. Not to mention what Trisha
Saunders told Karen she'd heard about us on the police scanner."

"Alright, alright," said Max. "So what're we gonna do?"

"Two of us will go into town, get some supplies to last a few
days," Mike said. "I say our best bet is canned food. Stuff that
won't go bad, maybe some burgers or hot dogs for tonight. And a
cooler with ice. We should also pick up a couple flashlights, and

some batteries." He paused to collect his thoughts as he paced back and forth across the porch, wringing his hands and running his fingers through his wavy brown hair.

"Unfortunately," he continued, "our budget is extremely limited for the amount of people we have, so if there's something you want, as long as it's within reason, then write it down, especially if you think we'll need it later on. Once the money's gone...well, I guess we'll worry about that when the time comes."

"What about my ATM card?" asked Karen. "There's got to be a bank machine around here somewhere, right?"

"I don't think that's a good idea," Mike said, shaking his head.

"How come?" asked Max. "You said yourself we could use the money."

"The cops can trace that stuff," remarked Rick. "Credit cards, bank cards, gas cards ...the cops will be keeping an eye out for those things."

"Okay," Karen said. "So we get some groceries. Then what?"

"Then we'll settle in. And eventually we'll call home and see if everything has blown over."

"And what if it hasn't? Then what?" Karen hugged herself despite the heat.

"We wait," Mike answered matter-of-factly.

"That's it?" Lou asked nervously, his brown eyes widening in disbelief. "That's your big plan?"

"What about calling the cops and telling them what really happened?" asked Rick. "Once they dust for fingerprints, they'll know we weren't the only ones in that house, right?"

Mike shook his head. "I already thought about that. The only problem is, how will we know if they're telling us the truth? I don't know about the rest of you, but I don't wanna wind up in jail while that...that bastard is still running loose. Until we sort shit out, it won't be safe to go home."

"What about Mom and Dad?" asked Lou. "What if he goes after them?"

Mike shook his head. "Don't worry about that. It'll be all over the news that we skipped town. It wouldn't make sense for him to go after any of our parents."

"So who's gonna make the first trip?" asked Max.

"Me and Karen."

"Well, let's start a list," Karen said. "Anyone got some paper?"

Before anyone could reply, Max farted and grunted at the same time. "Speaking of lists," he said, "I gotta drop a mean friggin' bomb. Who's got the toilet paper?"

The others looked at each other and shrugged.

Mike chuckled. "We don't got any. You'll have to wait until we get back from the store."

Max took a step back, made a sour face. "Aargh! You gotta be shittin' me! You don't got nuthin' in your car? Napkins? Paper? Anything!"

Mike shook his head, laughing. "Sorry, dude. Looks like you're shit out of luck."

"Look out!" Max grunted. He pushed Lou out of the way and vaulted over the porch steps, shouting out obscenities as he made a beeline for the nearby woods.

His friends laughed as they watched his desperate flight for privacy.

"HEY, MAX!" Mike hollered after him. "WATCH OUT FOR POISON IVY!"

They all laughed a little harder.

"What about the girl?" Karen asked, after their laughter had died away. "Shouldn't we get her to a hospital?"

Mike stared off into the mountains while he considered her question. "Honestly, I don't know. What do you guys think?"

Lou chewed his bottom lip and shrugged.

"She could be seriously hurt," Karen said.

Mike turned around to face her. He was frowning. "I know. I've been thinking about that."

"She sure as hell didn't act like she was hurt," Rick said, remembering her wild behavior in the back of the Thunderbird. His fingers went to the scratches on his face. "Then again, we can't hold her here against her will. That's kidnapping."

"How 'bout this," Mike said. "We wait until she wakes up and then we'll decide."

If she wakes up, thought Karen. But she kept that thought to herself.

And so it was decided.

"Good," Mike said, sounding rather pleased. "Now let's get going on that list."

~Fourteen~

The road leading back to the center of Willow's Creek was both a speedster's dream and a trucker's nightmare, an endless ribbon of steep inclines, rapid declines, and hairpin turns.

Mike Swart drove slowly, fighting his natural thirst for speed. He did not want to get pulled over. Besides, Karen was with him, and it made her nervous when he drove too fast, especially after Lori's fatal crash. Mike eased up on the gas pedal as gravity pulled them to the bottom of a tall hill. He glanced down at the speedometer and saw that they were already going 65 mph. Even the Thunderbird seemed eager for acceleration.

"You're awfully quiet," Karen observed, brushing the hair back from her face. "Is there anything wrong? Well, besides the obvious?"

Mike squinted for no reason. "No," he said too quickly, "I'm fine. How you holdin' up?"

Karen gave him a look.

Mike bit his lip. "I was just thinking..."

"About what?"

"About last night. I still can't get that dead girl out of my mind. It was horrible. Just fuckin' horrible, what he did to her. Everything happened so fast. I didn't really have time to think it over, us coming here."

She squeezed his arm. "Better to be safe than sorry."

119

"Uh-huh. But still, maybe it wasn't such a good idea. I mean, who knows what's going on back home, what kind of shit they're saying about us."

The road flattened out, and they soon arrived at a traffic light. The light was red, and Karen turned to him as they came to a stop. She took his hand and held it.

"You didn't have much of a choice," Karen whispered, as she lovingly stroked his hand. "You were forced into making a decision. So you made one. Nobody should have to make those kinds of decisions, Mike. Nobody. But think about it: Everyone's together. Everyone's okay, thanks to you. Just remember, your friends trust you. You didn't force them to come here. They believe in you. I believe in you."

Mike smiled, looked deep into her eyes, and gave her a kiss on the forehead. "Thanks," he said. "I mean that."

Just remember, your friends trust you.

They believe in you.

I believe in you.

That's what scares me the most, he thought.

~ Fifteen ~

Later that morning, after a brief tour of the Moody house, Officer Bailey and Agent Ferren were sitting at a corner booth in Donut Hevven, an all-night coffee shop nestled in the heart of Hevven. Bailey was watching Ferren, who sat hunched over a notebook, going over the notes he had taken while at the crime scene.

"Let's see," Ferren continued. "So far, your detectives have taken several blood and urine samples, as well as several sets of fingerprints, and casts of the tire marks which were presumably left by our suspect's car. Hmmm. What does that leave us with? Oh, yes, the fingernail fragment we found, which may or may not..."

While Agent Ferren continued, an attractive young blonde rollerbladed by the window, seemingly oblivious to the wandering eyes that followed her. On the opposite side of the street, a greasy-looking man in a beat-up Datsun turned his head to watch her, unaware that the cars ahead of him were slowing down. At the last possible moment he slammed on his brakes, stopping three inches from the car in front of him, his face turning the very same color as the light for which the traffic had stopped.

"I was thinking about what you said before," Bailey spoke softly. "About there being more than one victim. What, exactly, did you mean by that?"

Ferren flexed his jaw. He gave the young officer a hard, penetrating stare. He closed his notebook. "This is purely speculation," he explained. "So if you tell anyone about this I'll deny this conversation ever took place. This is just between the two of us. If the media gets a hold of this, both of our asses will be in the same sling. Understand?"

Bailey nodded deliberately. This was the closest he'd ever come to real police work. Besides, he never much cared for reporters anyway. He watched as Ferren withdrew a folded piece of paper from his breast pocket and spread it out on the table. It looked like a map of New England, if New England had been stricken by a bad case of the chickenpox. Bailey took one last sip from his coffee and bent over to study the map. "What do all those red dots mean?"

"Those are all the places where people, mostly young women, have vanished over the past 10 or so years." Ferren tapped his finger on the map. "Five years ago, in Connecticut, 19 year-old Darlene Wiggins disappeared without a trace just two miles from her home." His finger continued across the map. "That same year, three other girls vanished from various parts of New England: Maine, Rhode Island, and northern Mass. A year later, Carla Peteit, 18, vanished from her parents' farm in Vermont. The same month, two girls, one from southern Vermont, the other from New Hampshire, disappeared as well."

"Runaways?"

"Their parents would like to think so. Hell, I'd like to think so. Then we could all sleep a little easier at night, couldn't we? But it gets worse."

Officer Bailey felt a tingle in his spine. He glanced out the window.

Several minutes earlier three young boys had parked their bikes in the bike rack, and they were now standing outside the window, munching on chocolate frosted donuts and looking at Pokémon cards.

Agent Ferren continued, "Skipping ahead to this past month, and we have three more unexplained disappearances. The first was 21 year-old Julie Tarring, a waitress from Brockton. She disappeared from her employer's parking lot after her shift ended at 11 o'clock in the evening. She left her car, her purse, her driver's license; everything. Then, a little over a week ago, 19 year-old Anna

Hartsoe, a local college student, vanished on her way to Martha's Vineyard, where she was supposed to be spending the summer with a friend. She packed her bags, said goodbye to her roommate, and no one has seen her, or her car, since. Judging by the description her parents gave when they filed her Missing Person's Report, Miss Hartsoe could be our victim from the Moody house, which would probably mean that fingernail we found was hers. We won't know for sure until the results come back from the crime lab."

"And the other girl?" Bailey asked.

Ferren sighed, but his eyes remained steady. "The other young lady, Stacey Ann Mackinnon, was attending the summer semester at Quincy College. She was last seen jogging, roughly one mile from her apartment. She was last seen wearing a gray hooded sweatshirt similar to the one that was found in the room with the victim. I doubt if she's our vic, though, because their descriptions are nothing alike. Her parents also filed a Missing Persons Report. That was just a few days ago. But so far, nothing."

"So," Bailey asked nervously. "If that's not her body we saw, then where is she?"

"Oddly enough, it seems as though our suspects may have taken her with them."

"Do you suppose they're looking for a ransom?"

Agent Ferren shook his head. He traced an imaginary circle on the map. "It just doesn't add up. We have one body, and three girls, all gone without a trace within weeks of one another. All within a 20-mile radius of here. And I have no idea how our suspects fit into all of this, if at all. If they're looking for a ransom, why didn't they leave a ransom note? Why kill the one girl and take the other with them?"

Bailey looked skeptical. "But there must be like, what, 20 marks on this map? And you think they're all connected?"

"Twenty-seven," Ferren corrected him.

"Shhhit," Bailey said breathlessly.

"Twenty-seven girls in 10 years," Ferren continued, "all gone without a trace." He took the map, folded it, and tucked it back into his pocket. "And that's a conservative number. I'm sure there are others, ones we don't know about. And yes, I believe the same person is responsible for all of them. I've been following these cases for several years now, mostly on my own time, and I still haven't found a single piece of solid evidence to convince the STF to open a full investigation. Now, let me ask you something. What do you know about The Hacker?"

Bailey almost laughed in spite of himself. "Rumors, mostly." He slouched back against the seat, pausing to drink his coffee. After a moment, he went on. "Back in the 70s the body of a local girl was found in a dumpster. She was just 16. As the rumor goes, her face had been cut up like a puzzle. Not long after, another body was found. Then another. The town went nuts, and the Department ordered a 10 o'clock curfew for anyone under the age of 18. A couple weeks later, Moriarty nabbed a drifter from Texas who had a history of violent crimes. Pennington, I think his name was. Something like that. Anyway, he confessed to the murders and was shipped off to Walpole. A week before trial, he hung himself with a blanket. The locals kept the story going by turning it into one of those what-do-ya-call-its?"

"Urban legends?"

"Yeah," Bailey nodded his head. "Most people don't believe it ever really happened. And the folks who were around back then refuse to talk about it. Probably afraid it would lower their property values or somethin'. You think that has something to do with all this? Maybe these kids were actin' out some kinda weird-ass fantasy about The Hacker, copy-catting his murders?"

"No," Ferren said flatly. "What I know is that, for the past 10 years, someone has been abducting young girls from this area. For lack of evidence these girls have been catalogued as runaways, despite the fact that most of them don't fit the profile."

"Hold on a minute. I don't get it. If none of these girls fit the profile, how come the STF never bothered to investigate before now?"

Ferren smiled grimly. "You said The Hacker's first victim was 16, and her body was left out in the open?"

Bailey nodded emphatically, "Yeah, that's right."

"He probably didn't plan that murder the way he planned the other ones. That one was spontaneous. You could say it was his practice run. The media probably had a field day with it. It made him cautious. Cautious enough to go undetected all these years. It made him a better killer."

Bailey nodded thoughtfully and tilted his head back to take a sip of coffee.

"Don't you see?" Ferren said quietly. "That first murder made him smarter. After that, almost all of his victims were 18 or older. After that, he made damn sure no one would find the bodies."

Bailey's eyes brightened above the rim of his white Styrofoam cup. "And because of their ages, their parents couldn't report them as being missing. At least not right away, because once you turn 18 you have a legal right to go anywhere you want."

"That's exactly right," Ferren frowned. "Unless there's some sign of foul play, there's not a helluva lot the authorities can do, except to file a report."

"So instead of leaving his victims' bodies where someone will find them, the way most serial killers do, this guy hides them somewhere safe?"

Ferren nodded. "Which makes him rather unique. You see, most serial killers want to see their stories on the news, and in the papers. They leave their victims where they'll be found, not necessarily because they want to get caught, but because they want to prove to the world that they're smarter than the police. But not this guy. He's possessive of them. He keeps them for himself. And he's done a damn good job up until now. Something must've gone wrong. After so many years, why would he get sloppy now? No. This guy's too smart for that. It doesn't make any sense. This body was practically handed to us."

"It was?"

"You saw the crime scene. It was a slaughterhouse. It's not the first time he's killed there. Once we get some prints back from the lab, I'm sure we'll be able to rule out each of our current suspects. Like Moriarty suggested this morning, although it didn't sound like he really believes it, I doubt if those local boys had anything to do with this girl's murder. I think they just happened to be in the wrong place at the wrong time."

Bailey squinted his eyes. "But what about that guy Pennington, the one who confessed to the original murders? Where did he fit in to all this?"

"That," Ferren said, "is a very good question."

"And if Mike Swart and his friends aren't guilty, then where are they? And why did they run?"

Ferren folded his hands and leaned forward across the table. "That's easy," he said. "Think about it. When do people usually run?"

Bailey narrowed his eyebrows and shrugged.

"When they're being chased," Ferren said at last.

~Sixteen~

An hour later, Mike Swart and Karen Sloan returned from the store with a back seat full of shopping bags and a full tank of gas. Mike had expected to find his friends still sitting on the porch, eagerly awaiting their arrival, but there was no one in sight. He parked the car and sat there thinking, worried that something terrible had happened in his absence. It wasn't until he'd gotten out of the car that he heard the tell-tale sound of their laughter coming from the river.

Mike grinned, relieved. "Looks like they decided to go for a swim. I can't blame 'em. Hey, what do you say we take a walk down there?"

Karen looked over at him with a boys-will-be-boys look and rolled her eyes. "Go on," she said.

"Huh?"

"Go on," she repeated.

"No. We gotta get these groceries inside."

"Don't worry, I can get them on my own. I'll make some sandwiches and meet you down there. Besides, I gotta find something I can wear into the water."

"Are you sure?"

She nodded.

Mike gave her his best smile. "You're awesome. I'll see you down there."

He dashed away to join his friends. Karen watched him for a few seconds, marveling at his speed. He was almost to the river by the time she had lifted the second bag of groceries into her slender arms. She heard someone whoop a greeting upon his arrival. *Probably Max*, she thought without realizing it. Their voices echoed across the valley, the distant sound of children on a playground. Karen smiled to herself and huffed a little as she hoisted the two bags of groceries up the porch steps. For the first time since yesterday, she felt totally at ease.

Nudging the door open with her sandaled foot, Karen entered the cabin with the overwhelming sensation that everything was going to be alright. Mike would see them through this thing, as always.

She had one foot in the kitchen when she realized that something was missing. From some faraway place, she heard the sound of glass breaking as the two bags of groceries landed at her feet. A jar of all-natural Teddy Bear peanut butter rolled across the wooden floor and stopped at the base of the coffee table.

The couch was empty. On the floor there was a crumpled blanket, also empty. The clothes she had left at the foot of the couch, untouched. *The girl*, thought Karen. *Where's the girl?* It occurred to her, as she crossed the living room floor, that perhaps the girl had awakened while she and Mike were at the store, and was at the river with the others. She was still considering this as she bent over to retrieve the runaway peanut butter jar. That was how she discovered her.

She was naked on the floor, holding her knees against her chest, cowering in the corner between the side of the couch and the wall. Her auburn hair was slick with sweat. Her body trembled as she tried to speak, but no words came out. She motioned toward her open mouth.

Karen understood immediately. She darted across the room and returned five seconds later. Remembering the scratches on Rick's face, she maintained a safe distance as she crouched down beside the girl. Karen twisted the cap off the Evian bottle and the girl drank with her eyes closed, the cold water dribbling down her neck and over her bare breasts.

128

"Go slow," Karen whispered, but the girl ignored her. She drank, stopped, panted, and drank again, like a baby nursing from a bottle.

After she had taken her fill, she wiped her mouth with the back of one hand, lips slightly parted. "Where the hell am I?" she asked in a raspy voice, blue eyes bouncing off the unfamiliar walls.

Karen leaned over and grabbed the T-shirt and shorts she'd left by the couch. "Here," Karen said, helping the girl to her feet. "Put these on."

The girl looked down at herself. She had been unaware of her nakedness until just now. On trembling legs she dressed herself slowly, wincing at the soreness in her limbs.

"Do you need to go to a hospital?"

The girl shook her head and stared at Karen for a few seconds. She rubbed her wrists; the skin was still raw from the shackles. "How ...did you get me out of that place?"

"Not me," Karen said gently. "My friends. What's your name?"

"Stacey...Mackinnon."

"You're far away from that house now, Stacey. You're safe, okay?"

Stacey Mackinnon bit her bottom lip and nodded, shuddering as her mind conjured up images of that dark room, where she had listened to the blood-curdling screams of those other girls, and the laughter of that hideous thing that had held them captive there. She only hoped that this place, this dark-haired girl, was real, that she wasn't back in that room, kneeling and praying for her life, insane with fear.

She had remained strong at first, convincing herself that help was on the way. In the end it was the screams which had broken her down. Those tortured screams of girls she could not see. And what of them? Where was the help they had so desperately prayed for in the darkness? When she spoke again, there was venom in her voice. "He ka-killed them all. F-fucking k-killed them like they were nuh-nothing. And I would have been next...he told me to pray...to pray for my sins, and not to stop or he'd kill me. I don't know how l-long I prayed. Hours? Days? I hope that bastard pays for what he did."

Me too, thought Karen. *Me too.*

129

"Can you take me home, please? I just wanna go home."

Karen didn't know quite what to say. She lowered her head. How could she tell this girl that the nightmare wasn't over, that the man she spoke of had not yet been apprehended by the police?

"What is it?" Stacey asked. "Is there something you're not telling me?"

Starting with the call from Trisha Saunders, Karen told her all she knew.

~Seventeen~

As the sun ducked down behind the mountains and the stars unfolded in the sky, four friends sat with their new acquaintance on a sandy strip of beach at the water's edge, warming their hands over a small fire. Max was not with them. He had mumbled something about the mosquitoes, and had wondered off in search of bug spray. It was quiet without him.

Stacey Mackinnon sat Indian-style on the grass, considering the flames. She had not spoken much since being introduced to her rescuers, save for a few small details about her abduction, her mind still wandering back to the events that had befallen her. After listening to their story, she had readily agreed to stay with them until they could straighten out the mess they were in. After all they had done for her, she felt she owed it to them. Such a strange feeling, owing your life to a bunch of strangers.

"Anyone want some chips?" Karen asked, holding up a bag of Cool Ranch Doritos.

They were momentarily distracted by the sound of footsteps.

"Lookee what I found!" Max smiled as though he had just won the lottery. He was holding a bottle of vodka.

"Where the hell did you get that?" asked Mike.

"In your trunk." He plopped down by the fire. He poured some vodka into a Gatorade bottle and passed it to Stacey. "Here, have some medicine."

Stacey smiled a little, showing her well-formed cheekbones. "Thanks," she said, and took a small, polite sip. It wasn't that bad, really. She could hardly taste the vodka. She took another sip and passed the bottle off to Karen.

"Are there any beers left?" Mike asked.

"Yeah, but they're piss-warm. I stuck 'em in the cooler," Max said.

The last rays of sunlight trickled away, and the vodka-flavored Gatorade continued to make its way around the fire. Soon Mike started telling jokes (mostly good ones), followed by Max, who also told jokes (mostly bad ones), while the others laughed and groaned, grateful for the distraction. Through the eyes of an outsider, they would have looked like any other teenagers, living it up on a Friday night. But hidden behind their smiling eyes, temporarily routed by their laughter, they struggled to repress their secret demons.

By the time she realized she was drunk, Stacey felt as though she had known them all for years. Such was the comradery of alcohol. After a while, she went over and sat next to Rick. "Do you mind if I bum a cigarette from you?"

"No." He drew one from his pack and handed it to her.

She bowed her head, rolling the cigarette between her fingers. "Karen told me how you got me out of that house…how you took care of me. I just wanted to say thanks. I know that probably doesn't mean much now, after all that's happened, but I had to say it anyway."

She raised her head and put the cigarette between her lips. Rick nodded, deliberately avoiding her eyes. "Don't worry about it," he told her in his soothing, gritty voice. "I'm just glad you're okay."

Her slender fingers fluttered briefly over his hand as he bent to light her cigarette. "I'm sorry," she said, exhaling the smoke from one side of her mouth. "About what I did to your face."

For a moment, their eyes met. Once again, he found himself admiring the sensuous curves of her mouth, her flawless complexion, and the stunning blue of her drowsy, almond-shaped eyes. He remembered the warmth and softness of her skin, from when he had touched her cheek in the back of Mike's car. Aside from the fact that she was a college student, and had been abducted

132

several days ago while jogging in a park somewhere in Quincy (all of which she had confided to them earlier that evening), he hardly knew a thing about her. Looking at her, he couldn't help but wonder: Where did she come from? What kind of life had she lived before their paths had crossed at the house on Roller Coaster Road? How old was she? Nineteen? Twenty? Certainly, she was more of a woman than a girl.

After a few seconds, he realized he was staring and quickly looked away.

"It was my fault," he said without looking at her.

She gestured toward the bandage on his wrist. "Did I do that too?"

When he did not answer, she decided not to press him any further. He seemed uncomfortable with her gratitude. She smoked her cigarette in silence, watching the sparks dance like fireflies, twisting, twirling up into the night sky. Although she felt safe with this quiet, thoughtful boy, she could not shake the feeling that he was hiding something from her. She thought she saw a trace of sadness in those kind hazel eyes. Was it pity? She wondered. Pity for her? Or was it the aftershock of all that had happened the night before?

When the fire had reduced itself to a pitiful heap of embers, and the insects swarmed in, becoming too much to bear, they headed back to the cabin together, eager for a good night's sleep.

As Mike made his way across the meadow, one arm over Karen's shoulders and the other holding a flashlight he had purchased at the store, a familiar chorus of voices buzzed inside his mind. Of course, he knew where these voices were coming from.

It was Uncle Jack's giants again.

Good night, Mikey.

Still walking, Mike made a quick backward glance, so as not to attract Karen's attention. There they stood, blotting out the sky; the jagged silhouettes of the mountains, the giants.

Good night, Mike returned with his mind's voice.

He and Karen were the last ones to enter the cabin, and as he bolted the door behind them, such strange feelings overcame him.

He felt that everything was in its place.

133

He felt protected and safe.

He felt like he was home.

Lou Swart looked up from his makeshift bed on the floor. Through the bedroom window he beheld the great ghost of the northern sky. The moon looked close enough to touch, its edges smudged by silvery wisps of clouds. He had never seen so many stars in his life.

After a while, he rolled over and stared at his roommate's back. "Hey, Max, you still awake?" he inquired softly.

"Would I answer you if I wasn't?" Max asked in a dry voice, not moving.

"Do you think people back home are...you know, worried about us?"

"Your parents are probably worried. Rick's parents are probably worried, too. Shit, Karen's parents are probably sticking up those missing persons posters all over town," Max said in a matter-of-fact manner. But when he continued there was a trace of sadness in his voice. "But my old man...he probably just thinks I'm in my room, or crashing over someone's house. He wouldn't give a shit, even if he knew the truth."

"I'm sorry. I didn't mean to..."

"Don't worry about it, dude. I'm just a little drunk, and I'm babbling. Now shut up and go to sleep, willya?"

"Alright," Lou agreed. He rolled onto his side, shifted his butt around a little, and closed his eyes.

"Hey, Max...you still awake?"

"Whatsit this time?"

"What do you think about that girl... Stacey?"

"She's pretty hot. Nice ass, too. And that tattoo is kinda sexy. But I think she's got a thing for Rick. You see the way she was looking at him?"

"Yeah," Lou sighed longingly. "But that's a good thing, right?"

"I guesso."

"I mean, it's almost like...fate that they met. And ever since Lori died..." Lou stopped there, already wishing he hadn't said her name.

"Yeah," Max answered, "I know what you mean." And he understood completely. Ever since Lori Shawnessy had died, Rick Hunter had become but a shadow of the boy he had once been. But tonight, at the campfire, as Rick laughed at their jokes, and made eyes at Stacey Mackinnon, Max had seen traces of the friend he once knew.

Hell, yeah, it was a good thing. Max still wasn't sure if coming to the cabin was a good idea, but he knew it was better than turning themselves in to the police. And if Stacey could somehow help Rick to forget about his pain, even temporarily, at least something good would come out of this mess. That one thing would make it all worthwhile.

Max thought about this as he closed his eyes, and the crickets sang him lullabies until he fell asleep.

~ Eighteen ~

The weekend came and went.

It passed by with the fluidness of a dream. Twice Mike, Rick, and Max had wandered off to explore the forest, each time returning with firewood and sap-stained hands and stories about deer tracks and the wildlife they had seen. They had scattered the ashes of their original fire and dug a deep pit in the same spot, and surrounded it with stones. Lou mostly kept to himself, hovering over the magazines Mike had brought back from the store: *Popular Science, Entertainment Weekly*, and a month-old copy of *Sports Illustrated*. Of the two girls, one was never seen without the other. They passed the hours talking, in that open and honest manner that was exclusive only to the sisterhood of women. They talked about clothes, music, movies, and Karen's obsession with Starbucks coffee. Stacey had just completed her first year at Quincy, and she spoke of the woes of higher education and the difficult transition from high school to college, the snobby professors and expensive textbooks, the wild parties and crazy roommates. Then they would all gather at the river, to swim during the day and to sit by the fire at night; a routine they would get to know quite well. How long before they could go home? Strangely, that question had somehow transformed itself into a different one: How long before they would *have to* go home?

On Monday morning, as they gathered by the river, Mike put those questions on the table. After some discussion it was agreed that they would first try to contact Kevin Chapman, in order to get

137

an honest perspective as to where they stood with the police. They weren't sure if Kev was still in rehab, but Mike thought it was worth a try.

It wasn't long before the somber mood of their discussion wore on Max's playful side, and before anyone knew what had happened, he had already scooped up Lou in a bear hug and had tossed the squirming boy into the river.

"Sonofabitch!" Lou panted as he stood waist-high in the water. "You sonofabitch! What the hell did you do that for?"

Max stood on the water's edge, doubled over with laughter.

"Yeah, that's real funny," Lou muttered. "Dickweed!"

"Call me dickweed again, you little dork, and you'll really be sorry."

"Dickweed, dickweed, dickweed!"

Max stripped down to his boxers and dove in after him.

Watching the two wrestle playfully in the water, even Rick seemed to enjoy himself, which made Mike enjoy himself all the more.

"Oh, it's so hot, I feel like I'm gonna faint," Karen said in a tired voice, as she fanned herself. "What do you say we all go for a swim?"

Stacey raised her expressive eyebrows and nodded wholeheartedly.

"I'm down with that," Mike said. "Anyone else coming? Rick?"

"Sounds good to me," Rick said, already starting off in the direction of the cabin. "I'm gonna go grab my bathing suit. I'll be back in a little bit."

Several minutes later, Rick was sauntering back across the meadow in a pair of blue and black swimming trunks, nibbling on a blade of grass, as he admired his new surroundings. It was the kind of day that made him feel as though anything, even life without Lori, was possible. Sure, they had other things to worry about. Sure, they probably should've been trying to figure out a way to get themselves out of the mess they were in, but what the hell? Those things could wait, he supposed. There was always tomorrow. Or so he hoped.

Things wouldn't always be this good; he was smart enough to know that. And he was smart enough to take the day as it was, and not ruin it by speaking his mind. There was too much beauty here, among the mountains and the evergreens, to let ugly thoughts run loose. He'd rather sit by the river, or smoke cigarettes in the shade below the cabin eaves, and let his mind wander lazily from one place to the next. Anything to forget about his life for a while.

Inhaling the fresh mountain air, walking barefoot through the tall cool grass, he reached into the pocket of his trunks to make sure his trusty Zippo was still there, and found that it was resting safely beside his cigarettes. It made him think of Kevin once again, and he wished his friend was there to share this moment of...what was it, anyway? Joy? Serenity? Freedom? Rick didn't know exactly, but whatever it was, it was enough to make him feel like a human being again (which was something he hadn't felt since the morning after the incident at Sundown Beach.)

He joined the others at the river, where they spent the better part of the afternoon in the water and on the water's edge, laughing and talking about everything under the sun, carefully avoiding what thoughts lay hidden in the back of their minds, ready to pounce and maim.

~ Nineteen ~

Max Kendall was alone on the water's edge, reeling in his precious cargo, when he suddenly stopped what he was doing and grinned around his cigarette. From between the dark jaws of the mountains, the dim reds and purples of the harlequin sky glittered on the surface of the river like flecks of light from a disco ball, and Max was fully captivated by the spectacle of his own reflection on the water, where his face resembled an aquatic being that could only exist in the tidal pools of some alien world.

From the shallow water he pulled up a plastic shopping bag, which kept his cargo, a 12-pack of Budweisers, from escaping with the current. Earlier, he'd decided it was too much of a hassle to carry the cooler back and forth from the cabin all day, and so his lust for alcohol injected him with a sudden burst of ingenuity, and he discovered that the river would suffice in keeping the beers cold.

Meanwhile, in the background, his friends sat in a circle around a small fire, cooking hot dogs on sticks they had whittled with Mike's pocketknife. They laughed, ate, and then laughed some more, and, competing with the crickets and the nightbirds, carried on their own conversations. Full darkness had yet to arrive, but the day was leaving in a hurry, and the mountains were blowing cool night breezes through the valley.

Guided by the rich, charcoaly smell of burnt hot dogs, Max returned from the river with a handful of beers, asking, "Who wants some cold ones?"

He didn't have to ask twice.

After handing out the beers, Max sat himself down between the two brothers.

"You want a hot dog?" Lou asked.

"Sure." Max took the hot dog and chomped it in half. "It's pretty good," he said between bites. "But it could use a little ketchup or somethin'. Maybe some hot sauce, too."

"You and your hot sauce," Mike said. "I don't see how the hell you eat that shit without burning a hole through your stomach."

Chomping down the other half of his hot dog, Max shrugged.

"You drink a lot, don't you?" Stacey asked Rick after he'd polished off his first beer.

He shrugged innocently.

"I can tell," she said, trying to make eye contact. "You drink so fast. It isn't good for you. I knew a kid in college who had to have his stomach pumped."

He smiled at the tenderness in her voice. "Everything that's good is bad for you," he said softly.

"What's that mean?" she asked, looking at him questioningly.

"He means," Max interrupted from the other side of the fire, "that all the good stuff—alcohol, cigarettes, drugs, fast food, fast cars, candy bars, loud music, even sex—all that shit's bad for ya." He waved his hands in the air, as if to emphasize this, and continued in a cynical voice. "Someday, they'll find out that microwave food gives you cancer, or that too many potatoes can kill ya, or some other stupid fuckin' crap. Scientists prove that everything's bad for you sooner or later; that doesn't mean you have to give up the things you like...what would be the point of living?"

"Thank you for those words of wisdom, Mister Kendall," Mike said sarcastically, and saluted him with two fingers. "It's a wonder you barely graduated."

"Okay, but that still doesn't tell me why you drink so much." Stacey looked at Rick, her eyes gleaming playfully.

Rick guzzled some beer, thought about it, guzzled some more.

Again, it was Max who rushed to answer her. "Some people drink to remember, I guess. Some drink to forget. Some people just like the feeling of a good buzz; it helps them to forget some of their problems for a little while. Plus, it's fun."

"Oh, I see," Stacey said sarcastically, and Max smiled at her as he walked to the other side of the fire, where he sat between Mike and Lou. Then she turned, leaning closer to Rick, so that their shoulders were almost touching. "And which one are you?" she said softly, studying his face in the flickering yellow light. "Do you drink to remember, do you drink to forget, or do you just like to get drunk for the heck of it?"

"All of the above," he answered quietly, and grabbed another beer. He looked up, and for a brief moment, their eyes met.

"Do you want one?" he asked.

Stacey stared at him for a moment, feigning indignation. Then she smiled warmly. "I thought you'd never ask."

~Twenty~

An hour later.

"Where's Max?"

"Over there, Ricky. By the river," Mike said, rising from his place by the fire. He dusted off his jeans. "I gutta take a leak."

"You're drunk, aren't you?" Karen called after him as he stepped away from the firelight and into the shadows. She picked up a flashlight—one of the three she and Mike had bought during their trip to the store—and directed the beam at his ass.

"Naw," Mike said, unzipping his pants. "Not me."

Karen leaned over and whispered to Stacey, "He's lying. He's drunk. I can tell by that dopey smile."

The two girls giggled softly.

"I heard that!" Mike said over his shoulder as he relieved himself, and the two girls erupted into a fit of laughter. "Hey can someone get me a smoke?"

"Mike!" Karen scolded. "You better not be smoking again! You promised me you'd quit."

Rick got up and found Max standing alone at the water. "What's up?"

"Nuthin'," Max said, his eyes hidden behind long strands of hair. He took out a crumpled pack of cigarettes and lit one with a match.

"I was just thinking the same thing," Rick said, and fired up a cigarette with Kev's Zippo.

Enjoying their cigarettes, they stood listening to the muffled voices and hushed giggles of their friends in the background.

"Do ya ever wonder why people turn out the way they do?" Max said after a while. "I mean, you don't have it so bad. You're smart. You're parents are pretty cool. You manage to keep yourself out of trouble...most of the time. And everyone knows Mike's gonna make something of his life...something good. Do you think it's fate, or do you think people can change their...what the fuck do ya call it?...their destinies?"

"I don't know," Rick said, surprised that Max would even consider such things as destiny and fate. "I guess it depends on the person."

"It's just that, sometimes, I wonder where I fit in with you guys. This is the first time I've ever been out of Hevven. I mean, really out of Hevven, y'know? I mean, my mom died when I was just a kid. And my dad, he never had the money for us to travel anywhere. Pretty much the only place I go is to Boston, and that's just to buy weed and shit. This is probably the closest thing I've ever come to a vacation, and God only knows what kinda shit we'll be in when it's over."

Rick stood beside him in the darkness. "I know what you mean, brutha. I..."

"No offense, man. But you don't know. If that guy from the house finds us here...I don't wanna die. I can't die, man. Not yet. I've pissed my entire life away, because that's what my father did, and that's what I knew was expected of me. I mean, my dad's the town drunk. Everybody knows it. Even when I was a little kid, when people looked at me... parents...teachers...I could see it in their eyes. They gave up on me long before I ever gave up on myself. So I stepped right into my father's shoes, 'cause I thought it would be comfortable there. But you know what? It's not. I've acted like an idiot all my life, and I don't wanna die and have people remember me like that."

Max paused to catch his breath. He ran his fingers through his long hair, brushing it back from his face and tucking it behind his ears. His blue-gray eyes burned brightly in the darkness, brighter than the orange tip of the cigarette he was holding in his hand.

"No one's gonna die," Rick said, trying his best to sound convincing. Then, almost as an afterthought, he added: "Who cares

146

what people think about you? Life doesn't start and stop in Hevven. There are bigger and better things out there, for all of us. So don't let anyone tell you who you are, don't let anyone else define you, because that's up to you. You can be anyone you wanna be, man."

Max bowed his head and nodded solemnly. He reached into his front jeans pocket, removing two neatly folded Ziplock bags. He held them up so that both he and Rick could see their contents in the moonlight. The larger of the two bags held three joints and some marijuana flakes; the smaller held a dozen or so pills of various shapes and colors.

It's my life in this bag, Max realized. *Every dollar I've ever earned. Every thing I've ever done. I never thought I'd end up like this. I'm a loser.* The truth now dawned on him: He was nothing but a useless piece of shit, just like his father always said. His father had told him, when he was very young, that his mother had left because she knew her son was nothing but a piece of shit. Max always thought his father had made that story up, but now he wasn't so sure.

Rick watched Max with steady interest, blocking out the detached laughter of his friends in the background. He'd never seen Max so down before. Something strange was happening inside his friend, and Rick could sense it. It was as though Max's mental gears were grinding down, seizing, and Rick thought when they stopped, Max would snap. *Or maybe*, thought Rick, *it's more like the gears are finally turning after so many years of being dormant. Maybe this is his awakening.*

After a few seconds, Max packed the two bags together into a single ball (*Pedro Martinez, eat your heart out*) and hurled it into the darkness, and into the river. There was no audible splash, no sound with which either of them would associate the moment later on; only silence. But the feeling of relief that washed over Max was as powerful as a tidal wave.

For a minute or more they stood in silence, each noticing how the dark outlines of the mountains rose to meet the starry sky, how the river gurgled softly downstream, reflecting moonlight as though its surface were made of diamonds, and how the full moon seemed so much closer to the earth than it did in Hevven. But above all,

147

what both of them felt, though neither of them had the need to discuss it, was peace. The two bags of drugs floated silently downstream and disappeared into the night.

"Can I ask you somethin'?" Max whispered after a little while. "And I want you to answer honestly."

"Go for it."

"Why do you guys bother with me? I mean, why do you guys put up with all my bullshit? I know I'm not a very good friend. I try, but ..."

Rick smiled in the darkness. "Because you're one of us."

"WHAT THE HELL ARE YOU GUYS DOIN' OVER THERE?" Mike called out from the fireside, and followed that with something they could not hear(probably something obscene) that made the others laugh hysterically.

Rick looked at Max. "Feel better?"

Max inhaled deeply and the tip of his cigarette flared orange, lighting up his face. "Yeah, I guess. But I could use a few more beers, that's for damn sure."

Rick chuckled. "Let's go get 'em before they're gone."

"Rick?"

"Yeah?"

"Thanks."

"No problem."

"And Rick?"

"Yeah?"

Max pointed at the bandage on his friend's wrist, the one that covered the suicide scar. "Don't you ever goddamn do that again, alright? There are bigger and better things out there, for all of us. You know what I'm sayin'?"

Rick nodded, and the two boys shook hands.

Soon they returned to the circle by the fire, and the small band of stragglers talked, joked, and told each other stories well into the night.

And in the distance, the giants sat and listened.

148

~Twenty-one~

"See you in the morning," Rick said, spreading a blanket on the oval carpet, which adorned the living room floor. He curled the blanket over his body like a taco, using his denim jacket as a pillow, under which he tucked his hands. As he rested his head upon the surrogate pillow, he closed his eyes, already feeling the gentle arms of sleep waiting to embrace him.

Stacey switched off the flashlight she was holding and set it down upon the coffee table. "G'night," she said from her place on the couch. An awkward moment of silence washed away her words. The others had retired to the upstairs bedrooms several minutes earlier, and it was so quiet she could hear the cabin creaking as it settled on its foundation.

"Good night," Rick whispered after a while, his voice muffled as he yawned into the makeshift pillow.

Stacey was the first of the two to fall asleep, and it came with unexpected ease as she thought of the boy sleeping on the floor beside her.

In the smaller of the two upstairs bedrooms, standing in the pale shaft of light that shone through the room's only window, Mike Swart stripped down to his boxers while Karen Sloan watched, admiring his lean body.

"Come to bed," Karen whispered from the floor, where she was wrapped in one of the sleeping bags she had brought from home.

149

She patted the empty space beside her, as if to emphasize her invitation, and to show that his place beside her was still waiting. *You will never, ever know how much I really love you, Mike Swart,* she thought. *Not even if we were married for a hundred years.*

Settling down, Mike pulled the remainder of the sleeping bag over himself and snuggled against her. "Love you," he whispered. He gave her a little kiss.

"You taste like beer." She giggled, her big, expressive eyes twinkling in the splash of moonlight which came from the window.

"Sorry," Mike apologized, and wiped his mouth with one hand. He put his head on her shoulder. "I love you, you know that?"

"You already said that," she teased.

"Life's too short. You can never say 'I love you' too many times."

"I know...I like to hear you say that."

He said it again.

She kissed him on the forehead. "I love you too, Mike Swart."

They said their goodnights.

I'm gonna marry this girl someday, thought Mike. He fell asleep with a dopey, drunken smile.

~Twenty-Two~

Stacey Mackinnon awoke to a cool darkness.

Lying still, she waited until her mind adjusted to the waking world. After a few moments she grabbed the flashlight from the coffee table and shined the beam on the floor where Rick had taken up for the night. Nothing there but the tangled mound of his blanket.

Concerned, she tossed her covers aside and rose soundlessly, despite her dizziness, pausing once to shake the remains of the alcohol-induced dreams from her head, and then moved on. The cabin door was open, and moonlight spilled across the threshold. She went to the open door and poked her head outside, where everything glowed a ghostly white.

Rick was leaning against the far railing, facing the river, staring off into the distance. Though it was dark and he was looking away from her, there was no doubt that he was grieving; it was in his posture, the way he was slumped forward, shoulders sagging, and how he trembled as he breathed. From this angle, had she not recognized him, she would have thought him a crippled old man.

He looks defeated, she thought. *And tired; so very tired.*

As she started onto the porch, a floorboard creaked, and the sound was magnified tenfold by the preexisting silence. Rick turned away from the heavens, and his tear-filled eyes fell upon her. With a trembling hand, he raised a cigarette to his lips and puffed on it restlessly. He sniffed a little, faked a smile that was too pinched to be sincere.

151

For a split second, the way the moon made everything pale and colorless, she felt as though she'd suddenly stepped into a black and white movie with a brooding, dark-haired James Dean. Perhaps it was the alcohol she had consumed at the campfire, but everything looked so incredibly surreal.

Stacey knew why he was upset. She knew all about Lori, the accident, and a lot of other things Karen had told her earlier that day as they sat on the sandy banks of the river.

"Rick, I..." She suddenly realized she was at a loss of words. She barely knew this boy, let alone his heart.

"I wanna be alone," he told her, bowing his head. But the sorrow in his voice wasn't so easily concealed, especially by someone who knew sorrow as well as she did. It made her heart ache with empathy. If only it was possible to ease his pain; to absorb his suffering with a simple touch. If only she could heal him. *So much pain*, she thought. *So much pain trapped inside.* She moved toward him, fumbling words in her mind.

"I just wanna be alone," he repeated, his voice trembling, rising higher. He bowed his head and tossed his cigarette away as if he hated it, as if it was the source of all of his troubles. When he lifted his head, he saw that Stacey was standing right beside him. Tenderly, she reached out and began to wipe away his tears with her soft fingertips. She looked like an angel in the moonlight.

She felt him trembling, felt the pain coursing through his veins, and the tide of emotions swelling inside of him. Before she even realized it was happening, she too began to cry. "I know," she whispered. "Karen told me everything."

Before he could object any further, he found himself holding her, this girl, this stranger, who had endured so many horrors beyond his imagination. She was crying with him, for him, for herself, her arms wrapped around him, head pressed against his shoulder, tears rolling down his jacket. It felt as though a lifetime had passed since the last time he had held somebody that way, or since he himself had been held. He could smell her skin, the faint fragrance of apricots and strawberries; he could feel her long, silky hair caressing his arms and face, the warmth of her body, the rise and fall of her chest as she breathed slowly, and it all felt so good.

Not just for him, but for the both of them. For a long time, they stood that way; two strangers holding one another, crying together.

"It's not your fault, Rick," she whispered, so lovingly that he began to cry even harder against her shoulder, stroking her long hair, wrapped in her arms like a child.

"She was there one night...then she was gone...we had an argument and I let her go, I let her go...I never shoulda let her go...I let her walk away and now she's dead and I can't live anymore...I just can't live...I wish it was me...Oh, God, why did she have to die?" Rick sobbed into her shoulder, his defenses broken down by her warm embrace.

"Everything's gonna be alright," she kept repeating, holding onto him as tightly as she could. "Everything's gonna be alright." Stacey was actually grateful to be his source of comfort, and she said these words for her own benefit as much as his; it allowed her to push her own thoughts and fears aside. The knifelike memories that surfaced, threatening to severe the last tethers of her sanity, whenever she closed her eyes—the terror of her abduction, the unspeakable horrors she had witnessed inside the abandoned house.

After some time the tears dried, and with a little coaxing on Stacey's part the two of them went back inside the dark cabin, where they slept together on the floor, still holding each other.

Soon, sleep found them once again.

It was the best sleep either of them had had in a long, long time.

~Twenty-Three~

It was getting close to midnight.

Kelly Brine stood inside the Futawam Grand Cinemas, gazing out into the parking lot, and could barely see her blue Toyota Camry in the darkness. If she hadn't known better, she would have thought some jerk had painted the windows of the theater as a joke. Painted them black. It was that dark.

She licked her lips nervously. If Kelly had known the name of the genius who had come up with the brilliant idea of having the outside lights shut off automatically after closing, she would have been on the telephone with that person right now, using language that would make her mother cringe. Though the name of that person was unknown to her, the thought of cussing him out made her smile just the same.

Still looking outside, she unlocked one of the glass doors that stood beside the ticket booth and stepped out, where it was not only dark but chilly as well. She fumbled her keys from her pocketbook and locked the theater door behind her. At the same time, she went through her nightly routine of running down a mental checklist of all the things she was supposed to do when closing the theater:

Did you make sure the cleaners did their jobs, that all the floors and bathrooms are clean? Are the rugs all vacuumed?

Check.

Did you make sure all of the candy and food was accounted for, and that any old food was thrown out?

Check.

Did you deposit the money in the night safe? Was the money all accounted for?

Check.

She turned and looked for her car on the far side of the parking lot, beside the dumpster. Still, she could not see it.

Did you lock all the doors?

Check.

Good, then it was time to go.

Taking a deep breath, she slung her brown Coach pocketbook over one shoulder, hooked one finger through her keyring, and started across the parking lot. For a moment she considered returning to the inside of the theater, where she could call one of her friends to escort her to her car. But pride made her continue. They would think she was just plain silly, afraid of going alone to her car, which was less than 50 yards away. And the comments they'd make, and the sarcastic remarks. It just wasn't worth the bother. Besides, she was already halfway there.

Kelly walked quickly, her keys jingling too loud for the stillness. She tried to tell herself to be calm. She tried to tell herself there was nothing to worry about. She was doing a pretty good job of it until...

Something moved.

She gasped, heart thudding so hard it made her chest ache. Okay, what the hell was that? She struggled to see, squinting, pushing her glasses further up the bridge of her nose, closer to her eyes.

She wasn't a supermodel, but she was far from being ugly. With short blonde hair, plump breasts, and shapely legs, she was certainly considered attractive. And though she wasn't conceited, she knew, looking like she did, walking alone at midnight in a dark parking lot, she was a prime candidate for rape.

She jerked in the direction of the sound, to her right, toward the dark woods that bordered the theater. The sound, whatever it was, was coming closer to her. Was it the rustling of clothes, perhaps? She pictured a fat balding man with a maniacal smile rushing towards her from the woods, his cow-sized pants rubbing together at the thighs, rustling, rustling, his sweaty hands extended towards her

156

as he prepared to fondle her private parts, and the image made her nauseous.

The sound continued towards her and she picked up her pace, now able to see the windshield of her car as it reflected a sliver of moonlight. Though frightened, she was sensible. It wasn't the first time she had been left alone to close the theater. And as far as she knew, no one had ever been raped in the small town of Futawam. As far as she knew, there had never been a murder, either. But in Hevven, Futawam's neighboring town, that was another story. Weird things were happening there all the time. In fact, just earlier that evening, she'd overheard two of her co-workers discussing a pack of young killers who had escaped from the police the day before, and about the body of the girl that had been found. The story was on the front page of every newspaper, and on all the local television stations. It was big news for a relatively peaceful community. Hell, they'd probably end up making a movie about it.

The rustling noise stopped.

Just an animal, she thought. *A cat or something. Here, kitty, kitty...*

She glanced back at the theater. With the lights off, the ticket booth empty, and concession stand void of the usual array of hungry moviegoers, it was a veritable ghost town back there. It seemed miles away, hours since she'd left there. As for the rest of the plaza—CVS, Payless Shoes, Happy's Music Store, the Fashionable Lady garment shop, and Bogart's Liquors—it, too, was dead.

She finally arrived at her car, feeling out her keys, trying to find the one that would open the door to safety.

The rustling began again. Faster than before. The fat balding man, with that fat smile and drooping eyes, was almost upon her. She could see him clearly in her mind. She whirled around, terrified, preparing to fight him off. Readying herself to claw out the bastard's eyeballs if she had to. And as the sound drew closer, closer, she finally witnessed the source of all her fears.

A crumpled piece of newspaper zigzagged in the breeze, rustling and scratching across the pavement. It stopped as the breeze stopped, just several feet away from her.

She sighed, smiling as she scolded herself for being so frightened. As she again set to the task of locating the key which would open the car door, the ball of newspaper was again caught in the wind, and scurried past her, disappearing in the darkness once again.

Still somewhat nervous, her trembling hands fumbled the keys and they crashed to the pavement with a metallic jing-jingle. Shaking her head in disbelief of herself, she knelt down and scooped them into her hand.

At last, she found it. It was hard to miss, really. Most of the other keys on the loop were house keys, which were all similar in shape and size, and each totally different than the thick, silver key that belonged to her Toyota.

She slid the key into the door lock, instinctively pulling the handle at the same time, and the door came open before she had a chance to turn the key. *Strange*, she thought. *I could've sworn I locked the door this afternoon.* In fact, just as a precaution, she always made sure to lock her car. *Lucky for me it wasn't stolen.* Then it dawned on her that she hadn't been paying attention. And with her back to the woods, she was completely vulnerable. *Idiot*, she thought. *I have to be more careful. After all, Hevven is only about a mile away.* She glanced quickly over her shoulder and saw...nothing.

From somewhere nearby, the rustling sound began again. Her heart thumped, then settled. *That damn newspaper again! Doesn't anybody clean the damn parking lot around here?*

She got into the car, slamming the door behind her, placing her pocketbook beside her on the passenger seat. Sliding the key into the ignition slot, Kelly started up the Toyota, turning on her headlights with a flick of her wrist. Out of habit, she looked up to adjust the rearview mirror, and as she did so, panic made her freeze.

There was a shadow in the backseat.

A shadow that was smiling.

Frozen, unable to scream, pure terror gripped her.

Then a hand gripped her as well.

By the throat.

~Twenty-Four~

"You killed me," the dead girl taunted. Maggots spilled from her open mouth and landed, squirming, on the ragged earth. She smiled wickedly, swollen lips and bloodstained teeth. In a blur, her face was three inches from his, her movements as erratic as a hummingbird's.

"I didn't kill you, Anna," Agent Ferren told the walking corpse. He tried to move away, but it was like trying to move under water.

They were standing in a seemingly endless graveyard, in the middle of a forest. There were bodies everywhere, as far as the eye could see. They dangled from the trees like Halloween ornaments, stared at the sky from shallow graves. Ferren looked from body to body. He could tell how they had died by looking at their wounds. Shot, stabbed, beaten, strangled, and burned...the list went on and on.

"You killed me," the dead girl repeated.

Her name was Anna Hartsoe, and she had been missing for a week and two days at the time her body was discovered in an upstairs room in the Moody house. Ferren knew her name because her parents had identified her body at the morgue, and because he'd spent countless hours staring at her photograph and coroner's report. Stabbed, repeatedly. Blunt trauma to the head. Severe lacerations to the neck, chest, and fingers.

"I didn't kill you," Ferren told the girl, speaking in his political tone. "But I can help you. Tell me who did this to you, and I'll make sure he pays for it."

Anna Hartsoe flashed a toothless smile. In a blur, she was facing away from him, and he could see her spine through a gaping hole in the middle of her back. A smooth black handle protruded from between her shoulder blades.

"Agent Ferren," she smiled at him over her shoulder. Her voice was schoolgirl sweet. "Can you please take the knife out of my back?"

And with that, he returned to his plain-looking room at the Holiday Inn, where he had fallen asleep fully clothed, and with the light still on. He remained motionless for a time, first trying to remember the details of his dream and then wishing he could erase it from his mind. He squinted into the too-bright light, glanced around the tiny room.

There was a bottle of Black Label on the nightstand. After no more than two seconds of consideration, he rolled over and poured himself a shot. The insistent red glow of a digital clock burned the time into his skull; it was 4:30 in the morning. He was about to nail down his second shot when the phone rang.

"'Lo?" Agent Ferren spoke into the receiver.

"Sorry to call so early, but I thought you'd want to know about this..."

Teeming with nervousness and excitement. Bailey's voice.

Ferren downed his shot. "What's going on?" he asked in his no-nonsense voice.

"Another girl vanished last night. Her name's Kelly Brine. She works as a manager at the theatre in Futawam. Her mother swears she's never been late without calling. Her car was found in the parking lot with the keys still in it."

"Any sign of a struggle?"

"I'm still waiting for the word on that. I mean, it could be nothing. She's only been missing for what? Four hours? She might've shacked up with someone. Hell, she could be out partying over one of her friend's houses. I just thought you ought to know."

"No," Ferren said. "That's good. You did good. See if you can contact the Futawam PD and find out who they've got working on this. I'd like to have a look at the car. Like you said, it could be nothing, but I want to make sure. I'll be at the station in an hour."

"Alright. I'll be waiting."

Ferren hung up the phone. He sat on the edge of the bed, staring into the big mirror that rested above the dresser, directly across from him. His dark hair stood up in shocks, showing more of his scalp than he had ever noticed before, and there was about 40 years worth of luggage under his eyes.

"When the hell did I get so goddamn old?" he wondered aloud.

After a few moments he opened the nightstand drawer, where his Glock 9mm and an extra clip of ammunition looked strangely at home beside the hotel Bible.

As he thought about God and bullets, he poured himself another shot.

~Twenty-Five~

It was late Tuesday morning, five days after Mike Swart and his friends had fled from their hometown of Hevven, Massachusetts, and Kevin Chapman, the World Class Fuck-Up, was coming home.

Kevin sat silently in his mother's white caravan, watching the blur of trees through the passenger window. His mother drove, her long brown and gray hair blowing in the wind, both hands wrapped firmly around the steering wheel, her face a strange combination of relief, sympathy, and concern. The concern was for her only son, who had apparently heard the shocking news earlier that same day.

Kevin knew he and his friends were considered misfits in the little town of Hevven. He knew Max could sometimes explode for no reason, that Rick had teeter-tottered on the edge of insanity, and that he himself had garnered a well-deserved reputation for being a pothead. But murderers? Hell, no! They were harmless in that regard. Well, maybe not entirely harmless. There was that one time when Max had beaten the crap out of Willy Grant after school...for no good reason other than the fact that Willy was fat, and Max always got a kick out of picking on fat people. If one of Willy's friends, along with a couple of brave teachers, hadn't been there to break it up, Max probably would've messed the kid up pretty badly, perhaps would have sent him to the hospital. But even Max knew when enough was enough, though sometimes he got carried away.

At the most, Kevin supposed, he and his friends could be considered troublemakers, but they were a far cry from the cold-blooded murderers the police and the media were making them out

163

to be. And they sure as shit didn't belong to a cult. He was certain about that.

But how did they get caught up in a murder? This thought had troubled him the most since he had heard the news. And where did they go? Where? Canada? Knowing Max, that's probably where they were right now. Just before Kevin was sent away, he and Max had had a very long conversation about Canada, about running away and starting their lives anew. But maybe, to Max, it had been more than just a topic for discussion. Maybe he'd been planning it all along, though Kevin doubted that was true. Max had never been much of a planner; that was Mike's job. Wherever they were, though, Kevin wished that he was with them, even with the trouble that would find them sooner or later.

It was better to know. Kevin Chapman needed to know.

What the hell had happened? Were they set up? Was it some kind of freak accident? What if...what if Max really had killed that girl, and the others were trying to cover for him? These questions would bother Kevin until he found some answers. Anything to assure him that his friends had not become killers overnight.

Now, his early departure seemed aimless. There wasn't much to look forward to, with his friends gone and his probation officer already breathing down his neck. His high hopes for another slamming jamming summer were shot out of the sky and were now dying slowly, waiting to be put out of their misery. Bang! Bang! Bang!

What the hell is happening to Hevven? Kevin wondered. The town was becoming a black hole of misfortune. Yet, there was another thought in his head that carried just as much weight and confusion as the others.

How the hell did I earn an early release? Why me? Why now? He knew it had something to do with the cops, particularly that new guy, Officer Bailey, whom Kevin had seen talking to Doctor Parker yesterday afternoon. But why would Officer Bailey give a rat's ass about Kevin? Bailey was a new guy; he hadn't been on the force long enough to have formed a grudge against Kevin, or any of the other so-called punks in Hevven. Kevin guessed it probably had more to do with Bailey's dickhead superior, Chief Moriarty.

Moriarty was a typical small-town cop, a ticking timebomb of piss and venom. Everyone who had and hadn't met him knew that, either by firsthand experience or by word of mouth. It was Moriarty who had helped send Kevin to Plymouth. Hell, that bastard was the one who had taken him there from the courthouse.

So what's that asshole planning? Does he think I can lead him to Mike and the others? Yeah, he probably thinks I know where they are. Either that, or he figures they'll come looking for me to join them sooner or later. Oh, shit, or maybe Moriarty's looking to bust me for drugs. That makes a lot more sense, doesn't it? They've been after Pepsak for years, but they never seem to find enough evidence to charge him with anything. That's gotta be it, there trying to find out where I get my weed. That's why they sent me to rehab instead of putting me in lockup.

When they arrived at their Cape-style house on Tower Street, Kevin and his mother unloaded his things from the rear of the caravan and moved them into the house. It wasn't the nicest house on the block, with its water-stained shingles, fading blue trim, and crumbling driveway, but it was home, and Kevin was glad to be back there.

"Are you hungry, Kev?" his mother asked, as she placed one of his bags on the kitchen floor. "We can order takeout, if you want. Chinese? Anything you want."

She still felt guilty for turning him in, and it showed.

"Nah, not really. I think I'm gonna clean my room or something. Maybe unpack some of my stuff."

Are you hungry, Kev? That's all she could say? He knew she loved him, and he loved her too, but really, Are you hungry, Kev?

Grabbing his bags, he shuffled down the hallway and into his bedroom. Curtains drawn, it was dark inside, which was just how he liked it. Instinctively his hand went to the wall and his fingers found the switchplate. He flicked on the dim bureau light. His room was exactly as he'd left it, which wasn't necessarily a good thing. The walls were plastered with posters of all kinds, everything from Pink Floyd's *Dark Side Of The Moon* to a life-size image of Lauren German. There was a small television on a wooden stand in the corner; below it, a Playstation 2 console and a dozen or so games had spilled onto the floor. With a sigh, he looked at the dirty mounds of clothes on the floor and kicked them into one large pile in the corner of the room, near his closet. He decided he'd confront the washing machine later that day. Right now, he didn't have the energy to do laundry.

When his room was as clean as he cared for it to be, he slid a CD into his stereo, hit the PLAY button, and flopped down on his waterbed. A Beth Orton song wafted through the speakers. His mind wandered, electric with thought. He'd had plenty of time for reflection while serving his time at the rehab center, and now it seemed he'd have plenty more.

Where were they? What happened? Were they alright?

He knew it would be some time before he'd find the answers to these nagging questions, but he went on thinking just the same.

Still in deep thought, and with Beth Orton's hypnotic songs still drifting through his head, he soon fell under a calming sleep.

When Kevin awoke, nearly three hours later, he was more than grateful that sleep had taken him. He crawled out of bed, changed into a pair of fresh clothes, kicked the old clothes into the corner with the rest, and went out into the kitchen to find his mother.

"Can I borrow the car?"

His mother, who was watching one of those afternoon talk shows he loathed, looked up. "Where are you going?" she asked, sipping on a cup of herbal tea.

"Don't know. Get something to eat, maybe. See if anybody's still around."

She nodded sympathetically. "The keys are on the table."

"Thanks."

"Kev?"

"Yeah?"

"If you knew where your friends were…you'd tell someone, wouldn't you? Their parents must be worried sick."

He lied her a smile, and nodded.

"Sometimes it's not so easy, Kev. Having kids, I mean."

He smiled sadly. "Y'know what? Sometimes it ain't so easy being one, either."

Fifteen minutes later, after stopping off at Cumberland Farms for a pack of Marlboros, Kevin found himself driving aimlessly. *No place to go, no one to see. Where did they go? Canada?* Hardly conscious of what he was doing, he turned onto Titicut Street. *Where the hell are they?*

He passed Rick Hunter's house, and noticed that both of Rick's parent's cars were there. For a moment he thought of stopping by, to see how they were dealing with things. But something made him drive ahead, to the barren section of Titicut Street—where trees rather than houses lined the road, and the decade-old pavement was marred with cracks, frostheaves, and potholes—and it was here, on this mile-long stretch that connected Titicut with Roller Coaster Road, that Kevin began to slow down. Surrounded by the greenery of the Hockomock Forest, he pulled the caravan into the tall grass that flourished on the shoulder of the street, and slid the shifter into the park position.

The engine of his mother's caravan rattled noisily as it idled. He sat there staring longingly into the lush forest, down the front of the narrow path, at the end of which stood the small wooden shack he and his friends had built so many years ago.

Are you hungry, Kev?

After a long time he killed the engine, pocketed the keys, and began into the forest. He was hungry after all...for some answers.

~Twenty–Six~

Mike Swart awoke upon the hardwood floor with the taste of beer still lingering in his mouth, and his mind in disarray. The dream world had taken the events of the past few days away from him, and had led him to believe that he would wake in his own bed, in his parent's house on Sunset Ave. As his eyes adjusted to the dusty light he found himself looking at a knotty pine wall, and he realized he was not at home but in his late uncle's cabin in New Hampshire.

Still sleeping beside Mike was his girlfriend, Karen Sloan, the one person he loved more than life itself, and when this part of the reality came he was thankful for it. After watching her sleep for a little while he kissed her tenderly on the forehead, careful not to wake her as he rose from the floor.

He shuffled across the room, still feeling buzzed, and quietly dressed himself with yesterday's clothes. The extra things that Rick had packed were being used up fast, and later Mike would have to decide whether or not another trip into town would be a good idea. But that was a decision (are you making the right decisions?) that could wait until later. Right now he had plenty of other things to worry about. Not the least of which included the granddaddy of all headaches.

He left Karen sleeping and shuffled across the hall, where Max and Lou shared the smaller of the two bedrooms.

He opened the door a crack and saw Max sitting in a decrepit rocking chair with a blanket draped over his shoulders, rocking slowly back and forth as he stared out the open window. His head tilted slightly back, he was trying to blow smoke-rings but was unsuccessful due to the breeze coming in through the open window. In one of his hands he held a can of Budweiser. After last night, the mere sight of it made Mike want to puke.

"You look like an old lady," Mike observed, perhaps a bit too loud for the otherwise quiet room.

Startled, Max nearly tipped over backwards in his chair. He turned and sighed in relief as he saw Mike standing in the doorway.

"Don't do that, man! You scared the living shit outta me!" Max scolded in his scratchy voice. He grinned sideways. "You hung over?"

Mike yawned, stretching his arms above his head. "My head is killing me. Hey, where's Lou?"

"Uh, I think he said he was going to sit by the river or somethin'."

"How'd you sleep?"

"Pretty good," Max said, tilting his beer can as he took a swig. "Back's a little sore. How 'bout you?"

Mike rubbed his eyes. "I feel like I was hit by a truck. I hope to God I have some aspirin in my car. How can you drink that shit this early in the morning?"

"What, this?" Max asked, as if he had forgotten about the beer can he was holding. "Ahhh, there's nothing like a piss-warm beer to chase away your blues. Sip?"

Mike rubbed his temples. "No, thanks. I'll be back in a few. Looks like it's gonna rain."

"Yep."

Mike left the cabin and went straight to his car and, much to his satisfaction, managed to find a few packets of aspirin in his glove compartment. He tore open two of the packets and swallowed three tablets dry, all but gagging on the chalky taste they left behind.

Shortly thereafter Mike was in the meadow, almost waist-high in the tall grass, as he strode down to the river to find his younger brother. The morning mist was rising from the sleepy earth, and the dew-soaked meadow sparkled like a vein of diamonds in its wake. Birds flapped lazily from tree to tree, occasionally swooping down to wrestle an unsuspecting worm from the moist earth, and then back to the safety of the foliage. Clouds made dark shadows that crawled across the mountains like giant insects. The only sounds were those of the birds chirping, the ringing of insects that defiantly continued their nightsongs, and the shush-shush-shush of the wet grass against his jeans as he made his way across the field.

Had Mike looked back toward the cabin at that moment he would've caught Max watching him through the bedroom window, but he didn't. Other things, beside his throbbing headache, were troubling him. Things that needed to be said. Things that needed to be talked about. Mike knew it would not be easy (he could not remember ever having had a serious discussion with his younger brother) but he knew it was something he must do.

Then there was Rick who, only seconds ago, Mike had seen sleeping on the cabin floor with his arms around Stacey, as if they had always belonged that way. Mike had taken special care not to wake them as he left the cabin. The two had looked so damn peaceful there, by the hearth of the fireplace. Still, Mike couldn't help but wonder how they had grown so affectionate toward one another without him knowing it.

They barely spoke at all yesterday, Mike reasoned. *Did I miss something? I wasn't that drunk, was I?*

Nevertheless, Mike was overjoyed for his friend. Rick had tortured himself for long enough, and it was time he got on with his life.

And time for decisions, decisions, some voices in his head reminded him.

When Mike reached the river he found his younger brother sitting on river's edge with his pants rolled up to the knees, his legs dangling in the shallow water. Lou's cherished New England Patriots hat, two Reebok hightops, two balled-up socks, and a few cigarette butts lay scattered in the sand around him. A fresh, unlit cigarette dangled from the fingertips of his left hand, and in his other hand he held a white Bic lighter.

Mike stopped short and watched him for a minute. In the strange green-gold of the morning sunlight, it appeared as though Lou had been frozen, like a photograph, before he could bring his cigarette to life with a single stroke of the lighter's flint.

A few more seconds went by, and Lou remained still, seemingly hypnotized by the dawn's swirling light. After a moment Mike had to speak up, just to make sure his brother was still alive.

"What's up, bro?" Mike asked, easing down beside him.

Lou snapped to life, and craned his neck to look up at his brother. "Nuthin'," he blurted, as if he'd been caught doing something wrong. He lit his cigarette and took a quick drag. Then he offered Mike a cigarette. Mike accepted it with a nod of gratitude.

"Lou, there's something I want to talk about. Something I've been meaning to say for a long time," Mike said, giving Lou a sideways glance.

"You guys smoke," Lou muttered defensively. "I'm the same age you were when you started smoking. I'm old enough to do what I want."

"No," Mike said, and raised one hand to calm him. His large gray eyes appeared luminescent in the sunlight. He half smiled, half pouted. "It's not that. Look, I know you're scared, we all are, and I'd be lying if I told you any different. But we did the right thing. At least, I think we did the right thing. If we had stayed in Hevven we would've been putting mom and dad in a lot of danger. Look, I know it's rough on you...being away from home. But we have to be careful. We can't call them, or go home just yet, until we know things are safe. I know they miss us, and I'm sure they know we miss them, too. I'm just trying to do the right thing, like they always tried to teach us. They know we'll be back. I'm sure they're worried, but that's what parents do best, y'know?"

Talking to his little brother was much harder than Mike had anticipated. Changing a play at the line of scrimmage, throwing a 40-yard pass into the endzone in tight coverage, getting sacked by a 300-pound infant on steroids; all child's play compared to this. He wiped his forehead with the back of his forearm and thought, *God,*

172

I'm sweating! After a moment, Mike took a deep breath and plowed forward.

"I...I know it's pretty rough on you, being the youngest of us all. But that doesn't matter. We give you some shit sometimes, but you're still one of us. Do you know what I'm sayin'? Up here, things are different. Things are...changing. Look at Max. I've never seen him so freakin' happy before. And Rick...did you see him with Stacey this mornin'?"

Lou puffed on his cigarette; he nodded and grinned bashfully. He was so happy for, and envious of, his friend.

"I haven't seen him look so happy for months," Mike continued. "He's my best friend, and he tried to kill himself. And now look at him. Look, what I'm tryin' to tell you is that we should make the best out of this situation. I know I haven't been...the best brother in the world, but I care about you, and I've been told I'm a pretty cool guy to have around." Mike turned his head and saw that Lou was smiling. "And I'm there for you if you need me."

For a few minutes they sat without speaking. The only sounds were those of the river gurgling, birds singing, and a few scattered insects still buzzing with their nightsongs.

"Mike?" Lou spoke suddenly.

"Yeah?"

"Where do you think the river runs? I mean, does it go to the ocean or something, or does it just keep going...forever? No one ever has the answer. No one ever seems to know."

"That's pretty deep, man. No pun intended. I don't know. Maybe Uncle Jack knows...now that he's gone..."

Lou stared off at the mountains in the distance, the wondrously tall teeth of granite, and said, "Do you remember Uncle Jack?"

"Yeah," Mike said, flicking away his cigarette butt. "Do you?"

"A little bit. Not much, though. Can I tell you something?"

"Shoot."

"Promise not to laugh?"

Mike nodded. "I'll do my best."

"Come on, seriously."

"Alright," Mike said, putting one hand over his heart, and the other in the air, as though he was being sworn in to tell the whole truth, the truth, and nothing but the truth. "I promise."

"I had a dream about Uncle Jack the other night, but it was strange because I couldn't see his face. It was like there was a cloud in front of him or somethin'. I guess, until last night, I hadn't really thought about him that much since he died. Anyway, he told me not to worry. He said I would be okay, because the giants would look out for me. Pretty weird, huh?"

Pulse racing, Mike swallowed hard. "Yeah, I guesso." How could Lou have found out about the giants? Surely, Lou was much too young to remember anything Uncle Jack might have told him.

Are you making the right...

"Do you think we'll ever know?"

...decisions? Are you? Are you?

"Know what?"

"You know, about the river? Where does it go?"

Mike shook his head. "I don't know. To the ocean, probably. That's one of those things ...one of those mysteries you don't know the answer to until you die. Wouldn't it be disappointing to find out it drains into a lake or something? Maybe it's better not knowing. Maybe we wouldn't appreciate things as much if we had all the answers."

Lou nodded thoughtfully. Then suddenly his face went dark. "You know why they call him The Hacker?"

Mike opened his mouth, as if to speak, but then closed it. After a second, he stood up and folded his arms across his chest.

"They say it's because he doesn't care how he kills people," Lou went on. "He just likes to kill. That's also why they can't catch him. Because he always changes the way he kills people. He's evil. Pure evil. He just kills for the hell of it, because life means nothing to him." He paused and looked up at Mike, who stood towering over him. "I don't wanna die."

Mike bent down and scooped the New England Patriots hat from the sand. He dusted off the hat and handed it to his younger brother. "You're not gonna die. None of us are gonna die. I promise."

Lou fell silent. His brother's words had relaxed him a little, although he still had that watery, petrified look in his eyes.

After a while Mike's growling stomach broke the tender silence. He thought he could feel the aspirin tablets bouncing around inside of him like a pair of Mexican jumping beans with teeth. "C'mon," he said, standing. "Let's go find somethin' to eat."

"Alright," Lou agreed. He was putting on his sneakers when a cold, dime-sized raindrop landed on his forehead, and rolled down the bridge of his nose. "Looks like it's startin' to rain, anyhow."

Beneath a molten sky, Lou followed his older brother eagerly through the field. Still wondering about the destination of the river and the many mysteries of life, his stomach rumbled with the anticipation of nourishment. Side by side they walked back to the cabin in the late-morning haze, a cold and gentle rain falling on their heads, the reflections of two different people by appearance and manner; a young dreamer and a maturing leader. Yet, in the subtlest of ways, they were very much the same.

~Twenty—Seven~

"You motherfuggglgr..." Lou's cry was cut short as Max tackled him and shoved him underwater; a continuation of the endless water-wrestling match Max had started several days ago.

After the morning showers had passed and the thunderclouds relinquished their claim on the sky, the sun began to smile at the earth once again. It was Lou, standing by the window, who announced the departure of the clouds, and the six hideaways bolted from the cabin as though they had never seen daylight before, running through the meadow like small children on the last day of school. Beneath a pristine blue sky they convened at their favorite spot; the soft, crescent-shaped sandbar that skirted the water's edge. As the day wore on, it was impossible to tell that the storm had ever been there in the first place.

After a brief swim Rick sat down on a blanket near the edge of the water, and lit himself a cigarette while he watched the others play. A few minutes later, Stacey got out of the water and plopped down beside him.

"Everything alright?" she asked, resting her head on his shoulder.

"Mmm-hmm. Just taking in the scenery, that's all."

About half an hour later Mike climbed out of the water, shook his hair dry, and stood beside Rick. For a moment he didn't speak, watching Karen as she bathed herself in the deep water. She was holding a bar of soap in one hand and a bottle of Summer's Rain shampoo in the other. Meanwhile, Max and Lou were laughing hysterically as they wrestled one another in the shallows.

"I think maybe we should..." Mike's voice trailed off. He found himself captivated by the sight of Karen in the water. All he could think about was how much he wanted to hold her in his arms, how much he wanted to make love to her and kiss her and tell her everything was going to be all right. All he could think about was how much he wanted to protect her from the world.

"Earth to Mike," Rick repeated.

"Huh?"

"You were saying?"

"Oh," Mike said, looking rather dazed. "Yeah, I was gonna say that, well, maybe we should take another ride into town."

Rick squinted up at him. "Do you think that's a good idea?"

"I don't see why not." Mike rested his Coke in the soft sand so he could remove his T-shirt. "We need some extra clothes and stuff." He ran his hand down the side of his face, where two days' worth of stubble had begun to form a shadow. "And it wouldn't hurt to pick up some razors and shaving cream, either."

Rick nodded in agreement, rubbing the small, sandpapery whiskers on his own chin.

Stacey leaned over and used her fingers to trace the five o'clock shadow around his mouth. "Actually," she whispered, "I think it's kinda sexy."

She had tied her long auburn hair into a ponytail that rested between her shoulders, and her heart-shaped face looked radiant in the sunshine. Now, as she ran one finger over his lips, he began to smile. She wanted to tell him what that smile did to her, how it made her weak inside, how it made her want to kiss him, but she was unable to put her feelings into words. Besides, it was not the right time. She hardly knew the boy. She knew those things, but still she sensed that he could read her mind; it was in the way he looked at her, the way he touched her, so tenderly, that seemed to say it all.

Rick felt his face heat up. It wounded him, both physically and mentally, when Stacey touched him like that, because it constantly reminded him of Lori's own sweet touch. He looked at the river in an effort to distract himself, but all he could think about was Stacey and Lori, Lori and Stacey. For a few seconds, he forgot all about Mike's idea to make another trip into town.

Several feet away, Lou came up from the river gasping. Max had been holding him under, and Lou now grabbed Max in a headlock and began to turn the tables on the larger boy. This time they both went under. The water bubbled and foamed over and around them. Farther away, near the middle of the river, Karen was peacefully caressing herself with the bar of soap.

"If you want, I'll go," Stacey volunteered.

"Actually," Mike said, "I was thinking me and Rick will be making this trip ourselves. That okay with you, Rick?"

"What for? We got everything we need for now." Rick squinted as he looked up at his friend. Mike's voice was almost robotic, Rick noticed, and his attention seemed focused on Karen as she bathed herself. But there was something else, something in Mike's eyes as he watched his lover gliding through the water. He looked older, somehow.

"I'm thinkin' we should call Kevin," Mike replied. "Find out what's going on back home." He kicked off his shoes, watching Karen as she massaged the soap onto her arms and shoulders.

"Do you think that's a good idea?" asked Rick. "I mean, what if his phone is tapped or something. Besides, I don't think he's out of rehab yet."

"I heard somewhere that you get something like 30 seconds to talk before they can trace your call," Mike said.

"Are you sure?"

"Sure, I'm sure," Mike said, shrugging his shoulders and eyebrows. His jaw twitched ever so slightly, as if he had something on his mind, but wasn't quite ready to say it. He didn't want them to know his knowledge of phone taps came from watching spy movies, and cop shows on television.

Max and Lou splashed up from underwater, gasping for air, laughing and choking at the same time. "You're mine!" Lou howled.

Max cackled between breaths. He spat out some water. "Go for it, bitch-boy!"

They stood waist-high in the water, panting, bodies glistening in the sunlight, both too tired to make a move.

"Still, do you think that's a good idea?" Rick repeated.

"Yeah," Mike answered with some degree of uncertainty. "We'll go tomorrow. Just the two of us."

Pondering Rick's question, Mike folded his arms across his bare chest. Karen was tilting her head to the side, working the shampoo into her hair. As if she suddenly sensed that she was being watched, she looked up and offered Mike a cute little smile, and that was enough to chase his worries away for the moment.

Mike smiled back at her as he stepped into the shallows, wriggling his toes in the sandy bottom, watching the silver flashes of minnows as they darted to and fro. When the bottom eventually dropped off a few feet away from shore, and the water was sufficiently deep, he dove under and came up with his hair matted down against his head. He swam over to Karen, lifting her up into the air as he reached her. Karen laughed hysterically as she kicked her legs, and Mike let her down slowly into his arms and held her tight.

"You're nuts," she giggled.

"But do you love me?" Mike whispered.

"You know I do," she replied, and kissed him gently on the mouth. "Let me wash your hair."

"You wanna wash my hair?" Mike chuckled. "How 'bout I wash yours, then I'll think about it, okay?"

Holding her by the waist, he guided her back until her hair was under, and only her face was above the surface. He then leaned forward, kissing her tenderly on the lips, moving slowly up and down her neck.

"Mmmm..." Karen moaned, closing her soulful brown eyes.

"I'm not hurting you am I?" Mike asked, raking his fingers through her thick hair.

"Nooo, that feels good."

Mike continued to kiss her neck, supporting her weight with one hand between her shoulders and the other under the small of her back. Stroking her hair, he pulled her smooth, wet body against him.

"Now, when do I get to wash your hair?" Karen giggled, and Mike quieted her with another kiss.

It's going to be alright, Mike thought as he kissed her shoulder and the side of her neck. *Everything's gonna be alright. I'm gonna get us all outta this, Karen. I promise you, I will.*

On the riverbank, Stacey got up from her blanket and looked at Rick. "Feel like taking a little walk?"

"Sure," Rick said, wiping the sand from his hands. "Where are we going?"

"Up there." She nodded in the direction of the hill that towered above them. "Let's go check out the view."

Rick stood and followed Stacey up the grassy slope. When they reached the top Stacey sat down in the matted grass near the edge of the cliff, and Rick sat down beside her. Below, the others continued to frolic in their separate ways, in the place that was now the nucleus of their lives.

Although the cliff was no more than 20 feet high, the river, the fields, the forests, and the mountains beyond seemed to lie before them like some intricately detailed board game. And the four people in the water below were, of course, the players. The game, Rick supposed, if there had been such a thing, would have been appropriately titled *Taking Chances.*

If anything, it was one game they were all good at.

But could they win? That was the million-dollar question.

"It's so beautiful here," Stacey said in a dreamy voice, and leaned against him. "So peaceful..."

Rick was silent. He wanted to tell her that she was beautiful, and smart, and sexy, even though he hardly knew her. He wanted to tell her that she made him feel alive. But he knew it would be better just to tell her to leave him alone, because he had a promise to keep with a dead girl. A promise that he would never love another person as long as he lived. Besides, she was a college girl; what would she want with a boy just out of high school?

"Rick, about last night..."

He looked at her guardedly.

"I just wanted to tell you, it's not your fault. I know how you must feel. Karen told me the whole story, and..."

181

Rick stood up in a hurry. "How I feel?" he asked sharply. "God, I'm so sick of people telling me they know how I feel. You can't possibly know how I feel."

"I-I'm sorry," Stacey stuttered in surprise. She rose to her feet. "I didn't mean to..." She reached out to touch his shoulder, but he pulled away.

"Don't."

"Please..." Stacey pleaded, her eyes welling with tears. "I didn't mean to..."

"You wanna know how I feel? Huh? I feel like I'm dead. Is that what you wanted to hear?" Rick muttered, and with that he started across the meadow, in the direction of the cabin.

Tears surged down Stacey's face as she stood atop the cliff, watching the angry boy as he walked away. There was something about him, something she could not quite explain, that made her want him more than anyone she had ever met before. Sure, he was handsome and tall, but it was more than just that. His mere presence had opened a floodgate of feelings in her, the likes of which she had never felt before. Feelings she never knew existed until a few short days ago. The simple truth was, until she met Rick Hunter it had never occurred to her that she'd never truly been in love before.

When he was no longer in view she sat down in the tall grass, not wanting the others to see her cry. *All I've ever wanted,* Stacey realized, *was to be loved by someone, and to love that person in return.* "I'm sorry," Stacey whispered to no one.

Below her, like an undulating road to nowhere, the river wound its way through the valley. And the game of life went on.

182

~Owenty-Eight~

Twilight penetrated the forest in murky yellow rays, shimmering with pollen and dust. The sun was almost gone, and the forest hummed with life.

He was in the forest again, hovering over the dark, scum-covered pool as it consumed the girl he had taken last night from the parking lot of the Futawam Theater. She floated, face down, as the water flowed over her naked buttocks, her narrow shoulders, her plump calves. He knew he was safe here, in the forest.

The state and local police were still looking for the missing girl named Kelly Brine. Although they would not admit it to the girl's family, or to the media, they had already called in the cadaver-sniffing dogs. After all, there was no reason to believe she was still alive. These were killers they were dealing with, not kidnappers. All they could hope for was to find the body, and possibly some clues that would lead them to their suspects.

But that didn't bother him. The truth would never be told, because he'd find the missing youths before anyone else. They were kids. Just stupid kids. It was actually quite fascinating to think that they had made it this far. But they were bound to make a mistake sooner or later. And it would be the last mistake they would ever make. He'd see to that.

He looked at his reflection on the water as the body bobbed onto its side. Even from his distance, he could see the bruise he'd left on her neck. It was dark and puffy, in the shape of his hand. Most of

183

her face was submerged, but one wide, unblinking eye stared at him accusingly. He had liked her eyes. They were green and expressive. But she was a sinner. The pool had told him so. It told him that, sometimes, sinners look like angels and angels look like sinners.

"Sorry, angel," the man said in a grim voice. "But I had to do it. I saw the devil in your eyes."

The eye showed him no sympathy. It continued to stare at him. He looked away, then back again. He admired, from where he stood at the edge of the water, her one visible breast, the curve of her thigh.

"You look so beautiful now," he whispered. "So clean."

As if responding, the body rolled slowly onto its back, exposing both of her breasts, her firm stomach, and her neatly trimmed pubic hair. And, of course, her eyes.

Though she was now on her back, her eyes still seemed to be looking at him, trying to unravel him.

The pool's trying to test me, he thought. *It's using her to try and seduce me. Well, I'm not gonna fall for it. I'm not gonna wade out there and fuck her dead like it wants me to. No way! No way you're gonna get me to do that. Not now, not when I'm so close…*

"YOU CAN'T TRICK ME!" he screamed, pointing a thick finger at the black liquid. His voice echoed through the forest. The pool was testing him, trying to tempt him.

He watched as the pool pulled the body down slowly, so that only the girl's face and breasts protruded from the surface. Panting, he looked at his reflection on the surface and smiled at that other, younger, more beautiful image of himself. He would look that way soon, when the pool allowed him to enter its secret realm, where his parents would be waiting. It promised him it would ease his pain in time. It would lead him to The Truth.

He sat his bulky frame down on the bank near the pool, swatting mosquitoes away from his face, and watched as the pool finished devouring his offering. He moaned in ecstasy as her nipples disappeared below the surface, where she would remain forever. Suddenly, he became envious of his master.

The pool sucked on her body all at once, he knew. It could have all of her, all of them, at the same time, without a struggle.

He could only have them one piece at a time. He could only undress them with one hand, because the other was needed to cover their mouths and noses, or to pin them down by their throats, or to hold their arms. Because of this, he could only use one hand to touch them. He wasn't allowed to kiss them, but the pool could kiss them everywhere at once. It could be in them and around them. It could make love to them without boundaries, which was something neither he, nor anybody else, could ever do.

As she vanished beneath a flotilla of bubbles, he promised aloud that he would not forget her beauty, and that he would be with her soon to make everything better. Closing his eyes, he envisioned each of the twenty or so girls that existed in the domain of the pool; their hair, their lips, their breasts, the way they smelled; which ones struggled, and which ones did exactly as they were told without so much as a whimper of protest. So many bad, bad girls. But he'd saved them all. Yes, saved them from themselves.

He imagined that he was the pool right now, flowing in and around them. Kissing them all over, sliding into all of their forbidden places as only liquid could. With his eyes still closed, he began to moan softly, licking his lips. He'd be with them soon. He could feel it. He'd just have to play it cool. Act casual, so that no one would suspect anything. And as soon as those nosey little shitheads in the T-bird were dead and gone, his job would be done. And the pool would keep its end of the deal by giving him a better life. By making him all that he had ever hoped to be, by giving him all that he had ever desired; all the secret pleasures that society could never understand.

The body disappeared completely from view about the same time as the sun disappeared completely from the sky. The surface of the pool smoothed over the place where Kelly Brine's body had been, as if she had never really existed at all.

~Twenty-Nine~

Mike Swart hesitated at the cabin door. "I'll catch up with you in a minute, hon. I wanna talk to Rick for a minute."

It was late at night, and a cool mist had settled in the valley. After swimming and lounging all day long they'd spent another evening by the river, cooking the remainder of their hot dogs, eating potato chips, drinking Gatorades and Mountain Dews, while engaged in deep conversations, such as those which were sparked by Karen's question: "What would you do if you won a million dollars?"

Such as those that followed Mike's question: "Do you think there's life on other planets?"

Such as the debate which arose over Max's question: "If you're considered a legal adult when you turn 18, then why do you have to wait until you're 21 to buy alcohol? It's so fucked-up! You can go to jail, and join the army and fight in wars, but you can't buy a six pack? You know, you have to be twenty-five to rent a fuckin' car! What the hell? Who comes up with this bullshit?"

And, finally, it was Lou's question which had brought on the most heated debate: "Who do you guys think is hotter: Britney Spears, Michelle Branch, Lauren German, or Eliza Dushku?"

Now, some twenty minutes later, the others had wandered off to their makeshift beds. Only Karen, Mike, and Rick remained on the moonlit porch.

With a playful suspicion in her eyes, Karen smiled and kissed Mike on the cheek. "Should I wait up?" she asked, raising an eyebrow.

"Yeah...I'll be there in a minute."

"Alrighty." She waved her hand. "G'night, Rick."

"G'night."

Flashlight in hand, Karen went inside the cabin, and the two boys on the porch could hear her footsteps as she pranced upstairs, speaking soft goodnights as she went.

Mike closed the cabin door after her. Then he walked over to the corner of the porch, and faced the river. "Got a smoke?" he asked, resting his elbows on the railing, looking out towards the chainsaw blade of mountains (giants) which rose in the distance. The moon gleamed like a pearl embedded in the black belly of the northern sky, transforming the valley below into a dreamland.

"Yeah, here."

Mike popped the cigarette in his mouth, and Rick lit it for him with the Zippo.

"Thanks," Mike muttered.

For a long time they stood silently, relaxing with their cigarettes, marveling at the beauty of the night sky.

Rick knew straight away that something was gnawing at his friend, and that it was only a matter of time before Mike would have to unburden himself of whatever it was that was bothering him. Nevertheless, it was a lovely night, and he truly didn't mind if Mike wanted to take his time. Whatever it was that Mike wanted to talk to him about, Rick knew it had to be very personal, and could only be told from one best friend to another, because they trusted each other more than they trusted anyone else in the world.

"Sometimes," Rick said, looking out at the moon and stars, "this world can be so pretty, it hurts just to look at it. And other times… it's so goddamn ugly, it makes me wish I was never born. Y'know what I mean?"

"I heard about what happened today, between you and Stacey," Mike said after a very long time. "You wanna talk about it?"

Rick lowered his head in shame. After a few seconds, he shrugged. "There's nothing to talk about."

"Then why do you keep avoiding her?"

"I'm not avoiding her." Rick's voice rose an octave.

"You know she likes you."

"Pfff...she doesn't even know me."

"How can she? You won't even give her a chance. You can't keep pushing people away for the rest of your life."

"I'm not pushing anybody away," insisted Rick.

Mike raised his voice a notch. "That's bullshit, and you know it. You've been pushing us away for months. She's gone, Rick. Lori is gone. You've got to let her go."

"How can I let her go?" Rick asked, throwing his hands in the air. "I killed her."

"That's not true," Mike said. "You didn't—"

"I know I didn't kill her directly," Rick interrupted. His voice was flat, emotionless. "But I'm the one who got her into drinking. I'm the one that talked her into it, even though I knew she didn't want to. She had never even taken a drink until she met me. I'm the reason she left the party by herself that night. If it wasn't for me, she'd still be alive." Rick paused. After a moment he said, "Did you know that I betrayed her, that after she left, I ended up fooling around with Rebecca Morgan?"

Mike flinched. Even in the darkness, he could not conceal the look of shock that fell across his face. He started to speak, but couldn't find the words.

"My girlfriend was dying," Rick said, with a trembling voice, "and I was kissing someone else."

"It's not your fault," Mike said, looking him in the eyes. "You were drunk and upset. There's no way you could have known. All I'm trying to say is that Stacey cares about you. She was only trying to help. I see the way your eyes light up when she's around. The way you smile—"

Rick looked up, his face as cold as stone. "I don't need her help. I don't need anybody's help."

"What's your problem, man? Why are you so mean to her?"

"Nothing. I don't even know what you're talking about."

"Bullshit."

Rick opened his mouth to defend himself, but sighed instead. After a moment, he muttered, "You wouldn't understand."

"Try me."

Rick chewed his bottom lip. "I made a promise...to Lori...that I would never love anyone else but her. So I can't. I won't. Jesus Christ, I owe her that much."

"You're right," Mike whispered after a time. "I don't understand. Lori is gone, but Stacey is alive. And after all the shit she's been through, I thought you were the one person I could count on to show her some compassion."

"It's not that simple." Rick tossed his hands in the air. "I just can't allow myself to get that close to someone again. I can't handle losing somebody else that I care about. I can't do it, Mike. I won't."

Mike answered softly, "I just don't wanna see you miss a chance to...to be happy again, y'know? I miss you, man. I miss my friend. And I need you now, more than ever."

It was a long time before either of them spoke again.

"Can I ask you something?" Mike said at last.

"Yeah. Go ahead."

Are you making the right decisions, Mikey? Are you?

"Do you think I made the right decision coming here? I mean, things were kinda crazy, and I felt like I had to act fast. I didn't realize that it might be the wrong thing to do. Maybe we shoulda gone to the cops."

"That's bullshit, and you know it. The cops wouldn't have helped us. They couldn't have helped us. You really think they care about protecting us, or our families? They probably would've used us to catch the bastard. That's if they believed us in the first place. Our asses could be rotting away in jail right now."

"Yeah, but..."

"But what?"

"Ahhh...never mind. It's getting late. I should head in. Karen's probably waiting up for me." He took one more drag from his cigarette and flicked it onto the earthen driveway. A trail of orange sparks glittered in its wake.

"I'm gonna stay out here and finish my smoke," Rick said, feeling somewhat hurt by Mike's reluctance to elaborate on his thoughts. *What's bothering him so deeply?* Rick wondered. *Or is he just acting this way because he's upset that I won't talk about the accident? Mike hasn't exactly been himself lately. He's been acting strange. Even for someone in our predicament.*

Mike was already heading for the door, footsteps heavy, shoulders slumped, walking with the posture of a person who had no purpose in life.

"Just remember, Mike," Rick called after him. "We could've backed out any time we wanted. You offered us a way out, and we took it. We made up our own minds. Right now, we're all safe. Just be grateful for that."

Mike stopped but did not turn around. He nodded silently, and then disappeared inside, where he was swallowed by darkness.

Listening to Mike's downhearted footsteps on the stairs, Rick decided it would be a good idea to keep a watchful eye on his friend. A good idea, indeed.

~Thirty~

"You think he'll find us, don't you?" Mike asked the next day, just moments after they had left the cabin, and the others, behind. It was Thursday afternoon, exactly one week since they had fled from Hevven, and now that the two of them were finally alone Mike saw the chance to start asking some questions.

"Whaddya mean?" Rick asked, preparing to light a cigarette with Kev's Zippo.

"Remember the other day, when I sent Max to get the crowbar out of my trunk, so we could take the plywood off the windows?"

Rick lit his cigarette, nodding. "Yeah, so?"

"He found the fuckin' shotgun, Rick. No one else saw it but him, and I made him swear he wouldn't tell anyone, but you know how Max is about keeping secrets."

Rick slapped himself in the forehead. "Damn! I'd pretty much forgotten about it myself until earlier today. I'm sorry, man. I thought you knew."

"Shit, I was so freaked out the night we left, you coulda packed a friggin' bazooka and I wouldn't have noticed."

Rick exhaled a smoky sigh. "It's just a precaution."

Mike looked at him uneasily. "But you think he'll find us here, don't you?"

Rick turned to look at him. "Maybe. Shit, I don't know. But he might. You never know, right? Better to be safe than sorry."

There was a long period of silence, except for the low rumble of the engine.

"Do you know how to use that thing?"

"The shotgun? Nuthin' to it," Rick assured him. "My dad took me to a firing range once, when I was just a kid."

They didn't talk for the rest of the ride into town. After a while Mike reached over, turned on the radio, and began to search the airwaves for some sign of life. After a full minute of static drizzle he found a strong signal, catching the tail end of a Jackyl song. When the song was over, the announcer came on long enough to inform everyone that today was a record-breaker (as if no one had noticed), with temperatures reaching the high 90s. The fire hazard was moderate to high, and was expected to remain that way for the next three or four days. On I-93, traffic was backed-up from Exit 3 all the way back to the Massachusetts' border, so the announcer warned that anyone who was planning a day at Canobie Lake Park, or Weir's Beach, was in for a very long day. A Connecticut boy had been taken into custody last night, following a two-hour standoff with police in Bartlett. According to one source, the boy, who was a minor, and whose name was withheld by the police, allegedly took his girlfriend hostage after finding out she had obtained a restraining order against him. After speaking to a police negotiator, the 16-year-old boy agreed to give himself up. When captured he was armed with a .22 caliber pistol, which was reportedly not loaded, as well as a hunting knife. The female hostage escaped relatively unharmed, and was treated for minor cuts and abrasions. On a lighter note, Matchbox-20 was playing a show at Loon Mountain next Saturday night. Tickets went on sale Monday, and were almost sold out.

"...But just keep listening to The Mountain Of Rock, and you could be the lucky winner of a pair of Matchbox-20 tickets, as well as a chance to meet the band! That's right, we will be giving away five pairs of tickets to see Matchbox-20, with special guest Bambi's Apartment, as well as one pair of backstage passes to party with the bands! All you have to do is tune in, and when you hear any two Matchbox-20 songs in a row, be the seventh caller, and we'll give you a pair of tickets to see Matchbox-20 at Loon Mountain next

194

weekend. It doesn't get any easier than that! Coming up next, we have the latest single from Third Eye Blind. You can only hear it here, on The Mountain Of Rock..."

There was no mention of the boys (and girl) from Hevven; no announcement that began with, "The police are on the lookout for..."

Still, Mike could not stop thinking about The Hacker, and how Rick had been worried enough to have stolen his father's shotgun. Was it an omen, that his best friend did not feel safe here? Or was it simply paranoia on Rick's part? Mike did not know.

While he pondered the answers to these questions, the dead girl's face invaded his mind and would not go away. The image was so powerful he could almost smell the decay, could almost hear the chainsaw buzzing of the flies which had hovered over her, could almost feel the weight of her lifeless eyes upon him. Remembering these things, Mike cranked up the volume on his stereo, trying to lose himself in the music, trying to dash the thoughts from his mind. But despite his best efforts, the dead girl's face remained in his mind's eye.

When they arrived at Atkins' General Store, Mike drove his Thunderbird around the side of the building and parked next to a mud-caked Chevy pickup, which was the only other vehicle in the lot. The two boys looked at one another solemnly.

"Let's go," Mike said, unenthusiastically, and they both got out of the car. "Oh, yeah. Try not to let me forget Max's cigarettes...and some hot sauce. Maybe that'll shut him up for a few days."

Rick nodded as he followed Mike up the uneven steps and across the cluttered porch, where they began working their way through a maze of broken wicker chairs, a pair of prehistoric Coca Cola machines, several stacks of newspapers, and various other items of antiquity and refuse.

Bells jingled above the old screen door, marking their arrival, as the two boys entered the store. Behind the counter, an old man snapped to attention. He greeted them with a fractured, buck-toothed smile as he gingerly set aside the issue of *Bass Fisherman* he'd been reading. The two boys smiled courteously and then

195

divided their shopping list, which read like something from a scavenger hunt: two packages of D batteries (for the flashlights), two packages of hot dogs, a 12-pack of Coke, a deck of playing cards, a dozen bottles of Gatorade, a tube of antibiotic cream (for Rick's stitches), a roll of gauze (also for Rick's stitches), some magazines (mostly for Lou), a carton of cigarettes, six cans of Spaghetti-Os, a jar of natural peanut butter, a box of paper plates, a package of Gillette For Women disposable razors, a can of women's shaving cream, eight rolls of toilet paper, three bags of chips, a pound of pre-sliced turkey breast, a loaf of bread, a half-dozen Slim Jims, three flannel blankets, a can of Off! insect repellent (it seemed they could never have enough), some more toothpaste (Karen had already bought some on their first trip, along with several toothbrushes), and…of course, hot sauce (for Max). On top of all that, Rick insisted on buying a fishing rod. Mike thought it was a waste of money, but Rick considered it a worthwhile investment, so long as it kept one of them occupied for a time, and especially if they ran out of money. *If worse came to worse*, Rick had said, only half-joking, *they could always survive on fish.*

Meanwhile, the elderly cashier had already returned to his magazine.

By the time the mid-afternoon rush poured in (mostly consisting of out-of-state campers looking for directions back to I-93, and a handful of regulars who came to replenish their daily supplies of Budweiser and Schlitz) Carl Atkins, long-time proprietor of Atkins' General Store, had already forgotten the two scruffy youths with the Boston accents. He would not recall the two boys until several days later, when the state and local police, as well as two men dressed in tailored suits, dropped by with half a dozen pictures and twice as many questions. After leafing through a small stack of photographs, Carl Atkins would finally admit that he had, indeed, seen two of the boys, although in person they had looked much older than they did in the photographs (which were actually enlargements of their high school yearbook pictures). At first, Carl Atkins would think they had looked older in person because of their facial hair, but would later change his mind. The fact was, there was something in the boys' eyes, a kind of hardness that was not present in the photographs. But Mr. Atkins would keep that information to himself.

"How would you describe them?" one of the two suits would ask him.

Carl Atkins, who didn't very much care for being interrogated, and who cared even less for stuffy men in suits, would lean forward, over the cash register, adjusting his little bifocal-style glasses on the tip of his nose. He would smile the buck-toothed smile that was a landmark in these parts, and say, rather sarcastically: "They weren't fancy fellars like yourselves, understand, but they was true gentlemen nonetheless."

When Mike and Rick had finished their shopping they thanked the old man behind the counter, and transferred their bundles to the trunk of Mike's car.

The day was pleasantly hot, tempered by the occasional breezes which drifted down from the mountains, ruffling the leaves of the trees that cast their shade along Main Street. Several tourists, easy to spot in their bright summer clothes, were picking their way along the shady sidewalk. They paused at the display window of each store, sometimes pressing their noses against the glass, sometimes talking quietly amongst themselves, and then moved on to the next one, as if chasing the illusion that something better was always waiting just around the corner.

When the last of the supplies had been deposited into the car, the two boys gathered up a handful of pocket change, and walked around to the other side of the building to use the pay phone.

"What if he's not out of rehab yet? What happens if his mother answers?" Rick asked as Mike punched the keys. Nervous as he was, Rick thought maybe a smoke would calm him down, but as he brought one forth from his pack, he found he was even too nervous for that; he tucked the cigarette behind one ear for later.

Mike shrugged. "If his mom answers, I'll hang up."

Rick nodded. Mike sighed, waiting.

A few seconds later, someone picked up on the other end.

"Hello?" Kevin Chapman's voice crackled. He sounded as if he'd been sleeping.

"Kev?"

"Yeah, who's this?"

"Finally made it outta the Funny Farm, hey, Chapman?"
The voice on the other end became lively. "Shit! Mike?"

"Yeah, it's me."

"Mike," Kevin blurted, his excitement giving way to urgency, "the fuckin' cops have been lookin' everywhere for you guys. They even tore apart the shack lookin' for clues. God only knows how they found out about that place. You've been in all the papers, on the fuckin' television. The other night some chick over in Futawam disappeared. Everyone's searching for her body in the woods and shit. You know how it is around here. They think you guys are part of some kinda cult or something. It's drivin' the cops crazy. Why the hell do they think you guys did it?"

"Slow down, man. I don't have enough time to tell the whole story. I think we're safe where we are now, but we're not coming back until things are all cleared up. We didn't do nothing. But we saw who did it, Kev, and he saw us. That's why we had to haul ass outta there."

"Who?" Kevin said. "Who'd ya see?"

"The killer. The Hevven Hacker, I think. Whoever it was, he saw us, too. "

"Whoa, waitta minute...Mike, did you say The Hacker? But The Hacker was..."

"Caught? I know, we thought they caught him, too. But I'm telling you, it's him. I saw the body, Kev. I don't want to get into details. Maybe they caught the wrong guy. Maybe there was more than one killer. I don't know. And there's another thing..."

"What?"

"I've seen him before. The killer. I've seen him somewhere, but I can't remember where. I think he may be a townie."

"Jesus," Kevin muttered under his breath. "Mike?"

"Yeah, I'm still here."

"Where the fuck are you guys?"

"We're in—" Mike stopped himself just in time. *Nice. Real smooth. I almost screwed that up,* Mike thought, feeling ashamed. "I can't say the name. But remember a long time ago, we talked about taking a camping trip? Good trout fishin', remember?"

198

"No," Kevin said. Then: "Wait a minute! Are you talking about that place up in—"

"Don't say it!" Mike cut him off. "Just in case anyone is listenin'."

"Oh, shit! I read you loud and clear, Mike."

"I gotta get going, but there's something I want you to do for us."

"Name it."

"I need you to call each of our parents and tell them we're alright. Use a pay phone and don't tell them who you are. And no matter what they say, don't you tell them where we are. Also, we have a girl with us. Her name is Stacey Mackinnon. I need you to write this down." Mike pulled a slip of paper from his wallet and read him the telephone number, which Stacey had jotted down for him the day before. "I need you to call her parents and tell them she's safe."

"Got it. Anything else?"

"Yeah, be careful. Don't trust anyone, you got that?"

"No problemo. Tell everybody I said to hang in there. This place sucks without you guys."

Smiling, Mike hung up. He wasn't sure how long it really took the police to trace a phone call, and he hoped to God that, if Kevin's phone did indeed have a tap on it, they hadn't talked long enough to give them a lead.

"What did Kev have to say?" Rick asked quickly as they returned to the Thunderbird.

They hopped into the car and Mike keyed the engine.

"A girl in Futawam disappeared last night. They think it was us. The good part is, they still think we're in the area. The bad part is, the cops're going crazy trying to find us." Mike shook his head in disgust. He put the car into gear and doubled back in the direction of the cabin.

"How come you never said nothing before... that you recognized that man at the house that night?"

No, not a man. A monster. A motherfucking monster.

"I don't know. I guess it kinda bugged me that I couldn't remember where I've seen him before. We wouldn't be in this mess

199

right now if I could've ID'd him." *But I have seen him*, he thought. *I'm sure of it. I know him. Somehow. But from where?*

Yes oh yes oh yes you do, the giants said softly. *And you know what, Mikey? He knows you, too!*

Remember, damnit, Mike thought. *Remember!*

"I think we should keep the shotgun in the cabin from now on," Mike said, and then flashed Rick a sideways glance. "When no one else is around, we'll stash it under the couch. Just in case."

Decisions. Decisions. Decisions.

Karen's not gonna like this. Not one bit.

Rick nodded. In his mind he heard himself work the shotgun action. *Chick-chick...*

And his smile was almost malicious.

Booom!

~Thirty-One~

Karen was nervous.

Mike had left for the store in his usual upbeat mood, and had returned quiet and impatient. Tonight, as they gathered at their ritual dining spot by the river, he'd seemed preoccupied by something. Several times she'd caught him staring into the fire with a distant look in his eyes. When she tried to ask him what was wrong, he only smiled and shook his head, barely acknowledging her presence. There was no doubt in her mind he was troubled.

Now he was standing at the bedroom window again, forehead pressed against the glass, looking out into the night, where the (giants) mountains loomed beyond the river. With a trembling hand, he ran his fingers through his thick brown hair, trying to make sense out of everything that had happened in the last few days. Was there any sense in their existence? If there was, he could not find it. Far too many questions were being left to him.

Decisions. Decisions. Decisions.

What was Mike, the great decision-maker, to do next?

The weight of responsibility was growing too heavy on his shoulders. His head throbbed, his muscles ached.

Decisions. Decisions. Decisions.

Karen was lying on a blanket on the floor, watching him closely with her expressive brown eyes. Naked save for a gray baby-T and

201

black cotton panties, her thin body was nothing less than beautiful in the moonlight.

"Are you coming to bed?" she asked in a seductive voice. She hooked a thumb under the elastic waistband of her panties, snapped it playfully against her hip.

He tried to ignore her invitation, and failed.

"In a little bit," he answered with a sigh, already wanting her more than he was willing to let on.

Her smile became a frown. "What's wrong?"

He shook his head and shrugged. Upon returning from the store, he and Rick were fortunate enough to have found the cabin vacant, the others having gone down to the river for a swim, and so the task of hiding the shotgun under the living room couch was an easy one.

At first Mike felt as though he and Rick should have told the others what they had done, that it simply wasn't fair to keep a secret from them, especially after all that they had been through together. But in the end, they had both agreed that the shotgun's presence in the cabin would only raise unnecessary concerns, and that it was best to keep it quiet; at least for now.

"Come here," she said, moving aside for him. "Please."

After a few seconds, he went to her.

"What's the matter?" she asked, as he lay down beside her.

"I was just thinking," he said, and that was all he offered.

"About what?"

"About my parents," he said, running his fingers through her hair. He was about to elaborate, but then he smiled and shook his head. "Naw, it's dumb."

"Let me be the judge of that," she said, and she closed her eyes as his hand caressed her face. She slowly opened her eyes. "Go on."

"Well, I was just thinking about a story my dad used to tell me and Lou when we were little...about the night he and my mother first met."

Karen smiled a little, and that was enough to keep him talking. He continued to trace her facial features with his fingers, seemingly unaware of what his hand was doing.

"He used to tell us how he was at this college dance...he was a freshman at Bentley ...and from across the room he saw this girl wearing the brightest red dress, and how he'd wanted to go and talk to her, but he was kinda shy."

"So what happened?" Karen asked. Her brown eyes were wide with anticipation.

"Well, because of her dress, he knew where she was the whole night. He just had to look around and he could spot that dress from anywhere in the room. He wanted to talk to her, but there were too many people around, so he waited until most of the other people had cleared out of the dance, and when she was putting on her coat he went over and introduced himself. And that's how they met." He shrugged a little. "I told you it was dumb."

"Well, I think it's sweet. But what on earth made you think of that now?"

"I know it sounds weird, but ever since my dad first told that story, I've always wondered how things might've been if she'd decided to wear a different dress that night. Maybe he never would've noticed her. Or maybe he would've noticed her, but would've lost her in the crowd. Some other guy could've approached her first. My dad could've even chickened-out. There's so many possibilities, so many different ways that night could've ended. It's crazy, y'know?"

"I was just thinking of that, and I was thinking, I wonder if I made the right choice in bringing us all here. I don't know...it's just...it's kinda hard being the one who makes all the choices...all the decisions."

Decisions. Decisions. Decisions. Are you making the right decisions?

"Everybody's depending on me in one way or another," he said, "and I'm just as lost as they are."

"Of course you are," Karen whispered, running her fingers along the side of his face. "But you're doing everything you can."

"Am I?"

"Mike, things are really crazy right now. You know that, don't you? They look up to you because you've always been the one with the level head. You're like a father to them."

203

He frowned. "I just…I just never thought I'd feel so old at 18. All those times we all shared together, all those moments that I thought would last forever…they're gone. Nuthin' I can say or do can bring them back. Why is that? Why do we have to lose everything we love? Why does time have to be such a dirty fucking bastard?"

Karen simply stared at him, lips parted, shaking her head. She'd never heard Mike talk like that before. Still shaking her head, she whispered, "I don't know."

Mike ran his hands down his face. He looked at Karen steadily, the sadness so apparent in his cool gray eyes. Thinking of how much he loved this beautiful girl he was looking at, he started to smile. "Do you really think I'm their leader?"

Some leader, he thought briefly. *I'll be lucky if I don't get us all killed.*

"Yeah, I do," Karen answered with a smirk, glad they had moved on to another topic. "And don't you forget it."

He turned to her. "I love you, hun," he told her, looking her in the eyes, and he'd never meant it more than he did right then. "You're the best thing that could've happened to a guy like me."

He leaned in to kiss her, but she put her fingers on his lips, stopping him. "Lou told me you got accepted to UMASS," she whispered. "He said you might get a football scholarship. Why didn't you tell me?"

Mike looked at her steadily. "I was going to," he said. "It just didn't seem like the right time to talk about it."

"He's so proud of you. We all are."

"It's not a big deal."

"Don't be so damn modest."

"I'm not. There's just more to life than football."

Karen nodded agreeably. "What about us?"

His voice softened. "I was sorta hoping you'd come with me. You know, we could rent an apartment or somethin'. You could always enroll with me, if you want to."

Karen was still looking at him with those gorgeous brown eyes of hers. Doe-eyes, as Mike had once called them. She frowned. "You promise?"

"I promise," he said, grinning. "I'm not goin' anywhere without you, babe."

Her smile was wide enough to catch the moonlight, accentuating her high cheekbones, her small, pouty mouth. Leaning into him, she pressed her lips against his. It was a long, loving kiss.

Mike climbed on top of her, using his elbows and forearms to support himself above her. Running his fingers through her long, silky hair, he supposed he could save his bad thoughts for another time. She looked up at him, and licked her scarlet lips, waiting to be kissed again. As he eased his body against her, his open mouth finding hers, they slowly began to undress each other.

In the fusion of shadows and moonlight, she was more than just a shape, more than just a body. She was a part of him. A part of him that he loved more than anything else in the world. As their naked bodies moved together, slowly, tenderly, quietly, so that the others could not hear them, he thought about the first time they had made love, on his parent's bed while they were away on vacation, which was probably the very same bed where his life, as well as the life of his younger brother, had originated. He thought of how tightly they had held each other at Lori's funeral, where Karen had been so shaken she hadn't had the strength to stand on her own. He thought of dancing with her at the prom, singing in her ear as he spun her around, and how she had tilted her head back, laughing, as he nearly tripped over his own two feet. These precious memories, along with a million others, came rushing back to him all at once as their bodies moved in perfect rhythm.

Karen also doted on these things. They were the kind of things two lovers would not and could not forget for as long as their hearts still pumped with life. Those bittersweet memories that even time could not erase.

It was shortly after midnight when they finally fell asleep in each other's arms, their bodies naked and warm. Sleep was kind, and gave them dreams instead of nightmares.

Dreams of the past, present, and future.

~Thirty—Two~

In the nightmare he was running, and the man wielding the machete was close behind. Lou could hear him laughing, could feel the cold steel slicing through the air at his back, but his legs were moving in slow motion, as if he was running through muddy water. He could not move fast enough. He could not hide. He could not escape.

In the darkness he stumbled and fell onto his hands, but they only served to cushion the impact. He collapsed onto his stomach, grinding his teeth together in anticipation of the pain he knew was coming, but there was none. *Strange*, he thought. Then he twisted around to face the man, The Hacker, and what he saw was something from a fairy tale gone awry. The Hacker's face was a madman's version of a grandfather clock, with one eye at 10 o'clock, the other at 2. The timekeeping hands sprouted forth from the tip of his nose, spinning like twin propellers.

Lou screamed.

The Hacker raised the massive machete high above his head, clenching it with both hands. The blade glowed as if it were made of fire, and for a moment the monster stood frozen, grinning, distorting the numbers that were printed on his flesh, savoring the moment, as the hands on his face spun out of control, rapidly ticking away the final seconds of Lou Swart's life.

"Hickory Dickory Dock!" The Hacker howled through the folds of a lopsided mouth. It sounded as though he were gargling mud. "Ya can't eshcape the clock!"

This has got to be a dream, thought Lou, *because I'm gonna die!*

Then the blade came down...

Swish!

And that's when Lou Swart awoke, screaming at top volume. A cold sweat had gathered on his forehead, trickling down to meet the tears that were already running down his face. As he choked for air, he could still hear the distant sound of the blade rushing toward him, to cleave his skull in two.

Swish!

Max awoke instantly and was now by his side, shaking him in the dim moonlight. Within seconds, the others came rushing into the room, wide-eyed and worried-looking.

"What the fuck happened?" Mike asked, brushing past Max.

"I don't know," Max said worriedly. "He just started freakin'. He must've had a bad dream or somethin'."

Some dream, thought Mike. He could still hear the distant sound of Lou's scream echoing through the valley. He knelt on the floor beside his brother. "Are you okay?" he asked, his forehead wrinkled with concern. He licked his lips. "Lou, it was only a dream."

Lou whispered something softly. Something they couldn't quite hear. His eyes were wide with fear. His lips quivered.

Everyone leaned in a little closer to him.

"What?"

"He's coming," Lou said, speaking loud enough so that they all heard him this time. Spittle flew from his mouth as he spoke.

"What the fuck are you talking about?" inquired Max, his voice rising shrilly. A match popped to life, filling the air with sulfur, filling the dark room with a sudden burst of light, illuminating Max's frightened face. He lit a cigarette and puffed on it nervously. He shook out the match.

"HE'S COMING!" Lou repeated in a shrill voice. "HE'S COMING!"

Outside, the wind was an angry creature, hissing and howling against the cabin walls, rattling the windows, trying to force its way inside.

~Thirty-Three~

Four days later.

Kevin Chapman was sprawled upon his waterbed that humid afternoon, arms crossed behind his head, staring at the dull white paint of his bedroom ceiling, wondering what his friends were doing at that moment.

They were hundreds of miles away, doing God-knows-what in the mountains of New Hampshire, and here he was in Hevven, probably the lamest cow-town in the entire nation, torturing himself with worried thoughts. They were together, though. At least they had that much. And he was alone. Always alone. He wished that he and Mike had had more time to discuss what had taken place at the Moody house. He wished he'd never agreed to commit himself to Mount Hope. But most of all, he wished that he was with his friends. At least then he would know whether or not they were okay. Because right now he was lonelier than he'd ever been before.

Four days had passed, and still no word from Mike. The police had finally showed up on the second day, Officer Bailey and some stocky little guy from the FBI who, contrary to Kevin's preconception, didn't look anything like Fox Mulder from the X-Files. The FBI agent had done most of the talking, casually reading his questions from a notepad, as though he was going over this week's grocery list. The interrogation was brief, almost anticlimactic. Kevin denied any knowledge of his friends' whereabouts, and the two men left rather quickly, as if they'd had more important things to do. As Kevin showed them to the door, the FBI guy had slipped a business card into his hand, and Kevin had a sneaking suspicion that the two men knew more about his missing friends than they were willing to let on.

Kevin supposed that the only thing that had gone according to plan was the calls he had made three days ago, from a payphone outside a 7-11 in Futawam. Each went smoothly, except for the fact that he'd been unable to reach Mr. Kendall, who was probably piss-drunk and passed out on the living room floor in a puddle of his own vomit, which was an all-too-common occurrence at the Kendall home. Not that Max's dad would've cared to hear about his only son, anyway. Kevin thought it likely that Mr. Kendall hadn't even noticed Max was missing. Although the ordeal had been somewhat nerve-wracking, Kevin had managed to bullshit his way through each and every explanation. And he was extremely careful to change the subject when the common questions arose: Where are they? Where's my son? Where's my daughter? Who the hell is this?

He had told them whatever he thought they'd want to hear, everything but his own name, just as Mike had instructed him to do. And, as usual, Mike's plan worked. Kevin had never doubted that it would. Mike's plans almost always worked.

Kevin got up and snatched a *Maxim* magazine from a stack on his bureau. He brought it back to his bed, and began leafing restlessly through its pages. Next to *Hustler* and *Club*, *Maxim* was his favorite magazine. The articles were interesting, the jokes were funny, and the women…well, they were almost too gorgeous to be real. But today, Kevin couldn't focus long enough to read any of the articles. And the jokes did not seem funny for some reason. Even the glossy pictures of scantily clad women did not interest him, as they usually did. He flipped through the magazine, once, twice, then closed it with a slap.

Impulsively, he bent over and opened the bottom drawer of his nightstand and removed a handful of the photographs that resided there. As he flipped through the various pictures, there was one in particular which captured his attention. It was a picture Mike had taken of Rick, Lori, and Kevin leaning against the front of Mike's T-bird. Lori was in the middle, an arm around each of their shoulders. Lori, with her cute shoulder-length hair, her squinty, carefree eyes,

212

and her winning smile stealing the scene. Rick, with his dark hair wild, blowing in the breeze, and his brilliant eyes gleaming. And he, Kevin, with his wiffle-style haircut, and his drunken grimace. Friends forever.

Still holding the photograph, with the perfumed summer breeze wafting in through his bedroom window, he closed his eyes, and the recollection of that day surfaced in his mind with astonishing clarity. Suddenly he was there, if not in body then in mind, watching the memory as it unfolded before him, no longer a participant, as he'd originally been, but a spectator watching someone else's life.

"...I'd wish for...shit, I don't know," he (the memory Kevin) was saying. "I'll pass for now. What would you wish for, Mike?"

Leaning against the hood of his car, Mike sighed dramatically, tilting his head back to the sky. "I guess I'd wish for wisdom," he'd replied after a pause. "Everything depends on the decisions we make. The roads we decide to follow, the thousands of possibilities that we pass by every day. I never want to feel like I'm missing out on life. I never want to feel regret...for anything. Wisdom helps you choose the right path; I guess that's my wish..."

"Now that's a respectable answer," Rick had interjected before anyone else. "None of that 'I'd wish for a million dollars' bullshit."

"What about you, sweetie?" Lori wanted to know. She gave Rick a playful nudge with her elbow. "What would you wish for?"

"I'd wish for time to stand still," Rick said simply. He looked at each of his friends. "So that we'd always be friends, and we'd always be young, and we'd never die. I want us to always be together. I never want the good times to end."

"I second that wish," Lori responded with her winning smile, running her fingers through Rick's long hair. It was obvious, by the way she had looked at him, that she would love him forever.

"Well, I know a way we can save at least one moment," Mike told them with a sly grin. He vanished inside his car, rummaging noisily and muttering to himself, and returned a few moments later with a disposable camera.

"Alright, everyone move in closer," he ordered.

"What should we say?" asked Kevin, with a goofy smile.

"Don't say anything," Mike had whispered. "Just think about the moment."

The entire moment, frozen on a simple piece of film.

As Kevin stared at the photograph that stared back at him, a single tear rolled down his cheek.

I miss you, Lori, he thought. *Why'd you have to die? Rick was so wild, so funny, so alive, before you left us. We were all so close then, just like a family. We were gonna take on this whole fucking world together.*

Together.

He looked at her smile. Stared at that smile.

There was no such thing as together anymore.

He wiped a teardrop from his face with the back of one hand, and it occurred to him that he hadn't looked at any of her photographs since the accident. Once again, Kevin wished he was with his friends.

"I won't forget," he murmured, and tossed the pile of pictures back into the open drawer, where they scattered like playing cards. He closed his eyes to hold back the many tears that would soon follow the first. He thought of being alone. He thought of the precious time wasted within the walls of the Mount Hope Rehabilitation Center. Time that could've been spent working, or just hanging out with his friends. He thought of how one night he was at the beach, partying with six of the best friends he had ever had, and how the next day there were only five.

Why is it so easy to die, and so hard to live?

He could remember everything; it was all there when he closed his eyes, like clips of an old home-movie. Elementary School: playing baseball in the park. Pretending they were soldiers on hot summer afternoons in the forest near Rick's house. Building forts to hang out in, tearing them down to make way for new ones. Going on field trips to Plymouth Rock in the first grade. The night his father died, and how it was beyond his comprehension that he would never see the man again. Junior High: scooping on girls at the local mall. Sneaking beers when Max's father had passed out for the evening. Riding their bikes everywhere, not a care in the world. High School: greeting each other in the halls between and during

214

classes. Playing hooky together to get high in the Cherry Street pits. Throwing popcorn at each other in the darkness of the Futawam Theater. Cruising Main Street in Mike's car while the younger kids looked on with envy and admiration. Kicking ass when someone started trouble with one of their own. Smiling faces, sad faces, laughter, and angry words, all swimming through his mind. He could practically smell those hot summer days—the preternatural scent of honeysuckle, pollen, and morning dew—just as easily as he could recall the clinking of their bicycle chains as they explored their little corner of the world.

He only wished he'd realized then, just how precious those moments were. But, like most kids, he'd thought they would last forever. He never saw time creeping up on them like a serpent in the garden of their lives, slithering slowly, waiting to sink its teeth into the delicate flesh of their innocence, filling them with poison, robbing them of their childhood dreams, making them sick with age and change. He never imagined the reality of losing one of their own, never saw Death waiting to slam Lori Shawnessy's car headlong into a telephone pole, robbing her of that winning smile forever.

Finally, thinking of all of these things, he let himself go. Through stinging tears of pain, he thought of his life, and the mistakes he had made. Until now, Kevin Chapman, the World Class Fuck-Up, had kept his feelings locked inside. And at that very moment, while lying on his bed, staring at the ceiling through watering eyes, he realized why Rick had changed so dramatically after the accident, because he had learned the horrible truth before the rest of them: That life was little more than a rollercoaster ride into nowhere, and that the ride could end at any given time, and without warning. There was no slowing down. No turning back. No second rides. Kevin Chapman understood that now.

Deep sleep had nearly pulled him under when he heard his mother's voice calling him from the parlor.

"Kevin, are you awake? There's someone here to see you."

Kevin jumped up from his bed and quickly began to wipe his tear-streaked face. "I'll be there in a minute!"

His hopes began to rise. It was Mike and the others. They came back for him! They came to take him out of this place, out of loneliness.

Don't get your hopes up, Kevin told himself. It was probably one of his friend's parents, coming to demand some answers. Maybe they had recognized his voice when he called. Or maybe it's that cop, Bailey, and that FBI guy, whatever his name was, coming to interrogate him again.

After taking a minute or two to compose himself, Kevin left his room. As he walked down the hallway, hoping for good news, preparing for bad news, he could see his mother standing in the parlor, her arms folded across her chest. She had that worried look on her face once again, causing her to look much older than her true age, and with each step Kevin wished he hadn't answered his mother. She would have told whoever was out there that he was asleep, and to come back some other time.

He didn't feel like dealing with his own mother right now, let alone Mike's, or Rick's, or Karen's parents. He especially didn't feel like dealing with the cops again.

As he came within a few steps of the parlor, he could see a single dark shadow stretching across the floor, just off to the right of where his mother was standing. Judging by the size of the shadow, Kevin knew it had to be Rick's father who was waiting to see him. Rick's father was a big guy. He'd once been in the Army, as Kevin recalled. Before Rick was even born, his father had risked his life to serve his country. Rick had always been so proud of that fact.

Looking at the unusually large shadow, Kevin suddenly felt about three feet tall. If it was Mr. Hunter, what would Kevin possibly say to the man? Could he really be expected to lie to the man's face? But then again, how could he break the trust that Mike and the others had bestowed upon him? How could he tell the truth?

This could get ugly.

This is gonna be a shittier day than I thought, Kevin mused, nearing the end of the hallway.

216

~Thirty-Four~

In many ways, the days that followed Lou's nightmare were no different than the ones that preceded it. Karen and Stacey passed the time by chatting on the porch steps, tanning on blankets by the riverside, and painting each other's nails, desperately trying to maintain an air of indifference while the outside world continued without them. Lou mostly kept his nose buried in the magazines and books his brother had brought back from the store, losing himself in an imaginary world of video games, sports, and science fiction novels. Fascinated by the prospect of living off the land, as Mike had put it, Max spent the days hunting worms, then walking up and down the river in search of the perfect fishing hole. Although he claimed to have hooked a large rainbow trout and a smallmouth bass, he had yet to supply his friends with any tangible evidence that would support his fish stories. Nevertheless, it seemed as though he'd finally discovered a harmless occupation, and for that they were all grateful.

Meanwhile, Rick secluded himself as often as possible, sometimes wandering the forest for hours at a time, refusing to tell the others where he'd been and what he'd been doing. And Mike, as always, continued to play the selfless host (and sometimes referee), bouncing from one person to the next, trying to keep everyone happy at the same time.

At night, they all gathered around their riverside firepit. Max repeating the same old jokes; Stacey and Rick playing hide-and-seek with their eyes as they stole glances at one another from across the fire; Mike wondering if he'd made the right decision; and so on. But a dark cloud hovered over those peaceful evenings, sometimes bringing them a silence they could not ignore.

The silence spoke of all the things that lingered on the back of their minds, things no one, including Mike, wanted to talk about. The dead girl. Stacey's abduction. The police. Their parents. How long before the money ran out?

As each day passed, Mike wondered how much longer they could keep these thoughts at bay before the dark cloud they had left behind in Hevven finally descended upon them.

In a tight red half-shirt and faded jean shorts, Karen Sloan sat on the front steps of the cabin, wiggling her bare toes as she gazed at the river, quietly humming the lines of a Sheryl Crow song. She was just starting to get into it, bobbing her head and mouthing the words, when she heard a creaking noise behind her. Feeling slightly embarrassed, she quickly stopped humming and turned around.

Mike was standing in the doorway, bare-chested, wearing only a pair of black swim trunks. Sleep had given volume to his wavy brown hair; it curled back from his forehead and rose like a pompadour. He looked at her and smiled.

"Nice hair," Karen said as he stepped out onto the porch. "Where's your brother?"

"He's gonna sleep in, I think." His muscles rippled as he yawned. He sat down beside her on the steps, knees bending slowly, like a tired old man.

She put an arm around his waist and leaned against him. "Again? Is he okay?"

He brushed her hair aside and kissed her on the forehead. "Yeah, he should be. I don't think he's been sleeping too well. I think he's still pretty shaken from that nightmare."

"That was what? Three days ago?" Rick interrupted from behind, and they turned their heads to look at him. He was wearing a wrinkled Calvin Klein T-shirt and a pair of Scooby-Doo boxer shorts. His black, medium-length hair was plastered against his head, and his mysterious hazel-green eyes were half-closed as he squinted in the bright sunlight.

Stacey was standing beside him in the doorway, rubbing her eyes. Once again she had tied her fiery auburn hair into a ponytail, and she looked just as sweet and innocent as a schoolgirl. She offered a tired smile and waved her hand to greet them, baby-blues glowing with that thoughtful intensity of which they had all grown fond.

"Four," Karen corrected him. "How're you two crazy kids doing this morning?"

"I feel like I could sleep the entire day away," Stacey answered for the both of them, and Rick nodded in agreement.

"Where's Max?" asked Mike.

"He's upstairs changing," Rick said, running his fingers through his long, dark hair. "I'm starving. What's left for food?"

"Well," Mike said, wrinkling his brow as he struggled to remember, "we got some potato chips, a box of cookies, half a loaf of bread, some peanut butter. I think there's half a box of Wheat Thins…"

Karen wrinkled her nose. "All the healthy stuff," she snickered, rolling her eyes at Stacey with a What-Do-You-Expect-From-Men? look.

Stacey shook her head with a crooked grin, understanding and agreeing with Karen's none-too-subtle message.

"…a few apples, a few oranges." He stopped to think, pretending not to notice Karen's sarcasm. "Oh, yeah, and a leftover pack of hot dogs that we should eat before they go bad."

"Water," Rick said. "I need water."

"There's some Gatorade in the cooler."

"That'll do."

For the next 20 minutes the four of them sat side by side, content with being in the presence of nature. They watched the red-hot sun change positions in the sky, drinking Gatorades and sweet summer breezes. Birds circled around them, squawking and tweeting as they searched the meadow for food. Stacey thought she had never felt more at ease in her entire life.

A little while later the serenity was broken as Max came stomping down the stairs, a towel over one shoulder, and a cigarette dangling from his mouth. "Hey," he said to no one in particular.

They were being so quiet, he felt as though he had just stumbled into a funeral with a cowbell tied around his neck.

"What's up?" asked Mike. "Is Lou still asleep?"

"No, he's up," Max said, casually scratching his ass. "He should be down in a few minutes. So, what's going on? How come everyone's so quiet?"

"We're just tired," answered Karen.

Nodding, Max went over to the side of the porch and leaned against the railing. From there, he took in the increasingly familiar view: the mountains draped with mist, the delicate pinkish hue of the sky, the river glowing like quicksilver in the morning light, beckoning him to come and play. Max was also tired, but he didn't want to sleep. He was hungry, too, but he figured he could wait a few more hours before he really needed to eat. God had given them another beautiful day, and it seemed like such a waste not to enjoy it.

"Well, I'm going for a swim," he announced. He hurdled the railing and began down the meadow. "See you guys later."

By noon, the others had joined Max at the river, where they frolicked for nearly two hours until hunger set in. Mike and Karen walked back to the cabin, still dripping in their bathing suits, and returned a few minutes later with a box of Wheat Thins, a box of Oreos, a leftover package of hot dogs, six rolls, six bottles of water, and a deck of playing cards.

"I'm starvin'," Max said, rubbing his stomach.

"Oh," Karen said. Eyes glowing, she reached into the back of her jeans pocket and removed a small bottle of reddish liquid. "I almost forgot. Mike got you a present from the store."

"Dumb Ass Hot Sauce!" Max said, reading the label. "Cool!"

"Great," Lou muttered. He turned to Mike. "You should've gotten him an air freshener instead. Our room reeks of the brown ghost."

Rick smirked. "Brown ghost?"

Lou rolled his eyes. "Don't ask. You're just lucky you don't have to share a room with him."

After lunch, they settled down on the beach for a game of cards.

"Scat!" Max howled, and laid his cards down on the sand so everyone could see he was telling the truth.

"You piece of shit," Mike said in dismay, gathering up the cards. It was his turn to deal. "Are you cheating?"

"I'm not cheating," Max protested, chomping down an Oreo. He made a dignified face. "I'm just good, that's all."

Mike shuffled the cards and dealt them quickly. Then he placed the remainder of the deck in the middle of their circle, and flipped over the top card. It was a 10 of Diamonds. He scooped up his own cards and rearranged them from the highest to the lowest, winking at Karen as he did so. "Okay," he said when he was ready. "Let's play. You go first, Lou."

Lou glanced long and hard at his cards, cupping them defensively so no one else could see them. Taking a sip of water, he looked thoughtfully at the 10 of Diamonds, then at his own cards, and then at the 10 of Diamonds again.

"Sometime today would be nice," Max groaned. He lit a cigarette and started humming the Final Jeopardy theme. He was tapping his bare foot anxiously, unaware that he was signaling the others that he had a good hand.

Lou discarded a 7 of Diamonds and picked up the 10, trying to maintain a solemn poker face. "Can you pass the Wheat Thins?"

Max grabbed the box and tossed it across the playing circle, his foot still tapping away.

Way off in the distance a car passed over the bridge, moving toward the next town, Potter's Bluff. Sunlight gleamed from its windows and chrome, and the sound of its engine droned throughout the valley.

The sun stared down at them like a sleepy eye. The air was muggy and still, the sky an endless ocean of aqua blue that stretched on forever above the arrowhead tips of the mountains. Due to the recent drought, the river had receded an inch or more from the bank, and the water bugs had arrived in droves to take advantage of the sluggish current. Like miniature race cars, they zigzagged across the placid surface at neck-breaking speeds. Every once in a while the water would swirl, and one of them would vanish, swallowed

221

whole by an unseen fish, and another bug would appear to take its place.

Beneath the hazy-hot sun the small assembly of friends played cards for nearly another hour, allowing Max the opportunity to win three more games. When boredom finally set in (after a while, even Max grew tired of winning), they turned their focus toward a more invigorating activity.

They swam.

~Thirty−Five~

Sighing uneasily through his nostrils, Kevin saw his mother as he neared the end of the long, dim hallway. Arms folded across her chest, Ms. Chapman's face was a knot of puzzlement. Her eyes grew wider as she looked at her son. Then her eyes shifted back toward the stranger, who remained concealed just around the corner.

Kevin didn't like the way his mother had looked at him, or the way she was looking at the visitor, but his curiosity beckoned him onward. He stepped into the parlor. His mother smiled worriedly.

Then came the shot.

It was a muffled sound, like a child's cap gun, but the result was far from make-believe.

Before Ms. Chapman had time enough to scream, she was lifted off her feet, and thrown to the carpet with a thud, several feet away from where she had been standing only moments before.

"Mom!" Kevin screamed. He ran to her side, oblivious to the large man whose shadow he'd seen while coming down the hall, the man who now stood in the corner of the room, with a smoking pistol aimed at the back of Kevin's left leg.

A second muffled shot—pooofft—and Kevin felt an explosion of flesh and bone ripping through his calf. He crumpled forward, arms flailing, as though a wrecking ball had struck him from behind. He landed within reach of his mother, who was lying on her back, whimpering softly as she inspected her wounded stomach with her hands. She lifted her hands up to confirm her suspicions, and Kevin could see it, too. Her blood was everywhere.

"You Punks are all the same," a baritone voice rumbled from behind. There was no emotion in that voice; it was cold, robotic. "Sloppy, mindless. You're garbage, all of you. And I'm the garbage man. God sent me here to clean up the mess. Oh, and what a mess you and your friends have made."

Smoke eased from the silencer on his Glock as he watched, indifferent, as the two people on the floor squirmed in pain. He inhaled deeply the smell of gunpowder, thinking that he was now closer than ever to satisfying the dark pool in the Hockomock Forest. The pool that had, so long ago, promised him freedom. And The Truth.

"Mom..." Kevin moaned, reaching a trembling hand toward her.

"I want to know one thing," the Garbage Man said. "It's quite simple, really. Where're your friends?"

Kevin's first thought was that the Garbage Man was one of his old drug contacts. *Pepsak*, he thought. Maybe this guy worked for him. But, no. He hadn't talked to Pepsak in over a month. And besides, Pepsak had no beef with Kevin or his friends. Then it dawned on him. This wasn't some street-trash looking to punish him for past actions. It sure as shit wasn't the goddamn garbage man, either. It was the man whom Mike had warned him about, The Hacker.

Kevin strained to look at him, but was unable to see the face of the man who'd shot him. But that shadow, that long, cold shadow, remained on the floor, looming over him. "I don't know...what you're...talking about ... "

The man who owned the shadow fired again, this time into the ceiling, and Kevin winced as crumbs of sheetrock rained down upon him. Sobbing like a child, he looked at his mother, his lower leg burning as it gushed onto the carpet. She was not moving. She was just lying there. Still.

"Don't fuck with me," The Hacker said calmly. "I haven't come this far to let a little shit like you ruin it for me. The next shot will be in your mother's head. You can't see me, but that's where I'm aiming right now. You'll just have to take my word for it."

224

Again Kevin attempted to lift himself to see the man who had shot his mother, who had shot him, but failed miserably. Even though his arms were strong enough to bring him to the push-up position, his mangled leg sent tremors through his body to the point where he nearly fainted. He breathed heavily, falling back onto his stomach, helpless, wondering if his mother was still alive, wondering if there was any hope for either of them. He prayed for his friends. "They're in New Hampshire..." Kevin spat through clenched teeth.

"That's not good enough," the voice sang out. "And don't lie to me, because I'll know. I'm good at picking out liars. If you lie to me, you can kiss your momma goodbye."

Kevin wanted to scream. He raised his eyes to his mother. Did he see her chest rise and fall? Or was it just nervous spasms? How could he let her die? She was his mother, for God's sake. How could he live with that? And what about his friends, who had trusted him? How could he sell them out? How could he sic this goddamn lunatic on them?

"Quite frankly," The Hacker gloated, "I find your reluctance rather charming. Your mother is over there, bleeding to death, and all you can think about is your precious little friends? And here, I thought your generation knew nothing of the word 'loyalty'..."

"FUCK YOU!"

"Run-ning out of ti—iiime..." The Hacker sang out. Then his voice turned cold. "Better listen to me, you pathetic piece of shit. They took something that belongs to me, and I want it back. So you better tell me where they are RIGHT FUCKING NOW!"

"Wuh-wuh-willow Cr-creek...Wuh-willow Creek." Kevin sobbed, closing his eyes.

The man with the gun stepped closer, his feet sounding heavy on the carpeted floor. Kevin watched him through the corner of his eye, watched his merciless shark eyes, watched his crooked teeth separate his face into a lunatic's smile. Watched him, and recognized him. Still wearing that smile, The Hacker saluted Kevin with the pistol, as if to say farewell. Kevin saw that he was wearing gloves, the kind worn by surgeons, and by criminals who did not want to leave behind fingerprints. His casual manner showed he was a man who had done this sort of thing many times before, and took pleasure in doing it.

I've seen him before, Mike had told him over the phone. I recognized him from somewhere. I think he might be a townie. So be careful. And don't trust anyone.

Damn right he's a fucking townie, Kevin thought, looking up through watering eyes.

"You think you know who I am?" The Hacker smiled wickedly. "Don't you?"

Kevin nodded, barely able to lift his head from the floor.

"You don't know shit," The Hacker said, standing directly above him. His enormous biceps flexed as he extended his arm, pointing the Glock at the boy's chest. Smiling, he squeezed the trigger.

The bullet rushed down the dark barrel of the Glock, through the silencer, and out into the light, where it briefly tasted the air before it nosed its way into Kevin Chapman's soft, pliant flesh.

But it didn't stop there.

It was a hollow-tipped 9mm bullet, and it was hungry.

After puncturing one of Kevin Chapman's lungs it ricocheted off his spine, exploding through a fist-sized hole in his back, and its coup de grace ended as it lodged itself into the hardwood floor beneath the living room carpet. There was no need to shoot the woman. Judging by the way that she was breathing, one of her lungs had been punctured, and she'd probably drown in her own blood...if the pain didn't kill her first. Either way, she was already as good as dead.

After a few minutes passed, he poked his head out the front door, scanning the neighborhood for any potential witnesses. He saw there were none. He stuffed the pistol into his pocket and went outside to his car, an '82 Buick freckled with rust. From the trunk he retrieved a long-handled axe. By the time he returned to the living room, his prediction had come true. Ms. Chapman was dead.

Lucky for her, he thought.

Brandishing the heavy weapon, he dismembered both bodies, piece by bloody piece. When he was done he put the warm, twitching remains of Ms. Chapman and her son into two Hefty trashbags and hauled them out to his car, where he placed them in

226

the trunk. But before he left he removed Lou Swart's missing wallet from a Ziplock bag and tossed it onto the bloodstained carpet, out in the open, where the police could not miss it. Lou Swart and his buddies would be blamed for the murders of the Chapman woman and her son, just as they were blamed for the murder of Anna Hartsoe and the disappearance of Kelly Brine. The police lacked no imagination when it came to recreating crimes. They would speculate that Kevin had threatened to turn in his outlaw friends (or something to that effect), and that the young psychopaths had kept him from doing so the only way they knew how; by killing him. And then, of course, they had killed Ms. Chapman because she was a witness.

The beauty of it all was that no one would ever know what had really happened, because he was going to kill every last one of them, kill them like animals, and hide their bodies where nobody would ever find them. The police would never have the opportunity to arrest them, interrogate them, or take them to trial. Therefore, having no further suspects, there would be no doubt that Lou Swart and his buddies were, in fact, the killers. Sure, the police would continue their investigation. Hell, they'd probably even get an episode on *America's Most Wanted*. But they'd never find Lou Swart and his pals, because no one—he was certain—could find the pool but him.

I tore through the walls of that other world, and they showed me the way to The Truth. The Truth is what I need...what I've always needed. The pool told me what to do. Nothing will stop me. Nothing. I've got a seasoned heart, that's what the voices whispered to me from that deep, dark place. They told me what I must do, and then they'll welcome me with liquid arms. They'll protect me. They'll love me.

The terms of his inception were quite simple, really: Get back that dirty little cunt who had escaped him, and kill those miserable little bastards who had helped her get away. She was his. His! They had no goddamn right to steal her from him. No goddamn right at all. They would pay for what they had done, taking what did not belong to them. He'd make them bleed. Make them beg for their lives. Make them suffer for interfering with his work. Make

227

them beautiful. Throw them in the pool and make them beautiful. Ahhhh, the pool!

He could smell their fear: It was deep and red and black. And he could see it in his mind's eye, their faces: so young and beautiful and dead. And still. Yes, finally still.

Snapping out of his blissful trance, he realized he was now sitting behind the wheel of his car, still parked in the Chapman's driveway. He looked down. His belt was undone; his zipper, too. He couldn't remember getting into the car, no more than he could remember unfastening his belt or his zipper. He could not remember fondling himself, either, but his hand was still there, still wrapped loosely around the withered nub that was his penis.

He continued to fondle himself, thinking of all the fun he was going to have, purging the six wayward angels of their sins. It was the only way he could excite himself.

(make them bleed make them beg make them suffer)

Oh, yes, enjoy tonight. Enjoy it while you can. Soon you'll join the others in the pool. He could almost see their gawking, floating faces.

(beautiful and cold and dead and still, sinking, sinking)

Imagining this, he finished inside his pants.

~Thirty-Six~

The golden yolk of the sun was dipping down, sliding off the hot red griddle of the northern sky, melting into the dark gray cones of the White Mountains. It was almost 9 o'clock, and the night was slow in returning from the other side of the globe, struggling to reclaim its seat at Mother Nature's table. Scarcely a star was visible in the sky, as if somehow during the melee the duty of laying out the constellations had simply been overlooked.

By the river, the six runaways enjoyed the prolonged moments of sunlight, as the valley rippled with a soft and steady breeze. Warming themselves by the fire, they told ghost stories and jokes, their laughter mingling with the peepers and frogs. After a while, Max and Lou broke the circle and walked a few dozen feet away, to the water's edge, where they began taking turns with the fishing pole. Whatever it was—the reassuring magic of togetherness, perhaps, or merely the fact that they were surviving on their own—there was something extraordinary in the way they looked at one another, the way they laughed wholeheartedly at each other's jokes, the way they could sit in silence for long periods of time, not talking, not laughing, somehow content, enjoying the mere simplicity of just being alive.

Their suntanned faces glowed, childlike, in the eventide. Other things were gone from their minds. Things that could ravage these pleasing moments. Things that were buried with little effort beneath the surface of the present but would inevitably rise up, unwanted, at some later time. At this moment, however, there was only tranquility. Even the giants, who were usually tiresome, had taken a break to enjoy the sunset, their voices becoming little more than whispers on the wind.

Sitting with his back to the river, Rick dug his feet into the cool sand and looked through the flames of their fire. That's when he noticed Stacey looking back at him with those sexy, drowsy eyes, the ghost of a smile tugging at one corner of her mouth. Rick looked down for a moment. When he raised his eyes again, he saw Karen whispering in Stacey's ear, and they were both looking at him, smiling with their secret.

"Damn!" Max shouted, a few feet away at the water's edge.

"Get one?" Mike called out from the other side of the fire.

"Almost!" Lou replied excitedly. "It got away."

"Next time you gotta yank the line harder," Max was telling him.

"No," Rick said over his shoulder. "You gotta be gentle. The fish won't bite until it's good and ready. Give it a little slack before you set the hook. Then reel it in slowly. You don't want to scare it away."

Stacey watched Rick steadily through the dancing flames. *How true*, she thought. *How true.*

~Thirty–Seven~

Standing in the small, cluttered conference room in the back of the Hevven Police Department building, leaning over the fax machine and listening to the steady hum of the fluorescent ceiling lights, Officer Bailey had time to consider all that had happened since his secret chase on Roller Coaster Road. Quite an adventure, these past few days.

In less than two weeks he had discovered more about the dark side of law enforcement than most veterans would ever learn in a lifetime. He had joined the Hevven Police Department because he had wanted to do something positive with his life. He'd wanted to help people, to serve and protect them, just as he'd sworn to do. But instead of feeling good about himself, he felt tired and dirty. There were so many things he wished he didn't know about the world.

During his investigation into the murder of Anna Hartsoe he had learned, perhaps too quickly, about the noxious smell of a decomposed corpse, and the names of the 20-odd missing girls whom no one seemed to care about, except maybe himself and Agent Ferren. After discovering the words KISS ASS FAGGOT scribbled on his locker in blue marker, he had learned the hard way about the jealousy of his coworkers who, in their small-town mentality, seemed to interpret his cooperation with the FBI as a kind of political betrayal to the department. He had learned about the proper way to collect evidence in order to maintain the integrity of a crime scene, and how the media could turn any police investigation into a three-ring circus. He had also learned a bit about friendship, for he had already developed a deep trust and respect for his temporary partner, who had willingly taken on the role of Bailey's mentor.

Ferren appeared in the doorway holding two Styrofoam cups. He was dressed in his usual, meticulous attire; a sharp black suit with a matching necktie and a white button-up shirt. "You looked like you could use a pick-me-up," he said, handing one steamy cup to the young officer, whose uniform was wrinkled and unbuttoned at the collar, showing the V of the white T-shirt he wore underneath.

Bailey nodded wearily. "Thanks," he said, without smiling. "Nothing yet."

Ferren nodded and sipped his coffee. He was used to waiting.

A few minutes later the fax machine whirred to life and coughed up a single sheet of paper. Bailey took the page, glanced at it briefly, and handed it to Ferren.

Ferren put down his coffee. He looked at the fax sheet and frowned.

"What is it?" Bailey asked.

"Hmmm. That's odd," Ferren said, still staring at the page in his hands. After a few seconds he looked up, still frowning. "The lab is still running a few more tests, but a preliminary diagnostic of that fingernail we discovered at the crime scene revealed minute traces of a medical grade silicon."

"Silicon? Isn't that what they once used for breast enhancements?"

Ferren raised his eyebrows at him, obviously impressed. "How'd you know that?"

Bailey smiled sheepishly. "Long story."

"The report only mentions one possible match. You wouldn't happen to know anyone around here who wears a prosthetic, would you?"

"You mean, like, fake arms and legs?"

"Among other things. Here, take a look."

Bailey looked at the fax sheet, his eyes blank. The text of the report might as well have been written in hieroglyphics. He rubbed his bloodshot eyes.

"Do you know of any factories around here that produce similar materials? Maybe a medical supply company?"

Bailey shook his head as he handed back the report. "None that I can think of off the top of my head. But I know one person who would know the answer to that."

"The good Chief?"

Bailey nodded unenthusiastically.

"Let's give him a call."

Bailey got the number from the dispatcher. He turned to Ferren with the phone still in his hand. "I'm tellin' ya right now, he's not gonna be happy, me calling him at home," Bailey said as he dialed the number. He waited as the phone rang. Hopefully, the Chief wouldn't answer. Then they could both go home and grab a decent night's sleep for a change. Well, they could try to, anyway. Bailey had found it increasingly more difficult to sleep these past few nights.

"No answer?" Ferren asked after a few seconds.

Bailey shook his head. "No machine, either." He hung up the phone. "He's probably sleeping, which doesn't sound like a bad idea, to tell you the truth. It's gotta be what? Ten o'clock?"

"Ten-thirty," Ferren said. "Does he live alone?"

"Moriarty? He's not married, if that's what you mean. No, from what I understand, it's just him and his brother."

"Brother?"

"Yeah, he's got some kind of disease or somethin'. Never leaves the house, from what I've been told. Moriarty's been caring for him since they were teenagers. You see that bruise on Moriarty's neck a couple of days ago?"

Ferren nodded. "His brother did that?"

"Probably. Moriarty's always coming in with bruises and scratches. I asked the dispatcher about it once, and she told me his brother has fits sometimes. Violent ones. You know, like those retarded kids who have to wear helmets, or else they'd bash their own brains in? Except he's only mildly retarded, from what I hear. Anyway, she said that's why the Chief's always in such a piss-poor mood."

Ferren nodded. He felt a pang of compassion for the older man. Caring for his handicapped brother had obviously taken its toll on the man. "Well, sleeping or not, we gotta talk to him. As soon as possible. You know where he lives?"

Bailey nodded.

"Good," Agent Ferren said, adjusting his necktie. "Let's go for a little ride, shall we? Or would you rather we wait until the morning?"

The young officer smiled at the temptation. "Naw, we might as well get it over with. The sooner this case is over, the sooner I'll be able to get a good night's sleep."

Agent Ferren tucked the report inside his breast pocket and grinned understandingly as they both headed for the door. He patted the young man's back. "Spoken like a true cop."

And with that, they headed out and into the night.

~Thirty-Eight~

An hour and a half after their friends had gone, Rick Hunter and Stacey Mackinnon found themselves alone on the grassy hump of the cliff, listening to the babbling river below them. Overhead, the moon looked like a jack o' lantern, grinning mischievously from the black window of the northern sky. The peaks of the mountains (or giants, if you prefer) beyond the river glowed eerily in the orange moonlight, like inverted rows of candy corn, a muddled blend of orange and white.

Trick or treat? the voices in Mike's head had asked him earlier in the evening.

Treat, he had replied.

Sorry, the giants had returned. *You're much too old for treats, Mikey.*

That was one of the reasons Mike Swart had decided to call it a day, because the giants were nagging him to the point of exhaustion. The second reason was that he wanted to give Rick and Stacey a chance to be alone. Thinking of these things he'd taken Karen by the hand, and they'd said their goodnights and headed back up the meadow in the direction of the cabin.

When Max and Lou finally retired the fishing pole, they had returned to find Rick and Stacey sitting side by side, quietly smoking cigarettes as they contemplated the burning heart of the fire. Eventually, it dawned on them that Rick and Stacey wanted to be alone this evening, and the two fishermen excused themselves and retreated to the cabin shortly thereafter.

Nearly twenty minutes had passed since then, and Rick and Stacey had scarcely exchanged a word since, but for his suggestion that they should extinguish the fire and view the night sky from the top of the hill.

Now Stacey was standing near the edge of the cliff, spellbound by the moon's reflection on the river below, and Rick was standing behind her, staring at her back, trying to read her thoughts. The way she was standing reminded him of a painting he'd once seen in the Museum of Nautical History in Falmouth. The painting had showed a sailor's wife in a state of bereavement, standing on the edge of a seaside cliff while she eagerly awaited her husband's return. Rick recalled the long white dress the woman had been wearing and how it, along with her long copper hair, had flowed to one side of her in the wake of an imaginary breeze. Although the painted woman had stood with her back perfectly straight and her chin proudly tilted, there was something in her delicate posture that suggested hopelessness, as though she wasn't really waiting for her lover, but mourning him. It was as though the woman in the painting knew that he would never return from his journey.

"Stace?" he said finally, unable to stand the silence any longer. She did not turn around. "Yeah?"

"What're you doin'?" he asked, stepping up behind her.

She was looking above the mountains, at all the endless, twinkling stars. She'd never been much of an astronomer. She did not know the names of these stars, but she loved them. "Just thinking about everything, I guess. You know, if I hadn't been stupid enough to go jogging alone at night, I wouldn't be here right now. It's kinda funny, isn't it? If it hadn't been for him, I never would have met you."

"I'm sorry," Rick said. "I shouldn't have yelled at you the other day. I didn't have any right to do that."

"That's okay," Stacey said. "It was my fault for pressing you. I just can't help the way I feel about you."

Rick kept silent; he didn't know what she wanted him to say.

"I can't explain it," she said, taking two steps closer to the edge of the cliff. "It's just a feeling I have, like you're my guardian angel or something. Like, if I was to fall over this edge, you'd save me somehow."

Rick took her gently by the arm, pulling her away from the crumbled shelf of granite. "That's far enough," he said softly.

Stacey turned and looked at him. Her eyes were almost luminescent in the darkness. "You still love her, don't you?"

"Yeah...I do." He looked down at his feet, as was his habit. It suddenly occurred to him that, despite the circumstances which brought them together at the cabin, there wasn't another place where he'd rather be right now, and it pained him to think that this moment, like all others, was only temporary, and that someday they would go their separate ways again.

"That's okay," Stacey said. She ran her fingers through his long, dark hair. He looked so sad, so distant. "But you have to learn to let go...sometime. Before it tears you apart. Before you lose yourself."

"I know it sounds strange," he said, "but I always felt like I should have been born in a different time, a different place. I guess I never really felt like I belonged in this world. And it hurts. It hurts that life keeps going no matter what, that nothing ever lasts." He continued in a different voice, as if speaking only to himself. "Not a day goes by that I don't wonder: Why? Why can't we all stay young forever? Why do we have to grow up? Why do we have to die? We're ghosts, Stacey. We're ghosts before we even die. Oh, we don't notice it, because it happens so gradually, but we fade a little every day. From the very moment that we're born, we start fading, wasting away. And little by little, we keep on fading, our loved ones, our memories, our bodies...until there's nothing left...until we're dust, until even the dust is gone. I used to think that there was a meaning to be found in everything, but not anymore. There is no meaning. It's all just...random. I know that now."

After saying this, his eyes still closed, he paused to run his fingers along the gauze bandage on his wrist, his mind wandering back to the day of his attempted suicide, and to the scar that would remain forever as a grim reminder of the life and death of Lori Shawnessy.

"There is meaning," Stacey whispered after some time, watching his eyes as they opened to the sound of her voice. "When I was alone in that house, I prayed for days for someone to come and save me. And just when I was about to give up hope, you came. So don't say that life has no meaning, because it does. When I needed you, you were there. And I know you're good because you saved my life. And I know you'd do it again. I feel it. I see it in your eyes."

Rick gave her a haunted look. Then he bowed his head. "I won't always be there to save you, Stace."

"Yes. Yes, you will. I don't know how I know that, but I do."

After a moment he looked at her bashfully and said, "I know this is going to sound really stupid, but I'm going to ask you anyway. Before…all this, were you, you know, seeing anyone?"

There was a tang of jealousy in his voice, and she relished it. "You mean, like a boyfriend? No. Not really. I mean, nothing serious. I guess that's the way it is in college. Why do you ask?"

"Just wondering, y'know?"

Her eyes shimmering with tears, she gently lifted his chin until he was looking at her. In the soft glow of the pumpkin moon they stood as if posing for the cover of a romance novel, Stacey with one hand resting on his shoulder, Rick with his arms by his side, their features dramatized by the shadows as they passionately gazed into one another's eyes. *Kiss me*, she thought. *Kiss me, please. My body aches for you.*

But he did not kiss her. He did not move. He only looked at her passively, mouth slightly open, as if ready to speak.

After a time she took his unshaven face between her hands and, standing on her toes, pressed her soft lips against his open mouth. Eyes closed, they kissed, slowly, longingly, lustfully. He pulled her closer to him, her body stiffening as his strong hands found their way under her shirt, rising slowly to discover her perfect, braless breasts. He could not stop now. She intoxicated him.

Moaning softly, she tilted her head toward the sky, as his tongue traced the soft, feminine contours of her shoulders and neck. Blindly, she reached under his shirt, hands caressing his solid chest, his lean abdomen. While his lips continued to dwell on the smooth, taut area beneath her chin, she unbuttoned his pants and lowered the zipper, her dexterous fingers working slowly as she stroked his hard, naked flesh. With the palm of her hand she rubbed him slowly, slowly, and then their eyes met again; hot hazel and bothered blue.

"Are you sure you're okay with this?" he asked, caressing her face with his fingertips. "Are you sure this is what you want?"

"Yes," she whispered, pressing her forehead to his. "It's what I want. What I need."

In the cool, enchanting moonlight, they continued to undress each other.

"Oh, Rick, please. Please, make love to me..."

Heart singing, ears still ringing with those simple, beautiful words, he laid her down upon the cool summer grass and positioned himself above her. She moaned softly as his mouth continued to explore her warm, salty body; the elegant curve of her neck, the soft swells of her breasts and their hard little nipples, the trembling goosebumped stomach, the fine mound of her pubic hair. As she tilted her pelvis toward him, he buried his face between her thighs, hungrily lapping at her sweetness until she danced in ecstasy on her back.

Even as her body still writhed with the aftershocks of her orgasm, she cradled his head in her hands and gently pulled him back to her awaiting mouth, thrusting her body against him as their eager tongues collided. Slowly he lowered himself between her legs and inside of her. Slick with perspiration, their bodies slid together effortlessly, their nerves vibrating, their muscles trembling with pleasure.

She wrapped her legs around his waist and locked her ankles behind him, hands kneading relentlessly as she worked her fingernails into his back. Muscles tensed, then relaxed, then tensed again. He smoothed the long strands of auburn hair away from her forehead, gasping as they kissed, quivering as she tightened her legs around him, pulling him deeper inside of her, as their hips gyrated in unison.

"Don't stop," she begged seductively.

Upon hearing those provocative words, a sudden tremor arose in his lower body, and he began to throb and swell inside of her. Quickening the motion of his hips, he kissed her wide-open mouth and she gasped, tossing back her head, trembling as they came together. As the liquid heat blossomed between her legs, she raked her nails down his back; wrapped herself around him like a straight-jacket; sank her teeth into his firm, muscular shoulder; shook uncontrollably.

Bodies quaking, they seized each other tightly, bathing each other in hungry kisses, as they wound down to a slow and satisfied stop. In the darkness she shivered in rapture, the wet heat of their lovemaking already cooling between her outstretched legs. Dreamily she sighed. Already she wanted him inside of her again. After a while, he rolled off of her and pulled her back into his strong arms.

They remained there for a long time, her naked back to his naked front, enjoying the warmth of each other. Their contented sighs punctuated the silence as they lost themselves in the shadowplay of the distant moonlit mountains.

Finding sudden artistic inspiration, Rick plucked a reed from the earth and used its fine tip to draw invisible tattoos on Stacey's naked back. Between her shoulder blades, he wrote a love poem; on her arm, he drew a map of the valley; on the side of her neck, he scribbled S-shapes and figure-eights, leaving only a trail of goosebumps in his wake.

"Mmmmmm," she purred, smiling with her eyes closed. "That tickles."

Grinning, he continued to use her body as the canvas for his masterpiece, finding further inspiration with her every giggle and ticklish twitch.

"Mmmm...let's go for a swim," she suggested out of nowhere.

"What? Now?"

"Mmmm-hmmm. What do you think?"

"I think it'll be freezing."

Stacey rolled over and faced him. "We'll keep each other warm," she said, eyes moving slowly up and down his body. Then her full lips curled into a tantalizing smile. "C'mon," she said, rising fully nude and holding out her hand to him. "C'mon," she repeated. "It'll be beautiful. I promise."

Rick smiled, eyes blazing with desire. He could still taste the salt of her body on his lips, and his manhood was twitching with anticipation. If he didn't have her again soon, he was certain he'd die. He needed her that badly.

At last he accepted her hand and she helped him to his feet and they stood, smiling, trembling, lusting in the strange orange moonlight.

"I need you sooo bad," he whispered, their mouths no more than a breath apart.

Stacey's heart grew hot as she kissed him. Her body tingled from head to toe. I need you sooo bad, he'd told her. *God*, she thought, *if I can't have him again I'll explode!*

They quickly gathered up their clothes, and the tall grass tickled their legs as they descended from the cliff. At the water's edge they dropped their belongings in the sand and waded out into the slow current of the river, where they made love again beneath the milky moonlight. It was everything Stacey had promised, and more.

Dizzily, they returned to the cabin with their clothes in their arms, and settled down together on a blanket, by the yawning mouth of the old stone fireplace.

For a long time, they stayed that way; staring into one another's eyes, not speaking; Stacey with one leg draped around his waist as she lovingly caressed his face with her slender fingers; Rick with one hand resting on her thigh while he stroked the long wet hair away from her forehead. They were so close, they could feel each other's hearts beating.

"Remember," he whispered at last, "when you told me that I saved your life? I think it was the other way around. There's no place in the world I'd rather be right now than here, in your arms. You make me feel alive again."

Stacey smiled as her soft lips brushed his. With tears of joy streaking across her face, she kissed him tenderly.

It wasn't "I love you", but it was good enough for now.

241

~Thirty-Nine~

Fifteen minutes later, Agent Ferren and Officer Bailey arrived at Chief Moriarty's dark gray Victorian-style house on Elm Street, a dead end street that lay on the eastern border of Hevven and the neighboring town of Lakeville. Bailey was quiet behind the wheel, the strange findings of the coroner's report still weighing heavily on his mind, and as he slowly maneuvered the unmarked cruiser down the long, narrow driveway leading to the Chief's house, he gritted his teeth uneasily. He'd thought his training at the police academy had prepared him for just about anything the world could throw at him, but only now did he realize he'd been sadly mistaken.

He was aptly trained in the procedures, regulations, and codes of law enforcement. He knew how to weed out criminals, how to apprehend them, and process them according to the laws established by the constitution. But did any of those things even matter anymore? he wondered. Not once had his instructors at the academy (or anyone else, for that matter) ever acknowledged, or even alluded to, the possibility of evil in this world. And that's precisely what this case was all about, wasn't it? Evil in its simplest form.

He could think of no better word to describe a being who could kill without motive, for the sheer pleasure of destroying life. But it was not death that Bailey feared. Rather it was the possibility that the evil he sought was, in truth, no different in appearance than any other man or woman he passed on the good streets of Hevven. And if that possibility were to become a reality, young Officer Bailey knew, from that point forward, he would never again have the privilege of seeing the world through hopeful eyes, if ever at all.

"Why don't you wait here," Ferren said, as Bailey parked in front of a small one-car garage. It was not a question.

Bailey looked at him, wounded. "Why can't I come in with you? I'm just as curious as you are, to find out what he has to say."

"Because," Agent Ferren said, "if Moriarty's gonna get pissed at someone for knocking on his door at 11 o'clock at night, it might as well be me. After this case is over I'll be on my way back to Quantico. But you'll likely be stuck with that prick until he retires. No need to make an enemy of him this early in the game."

Officer Bailey grinned, once again showing his age. If not for his uniform, Ferren could easily have mistaken him for a high school student. "Not for nothing, but I have the distinct feeling that the Chief and I are about as far from friends as two people can get."

Ferren chuckled as he opened the car door. "All the same, I'd prefer it if you kept the car running. I'll only be a minute."

Bailey nodded and sighed through his nostrils.

He watched through the passenger side window as Agent Ferren approached the house and rapped his knuckles on the front door. Almost a minute went by, and no answer. Bailey was just arriving at the conclusion that Chief Moriarty was either not home, or did not want to speak with them, when the front door opened and Agent Ferren disappeared inside.

"Come in, quickly," the Chief answered the door, reeking of alcohol and fear. His pockmarked face was slick with perspiration, his complexion the color and texture of cottage cheese.

Agent Ferren stepped into the dark interior of the house and into a large vestibule.

"Chief Moriarty," Ferren said politely, "I'm sorry to bother you at home, but..."

"Follow me."

Ferren sensed an urgency in the Chief's voice as he followed the larger man through the dimly lit house, through a drearily decorated living room, down a narrow corridor, and into a large but cluttered kitchen. Once inside the kitchen, Moriarty grabbed a small bottle of gin from the table and smiled wanly. "Drink?"

Ferren turned down the offer with a wave of his hand. "I'm sorry to disturb you at home, sir, but I wanted to ask you a few questions regarding the coroner's report on the Hartsoe girl. There were traces of an uncommon substance found beneath one of her fingernail fragments. Medical grade silicon. I was wondering if, perhaps, you were familiar with any local companies that might produce such a substance."

The Chief pulled a chair out from the table and sat down. Slumping forward, he unscrewed the cap from the bottle of gin. "It's my brother," he said. "My goddamn brother." He put the bottle to his lips and drank a quarter of its contents in one gulp.

Ferren took a chair across from him. He leaned forward on his elbows, cupping one hand inside the other. "Sir?"

Moriarty bowed his head. "I should have stopped him when I had the chance. But he's my brother. The only family I had left after he ki...after our parents died unexpectedly." His black eyes fell on Ferren. "What was I to do?"

"Sir, I'm not sure I understand." Agent Ferren removed one hand from the table. Beneath the table, and out of Moriarty's sight, he unsnapped his holster and rested his hand on the butt of his Glock.

Moriarty paused for another drink. "You can't stop him. No one can. He's hardly even human anymore."

"Your brother?"

"That's right." Moriarty smiled drunkenly. "My brother, The Hevven Hacker. I even came up with the name, all those years ago, after they found his first victim. But it wasn't his fault, you see. It was the infection that did it, the one that stole his face and forced him to wear that God-awful mask. People, women mostly, they called him a monster. But it wasn't his fault. He was just a kid, a boy. The doctors didn't know how to help him. They said it was some kinda virus that caused it, the decay. They didn't even have a name for it." He paused to take another sip of gin.

"Whatever it was," Moriarty went on, "it drove him mad. At least, I always believed he was mad. He used to tell me he heard voices. I always thought he was talking to himself. Said he was doing 'God's work'. Only recently, and I know you won't believe me, it seems like the voices have been talking back. Horrible things, those voices...”

“Did you say he wears a mask?” Ferren interrupted as he quietly slipped his hand around his pistol.

“That's right, Agent Ferren. A mask. A prosthetic mask to hide his face. That's why he only goes out at night. It's the only time he can pass for a normal human being.”

“What about that other fellow?”

“Who?”

“Christopher Pennington. The guy you sent to prison for The Hacker murders back in '75. The one who hung himself. Where did he fit in?”

Moriarty smiled without humor. “Oh, him. Innocent. He was a homeless man. A bum. I'd seen him around town a few times, had threatened to write him up for vagrancy, until I realized I had the perfect suspect.”

“So you set him up?”

“I had to help my brother out of an uncomfortable situation. So, yes, I set him up. I even paid one of the prisoners to take care of him before it went to trial, make it look like a suicide.”

“Why are you telling me all this?”

Moriarty snorted as he went in for another sip of gin. Before his lips reached the bottle, he paused. Doesn't matter anymore. I always knew it would only be a matter of time before someone traced the house back to me and my brother. It belonged to my grandfather on my mother's side. Harry Moody. I did what I could to cover my tracks, Agent Ferren. But now I'm tired of lyin'. Tired of always lookin' over my shoulder, especially when I'm in my own goddamn home. I can't control him. Never could. I know that now.” Finally, he put the bottle to his mouth and tilted it back.

“Sir, I think it would be a good idea if we take a ride to the station.”

Moriarty stopped and looked at him blankly. Then his face became twisted with fear. “Oh God, what time is it?”

“Almost eleven,” Ferren said, glancing at his watch.

"Oh, shit," Moriarty blubbered. He tried to stand and nearly tipped over in his chair. "Shit, shit, shit!"

"Whatsamatter?" Ferren couldn't tell if the man was laughing or crying.

"My brother..."

"What about your brother?"

Moriarty trembled, looked at him with dark, bloodshot eyes. "It's too late," he muttered. "He's home."

Agent Ferren heard the floor creak behind him. A heavy sound, which could only mean one thing: he and the Chief were no longer alone. Ferren drew his Glock from its holster and sprang from his chair. He whirled around toward the direction of the sound.

Then the world went suddenly black.

Now alone, Officer Bailey once again tried to get his mind around the odd findings of the coroner's report. He found it difficult to believe that the body of Anna Hartsoe, decomposed as it was, had offered no evidence as to the identity of the killer; nothing so little as a partial fingerprint, or a single strand of hair.

Aside from the body itself, their only other piece of evidence was the broken fingernail, which Agent Ferren had recovered from the floorboards of the old house, the results of which were equally baffling. If Anna Hartsoe had tried to fight off her attacker, then why hadn't the coroner been able to find traces of his clothing, or DNA? At what point had trace amounts of medical grade silicon found its way under her nail? Was that something the perpetrator had planted there, simply to mislead them?

Bailey was still thinking of these things as a much-needed sleep pulled him under.

Close to 15 minutes later, Officer William Bailey awoke with his head against the passenger side window. The glass was cool against his face, and he yawned as he tilted his head to look at the digital clock on the dashboard. He could not remember dreaming, and he was glad of that. He'd temporarily shaken off all of the many questions that had tortured him, and for the moment his mind was a clean slate.

What the hell's taking so long? he wondered. After a few seconds he shut off the patrol car's engine, pocketed the keys, and headed up the walkway for the front door.

Standing on the front stoop, Bailey knocked twice and waited. No answer. Other than the distant sound of a dog barking, Elm Street was darkly quiet, and he could hear no sounds emanating from inside the Chief's house, not even so much as the low din of conversation. Bailey knocked again, but even as his knuckles met the metal screen door, he knew there would be no answer. He was beginning to get the sense that he was unwanted here. All he wanted was to find Agent Ferren and get the hell out of here, so he could go back to his apartment in Futawam and get some sleep. He was tired of looking at photographs of dead people, and memorizing medical reports that read like horror stories, and obsessing about things over which he had no control.

After another minute had passed, he opened the screen door and stepped inside. "Hellooo," he called. "Chief? Agent Ferren?"

No answer.

Only darkness.

In fact, it was darker inside than out.

Thick velvet curtains, drawn tightly together, kept the moonlight at bay. The foyer was dark, but up ahead he could see a puddle of dim yellow light spilling onto the floor, apparently from some other room. Walking slowly, it occurred to him that he should draw his firearm, but the very thought made him feel ridiculous.

Oh, I'm sure the Chief would get a kick out of that, mused Bailey. *Me walking into his house with my weapon drawn! He'd probably have me directing traffic until my arms fell off!*

Bailey crossed the dark foyer. It was a creepy old place, that was for sure. Ahead of him a tall, gothic-looking lamp shone dully on the scuffed brown wood of the living room floor. Using the lamp as his guide, Bailey continued to move slowly through the house, half-expecting to find the two men at the kitchen table, discussing the coroner's report over a couple of Budweisers. But as he rounded the corner into the dimly lit living room, he saw the lumbering frame of the Chief kneeling over Agent Ferren, who was lying motionless, face down on the hardwood floor.

"Shit," Bailey murmured, rushing to aid his friend. Then his voice rose to its highest level of concern. "What happened?"

The Chief did not answer him. As Bailey rushed past him, dropping to his hands and knees, the Chief rose quietly, stepping back into the shadows.

"Ferren!" Bailey shouted, trying to roll the man over. "Are you alright?" Two words flashed through his mind as he searched for a pulse: heart attack. *No pulse! Shit! What am I supposed to do?* He was about to cry out for someone to call the police, when it suddenly struck him that he *was* the police. At the very same instant, Bailey realized that something in this house was very, very wrong. Why was it so dark in there? Why wasn't the Chief helping him? And why was Ferren, whom had entered the house in a $500 suit, now wearing nothing more than boxers and a T-shirt?

At last Bailey managed to grab him under one arm, his fingers brushing lightly over some-thing wet and warm and sticky, and rolled the lifeless man onto his back. Suddenly Bailey felt the static wave of panic coursing through his veins.

In the murky yellow light of the living room lamp, he found himself looking at Chief Moriarty's contorted, terror-stricken face. His mouth was wide, his eyes frozen. On the front of his white T-shirt was a dark and blooming blood stain.

If that's the Chief, thought Bailey, *then who the hell is standing behind me?*

Before he could discover the answer to that question, his ears were drawn to a scratching sound that was coming from somewhere off to the right of him, and at the opposite end of a long corridor, he spotted Agent Ferren squirming toward him on the floor. His arms and legs were tied together behind his back, and there was a strip of duct tape covering his mouth. His face was a river of blood, eyes bulging as he raised his head in desperation, silently screaming, trying to warn the young officer.

But it was already too late.

Bailey spun around, still on his knees, and found the man dressed in the Chief's clothes standing over him. He was about the same size as the Chief, perhaps even larger, with shocks of long white hair that seemed to glow in the dark. Until now, Bailey had always secretly wondered whether or not the rumors of the Chief living with an invalid brother were true, or if it was all a part of some half-baked rumor. But there was no denying the family resemblance, although the rumors of him being badly deformed were apparently just that. In fact, his face was unusually smooth, almost similar to that of a department store mannequin; quite unlike the Chief's craggy, pockmarked complexion.

Alan Moriarty leaned over and pressed the cold muzzle of the police-issue Glock against the center of Officer Bailey's forehead, face expressionless, eyes gleaming with cold indifference.

"Wh-what are you doing?" Bailey mouthed. His voice was less than a whisper. "Wh-why?"

With the Glock still pointing at the young officer's head, Alan Moriarty used his other hand to reach behind his own right ear. For a brief moment his fingers fumbled at something, until there was a barely audible snapping sound.

And then his face fell away to the floor.

As Officer Bailey trembled in sheer terror, from somewhere far away he felt the warmth of release trickling down his legs. It now dawned on him that it was not a man that stood before him. It was an urban legend in the flesh; the living, breathing embodiment of every child's nightmare-conception of evil; The Hacker was real!

Alan Moriarty watched the dark stain blossom between the young officer's legs, and the maw that was his face opened wider to form a death's head smile. As he began to laugh, with all the warmth and humanity of a funhouse clown, the curtains of flesh surrounding his smile trembled.

Yes, thought Bailey, *there is evil in this world.*

The Hacker holstered the Glock and withdrew a hunting knife from a brown leather sheath that was attached to his belt. The serrated blade was still wet with his brother's blood.

In an instant, Bailey saw that nightmare smile flash closer, as The Hacker bent toward him. Then a large, powerful hand grabbed him by the throat and lifted him into the air with the same swift motion. Bailey's legs danced uselessly above the living room floor. He felt something sharp and cold slide into his flesh, just above his belly button. There was a brief moment of silence and agony. And then the world went gray...and finally, black. But before the darkness came Bailey heard the static, papery whispers of voices fill his head...voices like a thousand angry wasps, all stinging his brain in unison, injecting it with their venom.

He heard two words:

The Truth.

And then, he heard nothing at all.

~Forty~

The sky was clear above the cabin, but in the distance, dark gray clouds were boiling over.

There was no doubt about it, a storm was brewing. Beyond the horizon, it had already begun in Potter's Bluff: a cold, sweeping rain.

On the edge of the porch, Rick and Stacey sat beneath the rippled asphalt sky, snuggling against each other as they waited for the others to awaken.

A hawk was circling the otherwise empty sky, and Rick raised his eyes to focus on it, lighting a cigarette with the Zippo lighter. Watching the bird of prey as it soared gracefully overhead, his mind slipped back to the night before, to when he and Stacey had made love under the stars, and his entire body tingled with the memory.

As if receiving his thoughts, Stacey turned to look at him, and kissed him gently on the cheek. He turned to her and smiled warmly. She had never imagined that she would find someone like him. His smile alone was enough to fill her heart with hope. And those eyes, those passionate hazel-green eyes, were full of the kind of magic she had always searched for, and had never known until recently. She loved the way he looked at her, the way it made her want him. Last night, it had taken but one look into those eyes, and her inhibitions had melted away into nothing. But now she wondered: Was he for real? And did he feel the same about her?

"Thank you for the flowers," she whispered. "They're beautiful."

It was the first thing she had seen when she awoke that morning—a small bouquet of daisies and tiger lilies, fastened with a white ribbon Karen had given him, set upon the floor beside her head.

"I'm glad you like them," he said.

"Where did you find them?"

"I can't tell you that."

"Why not?"

"It's a secret. A mystery. Women like that stuff, don't they? Mysteries?"

She smiled playfully. "Not me. I like my men mystery-free."

"In that case, I found them over there, on the edge of the forest."

Stacey felt her heart swell. The thought of him searching the forest for flowers in the early dawn nearly brought tears to her eyes.

"Do you regret what you said last night?" she asked shyly.

"No," he answered without hesitation. "Does that bother you?"

"Of course not," she said, inching even closer to him. She put her head down on his shoulder. "I just wanted to be sure."

He looked down at her. "Are you sure now?"

"Yeah, I'm sure," she answered, nuzzling her face against the side of his neck. And she meant it.

"How 'bout you?"

A flirtatious pause. "How 'bout me what?"

He smiled. "Do you regret anything that happened last night?"

She raised her head so that their faces were almost touching. She caressed his cheek. "No."

They looked into each other's eyes for what seemed like a very long time. Then she rested her head against his shoulder again. She took his hand and began to play with it, pressing her palm against his palm, sliding her fingers between his fingers. When at last she spoke, her words were warm against his neck.

"You make me feel safe, Rick. No one has ever made me feel safe. I know you probably think that's crazy. Part of me thinks it's crazy, too. I mean, I hardly know a thing about you. It's almost like we were supposed to meet. Like in a movie, or something. That's why. I can't explain it, really. It's like déjà vu, only stronger."

Rick could only squeeze her hand as they sat and watched the clouds roll in.

Half an hour later Max and Lou dragged their lazy bones downstairs, soon followed by Karen and Mike.

"I feel like shit," Max groaned, rubbing the small of his back with one hand. His long hair was matted against his head like a helmet.

Mike chuckled, stretching his arms above his head. "You look like shit."

"Oh, and you don't?"

"Not me," Mike grinned. "I look like crap. You, though, you look like shit. There's a big difference, you know."

Max only smiled, too tired to think of a comeback.

Karen and Mike sat beside each other, their backs against the outside wall of the cabin. Karen yawned. She looked as though she were still asleep. She wrinkled her nose. "Looks like it's gonna rain," she said, yawning again.

"Yeah. Maybe we could take a dip before it comes," suggested Lou. He raised his eyebrows in anticipation. "Might wake us up a little."

"I'm game," Max said. He lit a cigarette and offered one to Lou, who turned it down with a wave of his hand.

Almost directly above the porch, the hawk screamed, and continued to circle the empty sky in search of a meal.

After chatting for a little while about their current financial situation, including how long they thought the remainder of Rick's money would last them, they headed down to the river, surrendering themselves to its cold embrace. As the clouds rolled in, blotting out the sunlight, the water was even colder than they had anticipated. They stayed at the river for close to an hour, until the distant sound of thunder sent them packing. Together they grabbed their shirts, shoes, and towels, and hustled across the meadow, cold and hungry and eager for the shelter of the cabin. The tall grass whipped their bare legs, as a strong wind pushed its way into the valley.

"Maybe we should get some dry wood for the fireplace," Karen suggested, as they hurried up the porch steps.

"I'll go," Rick volunteered. He turned to Lou. "Wanna give me a hand?"

"Sure," Lou said, and the two started off for the treeline.

While Rick and Lou scoured the forest for firewood, Mike was inside the cabin, gathering up the brown shopping bags to use them for kindling. Meanwhile, the two girls discussed their options for lunch.

"Hey, Max," Mike said, as he twisted up a part of a brown shopping bag and tossed it into the fireplace.

Max, who was standing at the window, watching the storm shadows crawl across the mountains, turned his head.

"Think you can get onto the roof?"

"Yeah," Max said. "Why?"

"I want you to check on the chimney from the outside, just to make sure it's not blocked up."

"Alright," Max said, sighing. "I'll do it. But if I fall, I'm blaming you."

"Be careful," Stacey called after him as he stepped outside.

He paused at the threshold, imagining her on her hands and knees, giving him mouth to mouth. He grinned sharkishly. It would almost be worth the fall. "Thanks," he replied, and disappeared outside.

Rick and Lou returned five minutes later with their arms full of branches and small logs, which they dumped on the floor, near where Mike was kneeling.

"What the hell's Max doing on the roof?" asked Rick.

"Makin' sure the chimney's clean," Mike told him. He stood up and dusted off his knees.

Just then, a deep voice echoed down the chimney. "HO! HO! HO!"

Mike smiled. "All set, Santa?" he yelled into the fireplace.

"Yeah, looks okay," Max hollered back.

"Well, get your ass down here."

"I'm on my way. You should see the view from up here. It's fuckin' incredible!"

"Alright," Mike said. "Let's get this baby going."

Rick flicked open his trusty Zippo and lit the corner of one brown shopping bag. A few seconds later, a small fire cracked and snapped cheerfully as Lou began to feed it branches. A yellow-orange light flickered on the cabin walls, and the shadows momentarily shrunk away to the corners of the room.

Max returned a few minutes later, his hair all windblown, going every which way. He was only halfway through the door when he asked, in an excited voice, "Hey, Rick, do you think you could teach me to use that shotgun?"

Rick looked at Mike, as if to say *Oh, shit!*

"Shotgun?" Karen asked, pronouncing the word as though it were something that tasted sour.

"I was going to tell you about it," Mike said, shooting Max a dirty look. "I just wanted to find the right time."

"Oops," Max said, tiptoeing past the couple.

Karen frowned and bit one side of her lower lip. "So…where did it come from?"

"Rick brought it along…just in case."

Rick bowed his head, unable to look her in the eyes. This was his fault, and he knew it.

"You're crazy," she scolded them. "The both of you. What if the police had caught us, huh? How would that have looked, to have a gun with you?"

"Nice going, Max," Lou muttered from the kitchen, where he was currently in the process of making a peanut butter sandwich.

Max threw his arms into the air. "What the fuck did I do?"

"I don't think it's a good idea right now," Rick said, finally answering Max's badly timed question. "Besides, I'm starving."

"Aww, come on! I gotta learn sometime. Besides, this is lame. We can eat after. C'mon, just one shot! Please! Just 'cause it's gonna rain, it doesn't mean we have to sit here like idiots."

"I said, 'maybe'."

"Man!" Max whined.

For a few seconds, the cabin fell silent, save for the crackling of flames.

"Does...anyone wanna make popcorn?" Stacey asked, raising her eyebrows a little.

"Hell, yeah. You have popcorn?" Max said, momentarily distracted from the shotgun.

"Yeah." Stacey held up a container of Jiffy Pop.

"Jiffy Pop! I didn't even know they still made that stuff!"

"I haven't had Jiffy Pop since I don't know when. Mom used to make it for us, remember?" Lou turned to Mike.

"Yup. That was before they came out with that microwavable crap," Mike said. He went over to Karen and rubbed her arm. She was still stewing over the shotgun. "I'm sorry," he whispered.

Karen narrowed her eyes at him. "You should have told me."

"I know," he said. "I'm sorry. Don't be mad." He kissed the tip of her nose, and she began to smile reluctantly. He looked at her for a moment, as if seeing her for the first time. He smiled. Kissed her again.

"You jerk," she said, giggling, knowing it was impossible for her to stay angry with him for long. "If you weren't so cute..."

"Come on," he said. "Let's go eat some popcorn."

They sat by the fire while Max tended the foil popcorn container, occasionally giving it a shake. Outside, raindrops plinked against the roof, and an angry wind hissed and howled, but inside the cabin it was cozy and warm.

"I think you're burnin' it, dude," Rick said, sniffing the air.

"Yeah," Mike said. "Pull it outta there."

"Trust me. I know what I'm doing," Max said stubbornly.

"You better not pour that goddamn hot sauce on it."

Thirty seconds later, a thin column of black smoke rose from the tiny hole at the center of the Jiffy Pop container, filling the cabin with an awful stench.

"I told you," Mike said, snatching the popcorn container from Max's hands.

He set it down on the floor, and carefully pulled back the layers of foil. Then he looked inside, shaking his head in disgust.

"What?" snapped Max.

"It's fuckin' black," Mike said. "It's no good."

Coughing through the smoke, Stacey got up and went over to the kitchen, in search of some other snacks.

"That's the way I like it," Max said defensively.

"What about the rest of us, you selfish prick?" asked Mike. He sighed in defeat. "Here," he said, handing the container to Max. "It's all yours."

Shrugging, Max grabbed a handful of burnt popcorn and shoved it into his mouth.

"What else is there to eat?" asked Karen.

Stacey began to go through the list of food and, like Lou, they settled on peanut butter sandwiches, Frito's, and potato sticks.

When Max was finished with the popcorn, he got up and stood by the door. "Please," he begged Rick. "Just one shot!"

"You better take him," Mike said, sitting beside Karen on the floor. "He won't shut up about it until you do."

"When you come back, we can all play cards," Lou said.

"Fine," Rick answered at last. "One shot, then we come right back. Okay?"

"Damn straight!" Max boomed, overjoyed. He did a little dance. "Where is it?"

"Under the couch," Mike told him.

Max knelt on the floor beside the couch and pulled out the shotgun and the box of ammunition with a look of awe. "Oh, yeah!" He beamed. "Now we're talkin'!"

Karen looked at him, folded her arms. "You mean to tell me that thing's been there the whole time?"

Mike looked at her, shrugging innocently. "Well, not the whole time, exactly."

"We'll be back soon," Rick said to Stacey.

"Be careful," she said, in a tone that bordered on pleading.

"Yeah," Mike said sternly. "And make sure Maxi-Pad doesn't blow his friggin' foot off."

"Fuck off," Max said, grinning. He was too joyful to be offended.

Max opened the door, and cool air rushed into the cabin. Rick followed him onto the porch, and bowing his head to the wind, closed the door behind them. Outside, they stopped to light cigarettes, which took great effort in the increasing rush of wind.

"Gimme that," Rick said, and Max reluctantly handed him the shotgun. "You can carry the shells."

With that, they began across the wind-whipped meadow. In the distance, lightning ripped a jagged line through the sky. From the forest nearby, something screamed in fear.

"How many shells are in the box?" Rick asked, trying to gauge the progress of the storm. Thunder slapped the earth with several angry blows (or perhaps, it was the giants).

Max opened the box and looked inside. "Four. Let's hurry before it starts to rain."

"Give me a shell," Rick said as they reached the cliff. He aimed the barrel of the shotgun down, at the water. Max handed him a shell, and Rick loaded it into the chamber. "It's easy. All you have to do is load it like this, pump it, and you're good to go."

"Then what?"

"Then you pull the trigger, and whatever you aim at goes bye-bye. So don't you dare point that thing at me. And be careful with the recoil. Don't hold it too tightly."

Max smiled. He didn't know what a recoil was, exactly, but it sure sounded cool. "Yeah, yeah. Let me try this bad boy."

As Rick gingerly placed the shotgun into Max's excited hands, a cool mist began to drift across the valley. "Hurry up, before the rain comes."

With his best gangster face, Max aimed at the river, pumped once

—chick-chick—

and squeezed the trigger.

BOOOOM!

The river at the base of the cliff convulsed and splashed several feet into the air. Max whooped with pleasure. "That was so cool!" he hollered. His ears were still ringing.

"Alright Rambo," Rick said, "that's your lesson for the day. We should get going before..." His voice trailed off as he looked back at the cabin. His jaw dropped open, and his face became a twisted mask of concern.

Max turned, still holding the shotgun, and saw what had silenced his friend. Coming slowly down the dirt road, towards the cabin, was a gray Ford LTD. The two watched as it pulled off to the side of the cabin, where it parked several yards away from Mike's T-bird. Out of the others' field of view.

"What the fuck?" Max murmured. "Who..."

"Give me the gun," Rick demanded. "Now!"

Trembling, Max handed Rick the shotgun and the three remaining shells. Rick reloaded quickly, pumped once, and breathed heavily. His hands tightened around the weapon until his knuckles turned white and he could squeeze no more.

The driver's side door flung open on the Ford, and a tall man dressed in a dark uniform emerged from it. He paused by the side of the car, reached back for his hat and placed it squarely on his head, all the while looking steadily in their direction. The hat remained on his head for almost two seconds, before he realized the wind wanted it more than he. As an afterthought, he took off the hat, threw it back into the car, and slammed the door shut with both hands. Then he began toward them, moving through the wind and rain with a purposeful stride.

"It's a fucking cop!" Max said in amazement, straining to watch the man through the blurring rain and wind. "Shit! What should we do? Should we run?"

Rick pointed the shotgun at the ground. "No," he said calmly, quietly. "I'm tired of running." He was thinking of Stacey, and how much he cared about her; perhaps, even loved her. He wasn't certain about that last part, not yet, but he thought it could happen in time. He was thinking about his parents, and the pain he knew they had suffered when he left town without explanation to come here, to Willow's Creek. He thought about the time he and his friends had spent at the river, and how much their lives had changed since the night they found the body. He thought that, perhaps, this moment on the cliff was nothing more than a bad dream, and that he was really back at the cabin, sleeping on the floor in Stacey's arms, and would awake at any moment.

But the man in the uniform continued toward them, unmindful of the torrent, undaunted by the shotgun.

261

"I knew I'd find you boys sooner or later," the policeman said, almost cheerfully, as he stopped several feet away from them. He raised his bushy eyebrows, deepening the wrinkles on his forehead, as he waited for the boys to respond. The wind had whipped his snow-white hair into a tousled froth, giving him the appearance of a very old man. He was in his mid-50s, Rick guessed. But, judging by his size, he was in damn good shape for a man his age. His large right hand rested against the butt of his gun, which was in a holster on his side. "I'm afraid you'll have to come back to Hevven with me. The rest of my men are waiting just up the road a bit. There's a lot of questions we need you to answer for us."

"We didn't do nothin'," Max said angrily. He looked at Rick for guidance, but Rick was too busy looking at the cop.

"I'm not saying you did, son," the policeman said calmly. "I'm just doing my job. We just want to know what you saw at the old house that night. We need to know everything. Don't do anything you'll regret, son. Now, please, put down the gun."

I can't shoot a cop, thought Rick. *He's just trying to do his job. He's just some old-timer...probably got a wife...kids. Maybe this is the only way to clear our names. Damnit, if only we'd had more time.* In the back of his mind, he heard Mike telling everyone it was time for change, and Stacey whispering in his ear that they might never get a chance to make love again.

Rick bent his knees, slowly lowering the shotgun to the ground, and as he did so, a smile began to form at the corners of the policeman's mouth. It was then that Rick realized he'd been tricked.

But it was already too late.

Rick was quick with the shotgun, but The Hacker was quicker with his Glock. A silenced shot wheezed in the air, and Rick Hunter, with the shotgun still in his hands, let out a muffled cry of pain as he disappeared over the edge of the cliff behind a spray of blood.

"Noooo!" Max yelped in horror, bolting toward the place where Rick had been standing only seconds ago. Slipping across the wet grass, his feet flew up from beneath him, and he traveled the rest of the distance on his ass, arriving at a clumsy halt just inches away from the edge of the cliff.

Panting like a dog, he peered down, and his eyes grew wide as he saw the river sloshing through the valley; the water had risen several inches due to the downflow of rain from the mountains, and the current had already quickened its pace tenfold, working itself into a foaming frenzy. It was raining so hard that the drops were ricocheting off the river, creating a blurry white mist above its surface.

Rick Hunter was gone.

Max screamed incoherently, pounding his fists against the ground. When he turned around, he saw that The Hacker was grinning.

~Forty-One~

"What's taking them so long?" Lou wondered aloud, shuffling the deck of cards, and everyone looked at him.

Stacey was standing in the kitchen, using a plastic knife to smear peanut butter onto a slice of white bread. She set aside what she was doing to look out the kitchen window. Through the rain, she could make out the shapes of two dark figures in the distance. "They're just standing there," she reported. "It looks like they're arguing."

"That's all we need," Mike said. "Do you need any help with those sandwiches?"

Stacey smiled a distracted smile, moving on to the next sandwich; there were four lined up on the countertop. "No, thanks. I'm just about finished, anyway."

"Don't worry," Mike assured her. "He'll be back soon."

Stacey blushed. "Guns scare me," she confessed with a shrug.

"Me, too," Karen said from the couch, where she'd been watching Lou shuffle the cards. "What're they doing out there, anyway?"

Stacey made a face. "Like I said, just standing there."

"They'll head in soon," Mike said again, tossing a few branches into the fireplace. "They're probably soaked already."

"Does anybody feel like playing Scat?" Lou asked, and sipped on a warm can of Coke. He made a sour face. When no one answered he said, "Come on, you guys. You're not afraid of losin', are ya?"

"Might as well," Mike said, and sat down on the floor beside his brother. "What're we playin' for?"

Lou thought for a minute. "How 'bout...what do we have left for snacks?"

"Chips and cookies."

"What kind of cookies?"

"I don't know...chocolate chip."

"We'll play for cookies, then."

"Okay," Mike said, "your deal."

Biting his lower lip, Lou dealt the cards, wincing at the sound of thunder as it stampeded across the valley. It sounded as if the earth would split in two. The window panes rattled, and the rain fell harder, hissing down from the eaves. The cabin trembled on its foundation, as if in anticipation of the events that were about to unfold.

~Forty–Two~

Fueled by rage, Max sprang to his feet. "You wanna shoot me? Go ahead, you cocksucker! Shoot me! C'mon, you pussy, you piece of shit! You don't have the fucking balls!"

The Hacker retorted with a bullet.

Max suddenly found himself looking at the sky, and then the earth crashed against him, knocking the wind out of him. It was only after he had caught his breath, that Max realized he had fallen. Moaning, he tried to get up, but his body betrayed him. It felt as though someone had set his right leg on fire. *Oh, shit!* Max thought. *Oh, shit, what happened?* But he knew what had happened. He'd been shot.

He looked down and saw the dark stain on his jeans. There was a small hole in his pants just above the knee where the bullet had entered. Wincing, Max stuck his fingers into the hole, and ripped it open. What he saw was not a bloody knee, as he had expected, but something that looked like a smashed tomato. *Jeezus!* thought Max. *That's my fuckin' kneecap!*

Suddenly The Hacker was standing above him, kicking him over and over until the bloody boy lay still.

"Is that all you've got?" Max snarled through a mouthful of blood. He looked up and saw The Hacker grinning, and the very sight of it made his stomach turn. Max rolled over onto his side and vomited in the wet grass.

"I'm gonna let you suffer for a while…for all the trouble you've caused me. Then, after I'm done with the rest of you little bastards, I'm gonna come back here, and I'm gonna cut off your feet, and then your hands, and I'm gonna throw you in the river."

The Hacker holstered the Glock and drew a medium-sized hunting knife from his back pocket. Skillfully, he flicked open the blade, and ran its razor-sharp edge along the side of Max's face in a thin red line.

Max gritted his teeth to stifle a scream. Before, he'd been angry. Now he was terrified.

The Hacker, still smiling, licked the dark blood from the wet blade. Then he turned and headed off in the direction of the cabin.

The way to The Truth was near. The pool would soon be satisfied. And the Punks would finally be still.

Max lay on his back in the tall grass, staring up into the falling rain, wondering if he would be lucky enough to bleed to death before The Hacker returned. He could see The Hacker sneaking around the cabin, peeking in windows, searching for a way to get inside undetected. Watching this, Max was torn. It was a Catch-22. If he attempted to warn his friends, they would step out of the cabin and into an ambush. And if he didn't warn them, The Hacker would ambush them from inside the cabin. Max's own helplessness was far more painful than his actual wounds.

Not wanting to see what he knew was going to happen, Max closed his eyes. The rain was cold against his flesh, but it was almost comforting. His leg was beginning to throb with pain, like a giant heartbeat, giving him the sensation that he was falling. And his ribs, several of which were broken, seemed to grind together as he breathed; in itself, a task that was becoming harder by the second.

When he finally opened his eyes he thought for sure that he was dead, because Rick was kneeling over him like an angel of mercy.

"Max, it's me…Rick," he whispered. "Say somethin', damnit."

"Are we dead?" Max asked. Spittle flew from his mouth and he began to cough heavily, trembling with every breath.

"No, man. No one's gonna die."

Max looked up and saw a dark river of blood running down Rick's side.

"Oh, shit...you too?"

"Yeah. It hurts like hell. Can't move my left arm...but my right's still good. How're you doin'?"

Max tried to sit up, but was unable to muster the strength. "Me? I'm just dandy," he said with a worried smile, and the gash on the side of his face opened and closed like a gill. Blood streamed down his cheek.

"You just sit still, man. You'll be okay?"

"Rick?"

"Yeah, what is it?"

"I'm pretty fucked up, ain't I?"

"No," Rick said, shaking his head. "No, Max, you're gonna be alright."

Max was looking up into the rain. He wondered if he would be there soon, up in the sky, or if he was going to that other place.

"I've been an asshole all my life, and I'm sorry," Max said, starting to cry. "I love you guys. I don't know what I would've done if I hadn't met you. Tell them that."

"Don't you talk like that," Rick said reassuringly. "You're not going anywhere."

Max shook his head. He blinked slowly. "I..."

"Look at me," Rick said, and Max turned his glossy blue-gray eyes towards him. "You're not gonna die."

"You gotta help the others! He's gonna get inside the house!" Max exclaimed suddenly, again trying to get up, again failing. "Where's the shotgun?"

"Right here," Rick answered. He held it up so that Max could see it.

The gun held three shells. Three chances.

Max grabbed him by the arm, grimacing with pain. His teeth were stained with blood. "Kill the muthafucka!"

Lightning fractured the sky, and in the yellow-white flash the two gave each other a solemn look. In a sense, Rick knew, they were bidding each other farewell. He didn't like it. But they needed to. Just in case.

Rick nodded and gave Max's hand a squeeze.

He had three shells. Three chances.

There was little room for mistakes.

As he hobbled across the meadow, Rick prayed that the shotgun, soaked from his fall into the river, would not fail him.

He only hoped that God was listening.

~Forty-Three~

After searching around the back of the cabin for a way to sneak inside, Alan Moriarty discovered the wooden ladder Max had used to gain access to the roof earlier that day, and slithered in through an open window and into the upstairs bathroom. Raindrops pelted the thin glass windows, tap-tap-tapping against the roof. Hunting knife in hand, he hid in the darkness, waiting.

Through the crack below the bathroom door, he could hear the voices of the Punks downstairs, ranting on about the insignificant things that Punks always talked about, and he couldn't help but smile at their ignorance. Among them, he could hear the sweetly seductive voice of the auburn-haired girl, the one who had escaped him.

"Soon they'll be quiet," he whispered to himself. He would bring the girl back to the pool and finish what he'd started. And I'll be in that other place, because they promised me salvation. The Truth. They promised me The Truth, and soon I'll have it.

He waited, grinning.

Downstairs, Stacey Mackinnon finished making lunch, knowing that Rick and Max would soon return with their healthy appetites.

"Are all the upstairs windows shut?" Mike asked as he dealt another hand. He was already growing weary of Scat, but it was the only game Lou knew how to play.

Lou stood up. "I think so. I'll go check."

"That's alright," Mike said, laying his cards face down on the floor. "I'll do it. Just make sure you don't peek at my cards."

Karen went to the stairs and paused with one hand on the railing. "Sit down and finish your game, you two. I'll do it."

She began upstairs.

"God, I'm still starvin'," Lou said, warming his back near the fireplace. He rubbed his stomach, which rumbled in agreement.

"Me too," Mike said, watching Karen go.

"Mmmm…this is sooo good," Stacey said, sucking a glob of peanut butter from the tip of one finger. She pulled the wet finger from her mouth, and added: "Don't worry guys, the sandwiches are almost ready."

"Thanks, Stace," said Mike. Then, to Lou, "Okay, let's see what you…"

Suddenly there was a shrill scream, and Karen Sloan came toppling head over heels down the stairs. At the bottom, her head smacked the hardwood floor with one final, definitive thud, and then she was motionless, lying in a crumpled heap across the foyer.

"Oh, Jeezus!" Mike shouted, and ran to his lover's aid.

From the other side of the kitchen, Stacey let out a cry of surprise. "Oh my God! Karen!"

Mike was already kneeling by Karen's side, pressing her limp hand against his face. Stacey was rushing over to join him when a sudden peal of maniacal laughter stopped her dead in her tracks. Her mind went haywire. Her hands trembled. Her feet froze. She couldn't breathe. She could not even will herself to close her eyes against the waking nightmare that was unfolding before her.

"Mike!" Lou cried out, but Mike didn't hear him.

Mike was still gripping her hand, shouting deliriously, trying to bring her around. When that didn't work, he lifted one of her eyelids, saw that the eye had rolled back like a big white marble. Then something on her midsection caught his eye.

A tiny rosebud had appeared upon her shirt. To Mike's horror, its crimson petals bloomed into a shape the size of his open hand. Praying silently, he lifted her shirt to reveal a deep and bloody puncture wound. He was about to call for a bandage, a blanket, a rag, anything—

272

Then came a wrathful voice—no, it was more of a primal sound, a growl—like the sound of a wild animal, chomping at the bit.

"I've come a long way to kill you little bastards." Wet shoes squished as The Hacker came down the stairs. "You should have stayed in Hevven, where you fucking belong, and this would have all been short and sweet. Now, it's gonna be messy…"

For some reason, upon hearing that voice, the image of a man with the leering face of a clock flashed briefly through Lou Swart's mind, and he knew that his nightmare was unfolding before his eyes.

Time had finally caught up with them.

Mike didn't know whose voice it was, but he could guess. He grabbed Karen by the arms and dragged her away from the stairs, into the kitchen. Pressing his hand over Karen's wound, he listened closely to the voice of the man; it was hellishly familiar.

A hulking figure wearing a police uniform appeared at the bottom of the stairs, his face barely visible in the dim firelight, but Mike recognized him just the same. Back in Hevven, Chief Moriarty was the leader of the Punk Catchers. Of course, Mike did not know that this was not the Chief himself but his brother, though the family resemblance was enough to jog his memory.

"Ahhh, Lucien Swart, I presume. I really gotta thank you for leaving me your wallet the other night. It came in handy. Otherwise, I wouldn't be here right now."

Lou stood near the foot of the stairs, trembling in fear as he looked up at the figure in the gloom. But in Lou's mind it was not a man he was looking at; it was Death incarnate.

With calculated coolness, Alan Moriarty withdrew his Glock from its holster and pointed the muzzle at Lou's head. "Don't be afraid, my little friend. I want to save you. I want to wash away your sins."

Then he looked away from Lou, towards Mike and the two girls. "I'm gonna take all of you back to Hevven," he said, his voice rising and rising. "BACK WHERE YOU BELONG!"

Nostrils flaring, The Hacker turned his attention back to Lou, whose unspeakable fear had nailed him to the floor. The young boy's fear made The Hacker grin.

Mike stood up now, knowing if he didn't act quickly his little brother was going to die. From the corner of his eye, he saw Max's Dumb Ass Hot Sauce bottle resting on the counter, beneath the kitchen window. All at once, it was as if someone had flicked a switch in Mike's mind.

You know what to do, Mikey, the giants whispered. Their voices were matter-of-factly, surprisingly rational in light of the chaos that was taking place before him. *You've been here before, remember?*

And suddenly it occurred to Mike that he had been here before. Not here, exactly, but in similar situations on the football field behind Hevven High School; fourth-and-goal, when the odds were stacked against him, and his only chance of winning was to throw a 20-yard rocket into the end-zone, risking it all on hope.

Mike snatched the bottle in his hand and cocked his arm behind his head. This was not a game. There were no time-outs. There were no blockers to protect him. Just a wide-open field. The outcome of this moment relied entirely on him, the quarterback. But Mike had never been one to buckle under pressure. (He was a leader. A warrior. A goddamn hero in the pocket.)

His arm snapped forward in a blur. It wasn't the perfect spiral, but its aim was true.

The bottle smashed against the side of The Hacker's face, dousing him with the potent red liquid.

The Hacker howled in anger as the hot sauce scorched his eyes. The impact of the bottle had unhinged his prosthetic cheek, which peeled away from the raw cavern of receding flesh that surrounded one corner of his mouth and jaw, and curled downward toward his collar, still loosely attached to an invisible strap behind his neck. But the effect was only temporary. Though his vision was blurry, The Hacker's ears quickly relocated his whimpering target. He turned toward Lou and raised the pistol. Mike watched helplessly from the kitchen as The Hacker grinned. Pulled the trigger...

He was still grinning when the cabin door imploded. The force of the blast pushed him back against the stairs, the pistol falling from his hand, as a thousand splinters attacked him like a swarm of angry wasps.

As Mike covered his eyes against the raining shrapnel, he saw Lou looking down at the place where the bullet had thunked into the floor between his feet. *Thank God*, thought Mike.

He glanced behind him and saw Stacey huddled protectively over Karen. As the smoke cleared, he looked up and saw a stranger standing in the empty doorway. For a moment, Mike believed, actually believed without a doubt, that Uncle Jack had returned from the grave to save them from The Hacker.

Lightning flickered outside, temporarily illuminating the cabin. It was then that Mike recognized his battered friend.

Rick Hunter's clothes hung from his body in tatters. His bare legs were crisscrossed with cuts and abrasions. His dark, vengeful eyes peered out from behind a helmet of mud-caked hair. In his filthy hands, the shotgun gleamed murderously.

The Hacker wasn't grinning anymore.

He was sitting upright on the steps, looking for his Glock, which in the blast had landed somewhere by his feet. A long splinter, roughly the size of a broken pencil, protruded from his right eye. Blood and hot sauce trickled from his forehead and over his rotten, half-skeletal face. Finally, with one blurry eye, he saw the butt of his pistol gleaming in the firelight, and he snatched it up with a roar of triumph.

Crossing the threshold, Rick raised the shotgun and took aim, using his left elbow to level the barrel, as a thousand spots danced before his eyes like fireflies. He was about to black out. *Don't go out*, he told himself. *Don't go out. Don't go out.* Nauseous with pain, he squeezed the trigger.

Blood sprayed every which way as The Hacker fell backwards onto the stairs, his chest exploding into a maw of ravaged flesh. He fired his pistol one last time, into the ceiling, before it tumbled from his enormous hand. Then, looking up at the boy who had shot him, he smiled hauntingly. He began to laugh, gargling on his own blood. The way to The Truth was so very near.

Badly weakened by his plunge into the river, the recoil of the shotgun had sent Rick stumbling back, where he eventually lost his balance and toppled to the floor of the porch. Trembling, he used the shotgun as a crutch as he struggled against gravity. Ears still ringing, he paused a moment to catch his breath, waiting for the spots to go away.

Don't go out! Don't go out!

Suddenly, time itself seemed to slow down. Rick looked to his right and saw Mike and Stacey kneeling on opposite sides of Karen's crumpled body; Stacey was running her fingers through Karen's long dark hair in a loving, sisterly fashion. Her bottom lip trembled, her eyes leaking an endless stream of tears, trying to speak, but only cries could express her anguish. Mike sat in a trance, his hands held out before him, staring at his palms, which were covered in the blood of his lover. His mouth was open, screaming silently.

Rick looked to his left, and found Lou cowering in the corner by the fireplace. He was hugging his knees, mumbling to himself, eyes burning with hatred as he stared fixedly at The Hacker. It looked, to Rick, as if the boy had gone insane.

Teeth clenched, Rick aimed the shotgun at The Hacker's grimacing one-eyed face. But there was something in The Hacker's frozen fun-house grin that made him hesitate. It was as though he were saying, I'm far too evil to kill. But I dare you. I dare you to try it, anyway.

Then Rick heard Max Kendall's voice, whispering in his ear, which was impossible, because Max was still in the meadow, trying to crawl toward the cabin. Nevertheless Rick heard him. Right there in his ear, just as plain as day.

Kill the motherfucka, Max told him.

Rick envisioned Max lying on his back in the rain, his face slashed, leg bent at that peculiar angle, his knee reduced to a bloody pulp. His eyes—Max's wild blue eyes—as wide and violent as ever, and his bloodstained grin. I'm gonna die, Max had told him.

Kill the motherfucka!

"Do what you're friend said, and kill me," The Hacker taunted, but Rick could not hear him. He could not hear anything, or anyone, but Max. "Kill me," The Hacker said, spitting a dark glob of blood by Rick's feet. "Kill me, now, you worthless piece of shit."

No other sound but Max's voice: *Kill the motherfucka!*

Rick Hunter's final shot cracked the upper half of Alan Moriarty's skull apart as if it were a coconut, pitching the debris—

fragments of bone, bloody clumps of hair, grayish chunks of brain matter—back against the stairs with a sickening splat. The body twitched in violent, dying convulsions, hands and feet shaking rapidly, and then fell still. What was left of his head was tilted upwards, towards the ceiling. Although most of Moriarty's features had been eradicated, Rick could've sworn he was still flaunting that crazed, crooked-toothed grin.

Rick dropped the shotgun and collapsed to the floor. With a bump and a thud, he went out.

Alan Moriarty, a.k.a. Alan Moody, a.k.a. The Hevven Hacker, was now where he wanted to be.

He was with the others—his victims.

He was with the voices.

In the dark fathoms of the pool.

~Forty-Four~

It wasn't often that Mike Swart drove long distances without his usual entourage of friends to accompany him, but today was different.

Today, only the shotgun seat was occupied.

If it had been up to Mike, however, he would have made the trip alone, without his co-pilot, but Rick had insisted on coming for the ride, and Mike hadn't had the strength to argue.

It was now September, some six weeks after Hell came to Uncle Jack's cabin in a gray Ford LTD, and a brisk morning had embraced the small town of Willow's Creek, New Hampshire. The trees were ablaze with their autumn colors, and the dry leaves were speaking in their static whispers, their predictions of the coming winter.

Local meteorologists had already formulated their own predictions for the season, and the outlook wasn't good: It was going to be a damn cold winter. Perhaps the coldest one in recorded history.

Between police reports, media interviews, and the funeral services for Kevin Chapman and his mother (whose dismembered bodies were discovered in the basement of Chief Moriarty's house on Elm Street), Mike Swart and Rick Hunter had little time to keep up with the nightly weather forecasts. This was their first opportunity to return to the place where the nightmare had ended.

But the real nightmare, the aftermath of that last terrifying day, was far from being over.

279

Lou Swart was at home with his parents. He would be returning to high school as a sophomore if, in fact, his newly appointed psychiatrist decided he was fit to do so.

Karen Sloan was in the Intensive Care Unit at Mass. General Hospital in Boston, where she remained in a coma due to severe head trauma, as well as internal bleeding.

Rick Hunter's hearing, as well as his vision, returned to normal after several days' rest. His left arm had been severely traumatized at the shoulder by both The Hacker's bullet, as well as by his fall into the river, but after 23 stitches and two weeks of wearing a sling, he was healing faster than expected.

Stacey Mackinnon had temporarily dropped out of college and had moved back into her parents' house in Watertown, where Rick visited her often.

"How's Max doing?" Mike asked as they passed Atkins' General Store.

Max Kendall was at Good Samaritan Hospital in Stoughton, Massachusetts. The doctors said…

"He's doing okay. But he's gonna have trouble walking after surgery. They said he's probably gonna have a limp for the rest of his life," Rick said sourly, lighting a cigarette with the lighter Kevin had given him. He stared at the chrome Zippo, remembering his friend. He smoked his cigarette with a quiet intensity, choking back the tears that wanted to come.

Back in their hometown, Hevven, they had become heroes. Every television, newspaper, and radio station within a 500-mile radius was knocking on each of their doors, calling on their phones, pestering their parents, their neighbors, in search of any information they could use to feed the hungry public. It was sickening, really. But for their friends and families, it seemed the entire world had already forgotten Kevin Chapman and his mother, as well as the rest of The Hacker's victims; the search for their bodies had practically screeched to a halt. Everybody wanted a piece of the action, a piece of the story. What events led up to the youngsters finding the body? How did young Lou Swart feel about this and that? How did the charismatic Mike Swart lead his friends from the clutches of the serial killer known as The Hacker? Had Alan Moriarty sexually assaulted Stacey Mackinnon before she was rescued from the Moody house? Was it true that Karen Sloan was in a coma? Were they interested in a movie deal? A book deal? Would they appear on 60 Minutes? Oprah?

Bullshit. All of it was bullshit. People they'd gone to school with were even asking them for their autographs. Their goddamn autographs, as if they were movie stars!

But the truth of it was, the young group of friends were worse off than they had ever been before. Far, far worse.

"I saw on the news today," Rick said. "You know that cop and the FBI agent who were working on the case? Looks like they're gonna make it, after all. I guess, once they fully recover, they'll be continuing with the investigation, to see if they can find out what happened to all those other missing girls."

Mike nodded but did not respond. He couldn't find it in his heart to care about those other girls. They were dead, and nothing he did could change that now. He only cared about the one he loved, Karen Sloan.

They soon arrived at the cabin, and for a moment, the two lifelong friends remained in the idling car, their thoughts drifting back to a different time.

Rick looked over at Mike. *What now?*

"Do you think...maybe...you could wait out here?" Mike asked, drawing a fresh cigarette from a pack on the dashboard. It occurred to him that Karen wasn't there to scold him for his habit. She couldn't shake her head, frowning, and fold her arms across her chest in that motherly fashion. She was in a hospital far away, and she was...sleeping. Yes, sleeping. And she'd awaken, the doctors assured him, someday. Maybe.

"Are you sure?" inquired Rick. Mike didn't look so well. None of them looked so well these days. Lou was bad. But Mike, he was far worse. He'd almost lost his brother, and was still in danger of losing his girl. He looked pale and gaunt, and there were dark bags under his eyes.

"Yes," Mike responded too quickly, "I'm sure." He lit his cigarette, wishing to God that Karen were there to react, to be annoyed with him. To yell at him, even. It occurred to him how insane that was, to long for her company even if it was only to argue with him (which didn't happen very often). But Karen Sloan, the girl he loved more than life itself, wasn't there. She was sleeping.

"Okay," Rick whispered reluctantly. He found the power button on the stereo and pressed it. An acoustic song by Green Day came on, and he sat looking at the meadow, visualizing himself and the others as they were only weeks ago, swimming and splashing in the cool water, passing the time on the sun-baked sand. He could almost hear their voices floating above the whisper of the wind, their childish laughter, their deep conversations.

Rick Hunter thought about these things for a while, and as he stared through the windshield of Mike's T-bird, watching the river run its course, he soon became lost in a flood of memories. *God, why did we have to come back here so soon?*

Mike stood inside the cabin, looking at the playing cards that were strewn about the floor, just as Lou had left them.

We never did finish that game, Mike realized, as he slowly climbed the stairs, crossing over the chalked outline where The Hevven Hacker had met his violent end. He went to the upstairs bedroom that, for a number of pleasant nights, he and Karen had called their own. But Karen wasn't with him this time. She wasn't with him because she was still lying in a narrow bed, under cool white sheets, in a small cubicle in Mass. General Hospital, her body a circuit board of needles and tubes tied to machines that sustained her vital organs, keeping her neither alive nor dead, but sleeping.

Suddenly losing the strength to stand, he sank down on the pile of blankets that had been their bed, thinking of all the things that had happened there, at Uncle Jack's cabin. He clutched the blankets against his face with both hands, over his mouth and nose, and inhaled expectantly. Nothing; he exhaled. Frustrated, he inhaled again, as deeply as he could without choking on air, but the smell he was searching for—Karen's own sweet smell— was no longer there. There was only the dank, dusty air, the vague smell of mildew, and silence.

And—it suddenly occurred to him—many, many ghosts.

It was his decision that had brought them to Willow's Creek, a decision that had rendered Max a cripple for life. It was that same decision that had, perhaps, scarred Lou's mind forever. It was also his decision to involve Kevin, and if he hadn't, Kevin Chapman and his mother might still be alive right now. And, lastly, it was his decision to let Karen come along. A decision that had left her…sleeping, he told himself, even though he knew it was a lie. She wasn't sleeping, she was dying. And it was his fault, his...

Decisions. Decisions. Decisions.

Are you making the right decisions?

Mike Swart's world was shattered. It seemed as though even the giants were his enemies now.

He removed two items from the rear pocket of his Calvin Klein jeans, one of which he let fall to the floor. The other, he held firmly in his hand.

Uh-oh, Mikey, are you sure you wanna do that?

I don't know.

Are you making the right decisions?

I don't know. I don't care.

With tears streaming down his face, Mike Swart made another decision.

Just over 45 minutes had passed while Rick waited for his friend to return. He'd smoked nearly half a pack of cigarettes while he listened to the stereo, forced to remember all that had happened there. Finally, tired, hungry, and wanting to go home, he shut off the stereo and stepped out of the car into the cool autumn air. The treetops rattled eerily. The valley had become an empty place.

Crossing the earthen driveway, he wondered how long it would be before the landscape turned from green to gray, and the water would freeze on the riverbanks; how long after that, he wondered, would snow hide the valley beneath a northern quilt? His heart was already longing for the return of summer.

Taking one last look at the mountains, he headed into the cabin, where the smell of burnt Jiffy Pop still lingered in the air.

"Mike? Are you alright, man?" he asked from the bottom of the stairs.

283

No answer.

"We should be heading home," Rick called out. "I'll drive, if you want me to."

No reply.

Rick walked slowly up the stairs. He entered the large bedroom, and saw his friend in the corner, hunched over a pile of blankets. "It's okay, man. It's going to be o..."

God, no! No!

Rick ran and skidded on his knees across the dusty wooden floor. He rolled Mike over, onto his back. Mike's body was bloody and cold. Both arms were slashed vertically from the wrist to the elbow. Rick quickly felt for a pulse. Nothing! He began to perform CPR, which he had learned in his high school health class.

One-one-thousand, two-one-thousand, three-one-thousand...

Still not breathing. Still no pulse.

"C'mon, breathe, you sonofabitch!" Rick screamed hysterically, hammering away at Mike's chest. "Breathe!"

One-one-thousand, two-one-thousand, three-one-thousand...

"Oh, God! Please, Mike. Please, man. You gotta breathe!"

Nothing.

Still kneeling, he scooped the limp, bloody body into his arms, crying so hard that he felt as though he would explode, looking into Mike's gray unblinking eyes. And suddenly, a lifetime of memories came crashing through Rick's mind.

Suddenly it was five years ago, and he was in the woods with Max Kendall, Kevin Chapman, and the two Swart brothers, erecting the frame of what would later become their secret hangout and—God!—they looked so young and happy...further back in time, and suddenly he was a soldier again, one of the brave few who protected the Hockomock Forest with squirt guns and slingshots (though, in the world of make-believe, their squirt guns fired laser beams, and their slingshots could kill a swamp monster with one well-placed shot). And Lou, who couldn't have been any more than seven years old, was galloping along behind them through the meadow near the end of Titicut Street, hollering for them to wait up, and they were laughing, pretending they didn't hear him...a party at the Cherry Street pits ...it could have been any party...Mike and Rick and Max were leaning against the hood of the T-bird, passing around a joint, and Rick was telling them about a new girl he'd met in school, a cute little blonde by the name of Lori Shawnessy, and Mike was patting him on the shoulder, telling him to go for it, wishing him good luck...Lori stood between him and Kevin, an arm over each of their shoulders, smiling that bright smile, as Mike squinted one eye in front of them, ready to take their picture...Karen Sloan clinging to him, her face pressed against his chest, her body trembling fiercely...they were all dressed in black, and in front of them there was a coffin covered with flowers...and on the other side of that coffin, Lori Shawnessy's mother cried into her hands, while Mr. Shawnessy rested one arm over her shoulders, his face a ghastly white...they were at the river...the water flowing, pulling, pushing, cooling, relaxing, endlessly moving to a place unseen...the river knew no hatred, or love, or prejudice, it only knew its course...Lou and Max were wrestling and Karen was wading out to wash her hair...Rick and Stacey were lying down beside each other on a blanket near the water's edge, and Mike was standing beside them, watching Karen...there was a strange look on his face, a kind of strange look in his eyes, a bit of a smile pulling up the corners of his mouth (a reflection of the man he would never become)...

Rick hadn't paid much attention to that look before, as the event unfolded before him, because he'd been too busy enjoying the moment, but he paid attention to it now, as it played out in his mind, and he knew that expression.

It was serenity.

Then, as suddenly as they had come, the memories drained away.

Once again, there was only Mike's gray eyes staring up at him, unblinking. And, once more, for the very last time, there was serenity.

"Bre...eeethe!" Rick pleaded. "Puh-lease, jus-just breathe!"

As he bowed his head, whimpering helplessly, still holding Mike in his arms as if he were a doll, Rick noticed the bloody razorblade, which had fallen to the floor, probably released from Mike's hand as the life drained from his body. With dark intentions he reached out for the tool which had aided in his best friend's suicide only moments ago, certain his own destiny must also lay in that direction, and paused before his fingers found the blade.

Once again, Life and Death weighed on the scales of Rick Hunter's mind. Only this time, he found that the measurements had changed. He had once chosen Death, but not this time. In the end, it was Life that ruled the scales. He stopped his hand and brought it back slowly, leaving the razorblade where Mike had dropped it. It was then that he noticed a folded sheet of paper on the floor, just far enough away so that the blood had not stained it, and, with one trembling hand, he leaned over Mike's body and reached out for it. Before he even opened it, he knew exactly what it was: Mike's farewell letter; his suicide note.

Weeping softly, he smoothed out the paper, and read out loud, wiping away the tears with the back of one hand.

"Dear Rick, I wish things didn't have to be like this, but I can't change what has happened. Remember when we used to talk about finding a place to fit in? You've found your place, with Stacey. Maybe now I've found mine.

"You've got a good girl there. Don't let her go. I wish I could have been around longer, so that I could have gotten to know her better, but it just wasn't meant to be. Tell her about me someday. Tell her all about the crazy things we used to do, so she can know what I was like before things went bad.

"Kevin and his mother died because of me. Max is crippled now. Karen is in a coma, and I don't think I could face her, even if she did come out of it (I'm not kidding myself, man, because I don't think she will). And I just can't go on alone, not after all that has happened. But if by some miracle she does wake up, tell her I love her. And tell her I'll always love her, and that I tried.

"I really tried.

"It's a cold world out there, but you already knew that, I think. I noticed we haven't been quite as close lately, since Lori passed away, but I wanted to tell you this: you're the best friend a guy could have, Rick. Like a brother. I don't know what my life would have been like if I hadn't met you. You guys were like a family to me. We were always together, through the good and the bad, and I want you to always remember it that way.

"Watch out for everyone for me. Especially my little brother. He looks up to you. I'll bet you never noticed before, but it's true. Tell him I love him, because I never had the balls to tell him myself. Tell him I'm gonna go on looking for the end of that river. Ask him about it. He'll know what I mean.

"No matter what happens, don't let the memories die with me. Sometime in your life, that might be all you have. There are other worlds than the one we know. Better worlds. Someday, somehow, somewhere, we'll all meet again in one of those worlds. I promise. It's just one of them feelings, you know? Do you feel it, too? I'm missing you already, old friend."

Your friend,
Mike

Rick sobbed against the stillness of his best friend's chest. Trembling, he kept his eyes closed tightly, but the tears kept rolling down his cheeks from between his closed lids. The suicide note still in hand, he held Mike Swart in his arms the way a child might hold a doll, rocking, rocking, rocking, until finally he threw his head back to the ceiling and expressed his sorrow with a long and painful roar.

From somewhere outside, above the weathered cabin walls, and far beyond the reach of the blazing treetops, a hawk answered with a similar cry.

~Forty-Five~

In the days to come, the four remaining friends—Max, Lou, Rick, and Stacey—set time aside each week to go to the hospital where Karen Sloan, looking pale and on the threshold of death, lingered in a coma.

They took turns talking to her, and reading books to her, praying that she could somehow hear them, that somehow they were getting through to her. Each dreaded the one fearful day when she would finally let go, when the life-preserving machines that she was connected to could do no more.

But that day would never come.

It was a cold October night, nearly a month after Mike's tragic suicide, when the miracle happened.

Without warning, Karen slowly opened her eyes, and in the darkness of the tiny hospital room saw the blurred outline of a person sitting beside her.

"Mike?" she asked weakly. She felt as though her mouth were full of sand.

The figure sitting beside her moved closer.

"Mike?" she asked again.

"No," a gentle voice told her. "It's Lou."

"Lou," she said, smiling druggedly. She tried to reach her hand out to him, but was too weak to command movement. Her arm slid off the side of the narrow bed, hanging limply. "Where's Mike?"

Suddenly, Lou began to cry into the blankets. He didn't answer her question. For all the emotion that rocked him, he was unable to do so.

Nor did he have to.

Hot tears began to seep from Karen's eyes because somehow, some way, she sensed that Mike was no longer with her. Later, when she thought about that night (and she would think about it often), she would tell herself that she must have heard one of her friends talking about Mike's suicide while she was in her coma, and that her subconscious mind had somehow retained that information. But there was a part of her that would always disagree, a part of her that would whisper the truth, with a thin little voice in the back of her mind: You knew he was gone. Somehow, you already knew.

"It's okay, Lou," she whispered soothingly. She could feel him trembling against her.

"Nooooo..." he cried.

"It's okay," she repeated, her eyes burning with tears.

In the darkness, her trembling hand found his.

~EPILOGUE~

Only Rick Hunter and Stacey Mackinnon remained in close contact in the years that followed that tragic summer. Eventually, they moved in together and attended college at Stonehill. After some hard times, they were married in a small church in Middleboro, Massachusetts, and later had a son.

Little by little the remaining friends went their separate ways, and in time, the memories of their stay at Uncle Jack's cabin became cracked and blurry, like photographs slowly consumed by the heat of the summer sun. Faded, but not forgotten.

Once in a while, but not too often, the friends bumped into each other unexpectedly, either at the cabin, or at the Pleasant Pines Cemetery, where their loved ones had been buried. Soon even those meetings became scarce, for the friends now frolicked in a different river, a river whose inescapable current shoved them violently away from the past, leading them far, far away from Hevven, pulling them onward towards that golden distant shore known as The Future. A river that was often calm and peaceful, and sometimes as jarring as a rollercoaster ride—the inevitable river of Time.

But no matter how many years divided those brief encounters, no matter how many miles came between them, or how much their lives would change, they would never forget those special days spent together at the cabin, walking barefoot through the meadow, going down to the river. Nor would they ever forget the lives that were lost, the horrors they endured, or the many precious memories that would forever wander through the passageways of their minds, like the ghosts of long-lost friends, waiting to guide them back to yesterday.

The magic, the innocence, the dreams of childhood were over, but the scars they had suffered, both physically and mentally, would remain with them for a lifetime. They would never heal, never go away.

As for the giants...

They never spoke again.

About the Author

James Michael Rice lives in New England and is the author of *A Tough Act to Follow*. He can be contacted via his website at www.jamesmichaelrice.com.

F
RIC
Rice, James Michael
REBEL ANGELS

DATE DUE

JA 11 '10			
MY JE 5 '10			
JE 12 '10			
JE 23 '10			
AG 09 '10			
FE 13 '12			
OC 28 '14